MW01518751

WHERE

FUTURES

END

WHERE

FUTURES

END

PARKER PEEVYHOUSE

Kathy Dawson Books

KATHY DAWSON BOOKS
An imprint of Penguin Random House LLC
375 Hudson Street
New York, NY 10014

Copyright © 2016 by Parker Peevyhouse

Library of Congress Cataloging-in-Publication Data
Names: Peevyhouse, Parker, author.
Title: Where futures end / Parker Peevyhouse.
Description: New York : Kathy Dawson Books, [2016]
Summary: "Five interconnected stories that weave a subtle science-fictional web
stretching out from the present into the future, presenting eerily plausible possibilities
for social media, corporate sponsorship, and humanity, as our world collides
with a mysterious alternate universe"— Provided by publisher.

Identifiers: LCCN 2015022984 | ISBN 9780803741607 (hardback)
Subjects: | CYAC: Science fiction. | BISAC: JUVENILE FICTION / Science Fiction. |
JUVENILE FICTION / Concepts / Date & Time. | JUVENILE FICTION /
Social Issues / General (see also headings under Family).

Classification: LCC PZ7.1.P444 Wh 2016 | DDC [Fic]—dc23
LC record available at http://lccn.loc.gov/2015022984

Printed in the United States of America

1 3 5 7 9 10 8 6 4 2

Design by Maya Tatsukawa
Text set in Haarlemmer MT Pro

FOR ELIZABETH,
who plans for endless futures

CONTENTS

WHERE

FUTURES

END

1.

WHEN WE ASKED
THE IMPOSSIBLE

(one year from now)

DYLAN

Dylan asked his first Impossible Question when he was five, when he could still hear music in running water, still find gilded kingdoms trapped in beams of sunlight.

Why do I see things no one else can see?

Impossible to say, son, Dad had answered with a smile, closing the cover of the book they'd been reading, *The Blue Fairy Book.*

Are they real, the things I see?

Dylan's older brother, Hunter, hated questions like that. *Stop pretending you're special,* he would say.

In a storybook, an Impossible Question might be a riddle that could never be solved, a challenge that would bring the quest to a standstill.

In real life, an Impossible Question might be easily met with a shrug or a sigh. But it might also carve the whole world into pieces as small as dust motes so that you could hardly breathe for fear of scattering them all.

At the age of eleven, Dylan asked Dad an Impossible Question for the last time, when they were getting hot dogs at Alki Beach in West Seattle. It wasn't that Dylan never saw Dad again after that. It was just that there were no more jackets tied like capes, no more laughs that went sideways in the wind, no more perfect burn of salt spray and spicy mustard. The story of Dad and Dylan came to a standstill.

In the years since the day at Alki Beach, Dylan had become an expert at Impossible Questions. He would creep into Hunter's room after lights-out to ask, *What's at the bottom of a black hole in space? Is a red blanket still red in the dark? Why don't zombies eat their own flesh?* Hunter would pass one of his earbuds to Dylan and they'd let the Sonics or the Rolling Stones answer as best they could.

Why do I sense things no one else can? Dylan asked himself now, standing outside the prep school gymnasium where his brother's basketball game was taking place. He knew the crowd was about to roar. He felt the hum in his bones, without even seeing the action.

And sure enough, a moment later, the cheer erupted.

He opened the door and stood in the doorway. Gray-and-purple banners emblazoned with *Hevlen Preparatory* were slung on the walls. "Heavily Perspiring," Dylan and his friends had used to joke, sophomore year—before Dylan had gotten kicked out for cheating. Now it was fall of his junior year.

A boy in a gray Hevlen blazer edged through the doorway: Blaine, who used to sit with Dylan at lunch so they could program modifications to their favorite PC games. He tipped his carton of popcorn toward Dylan and said, "Is it true that some kids carry knives to class in public school?"

"That's why we get those metal rulers," Dylan said, reaching into the carton. "Levels the playing field."

The air in the gym was warm, but Dylan suddenly wished he'd worn a jacket, because Blaine was staring at the peeling letters on Dylan's T-shirt that spelled out *Put on Your 3-D Glasses*.

"It seemed cool in my mom's pawnshop," Dylan said. "Anyway, my old Hevlen uniform's too small now."

"I wish I didn't have to wear this thing." Blaine flicked the collar of his blazer. "Think I should defect? Try my luck with metal rulers?"

Dylan tried to laugh, coughed out a popcorn kernel instead. Blaine eyed Dylan's slouching frame. "Hevlen has to expel *somebody* at the end of each year. To keep the rest of us sweating." He studied his popcorn carton and shrugged. "Probably only picked you because you were on scholarship."

Dylan tried to give off an air of *sure, fine,* leaning back against the doorway. That odd electricity hummed in his bones again and then, what do you know, out on the court his brother sank another three-pointer. The crowd chanted his name: *Hun-ter, Hun-ter!*

The other team called a time-out. The hum in Dylan's bones subsided. He had a clear view of his brother standing a head taller than the rest of his team. Everything about Hunter's face was rugged—sheer-cliff forehead, wide chin. Even his sideburns looked like they were trying to reclaim territory ceded to his ears.

"Your grades weren't really that bad, though, were they?" Blaine asked. "You were on the team that went to math regionals."

"I cheated on my finals. Zero tolerance rule. Whatever."

Blaine's eyes widened.

"We actually debated the legality of that zero tolerance rule in philosophy class," Dylan said. "Whether it's really fair to kick someone out for a first offense."

"They have philosophy in public school? Huh, wow."

Dylan didn't answer.

On the court, Hunter slid past the point guard and flipped the ball up to the basket.

Blaine's mouth hung open. "It's like someone spliced dolphin DNA into his."

The air in the gym was way too warm, the popcorn smell stifling. "I'm gonna go," Dylan said. "See you online sometime?"

"You know my gamer tag."

Dylan strode toward the bench where the second string was watching the game and grabbed Hunter's jacket. It would be cold out in the parking lot.

As Dylan turned back toward the door, he was startled to see Dad sitting in the bleachers. What was *he* doing here? He never came to Hunter's basketball games. *Maybe I'm seeing things again,* Dylan thought.

Then the crowd shifted and he glimpsed another face that didn't belong: the face of a girl he hadn't seen in ages, except in his memories. His stomach twisted.

Definitely seeing things.

The buzzer signaled the end of the game. Dylan lost sight of both Dad and the girl as the crowd stood to cheer. He found a ski cap in the pocket of Hunter's jacket and tugged it on over his ears as he hurried outside, bristling with confusion.

Out in the parking lot: pale twilight. The cheers gave way to leaves skittering over asphalt, car doors popping open. The typical Seattle smell of rain and salt was in the air, plus a brewing wind. The tops of the distant maple trees shook as if a monster might charge through the branches at any moment, like something out of *Jurassic Park*.

That sound—leaves rustling in the dark. Dylan closed his eyes. Waited a beat, and then opened them. He half expected the trees to have disappeared, half thought he'd be transported to somewhere else. Where, he couldn't say.

Why do I see things no one else can see?

In his head, Dad's voice asked, *What kinds of things?*

He'd seen that girl in the gym before. Seen her face lit by sunlight. But where? Who was she? A phantom from his memory, someone he had known long ago. But who?

Dylan angled himself toward the doors to the gym. Did Dad come to Hunter's games all the time? Maybe he did and Dylan just never knew—snuck in and out without saying hi because he knew how much Hunter hated him. Not that Dylan was keen to see him either. Last week's phone call was as much as Dylan could take for this month: *Mom's fine, Hunter's fine, school sucks, bye.*

"Nice game, Yates."

Dylan turned at the sound of his last name, startled. Then he remembered that *Yates* was written on the jacket he was wearing.

"Thanks," he mumbled to the back of a guy in a school uniform.

What kinds of things do you see? Dad asked again in Dylan's head.

Blue light sparked along the skin of the guy walking away, and then fizzled out as he maneuvered around the cars in the parking lot: a physical manifestation of post-game excitement. Dylan had seen it before.

He had a name for his ability to see such things, one he'd come up with back in the first grade, when his teacher had read "Jabberwocky" aloud to the class. *The vorpal blade went snicker-snack!* Over time, he had somehow dropped the *blade*.

The vorpal went snicker-snack. That was the exact feeling he'd get. His vorpal would flicker and he'd sense something others couldn't: rain getting ready to fall, squirrels sleeping in nests of leaves, Mom's worry, Hunter's dark moods. He never told them about it. Only his dad had understood.

"Yates, nice job," someone said behind him.

Dylan turned, expecting disappointment or embarrassment: *You're not Hunter, sorry.* But it didn't come. The boy looking back at him was short, bad haircut, definitely a freshman. He kept on talking.

"That hook shot in the third quarter? The defender thought he had it until he almost got an elbow to the face."

Dylan waited for the kid to realize his mistake. Dylan was three inches shorter than Hunter. His shoulders weren't even as wide as Hunter's rib cage.

It was happening again. The weirdest thing: People mistook him for Hunter.

Dylan knew it was his vorpal's fault. It made him see things, hear things—but it also made people around him see things. Sometimes because Dylan *wanted* to change what people saw, and sometimes it happened by accident. He wasn't great at controlling it.

"Think we'll take Grady Prep on Thursday?" the boy asked.

"Our cheerleaders could take Grady Prep," Dylan said, because it was true. *Heck, I could take Grady Prep.*

Out of the corner of his eye, Dylan caught a flurry of movement among the parked cars. His mom darted around a BMW, flapping her hands at Dylan. "Sorry—I missed the whole thing, didn't I? I'm sure you were great."

She strode up to him and gave him a peck on the cheek, turned to the freshman. "Was he great?"

Realization finally dawned on the freshman's face: *That's not Hunter Yates.*

Dylan's mom turned to look at him. Dylan half hoped she wouldn't realize her mistake, that she'd keep seeing him as Hunter. She was always so glowy with Hunter.

But she jerked her hand away from his shoulder. "Dylan." Half surprise, half accusation.

Dylan's face went hot. Skinny as a spider monkey, but even his own mom mistook him for hulking Hunter.

Because of his vorpal.

His mom was looking at him, jaw clenched. Dylan ducked his head. "I'll wait in the car," he said, giving up the idea of watching for Dad. Over his shoulder, he called, "I can work at the store tomorrow," by way of apology; for what, he wasn't sure. Then he made for the Tahoe, his ears full of the sound of trees crackling in the wind.

The pawnshop was a trove of old guitars and DVD players and a pair of cracked leather boots that had Dylan's name on them if he could get ten more dollars. Everything in the store had once been great but was now only kind of cool, and only to someone like Dylan, who wasn't currently in a position to buy anything not-used.

He went to a shelf in the corner that held a row of fantasy novels everyone reads by the time they're twelve. Wizards and monsters and magical relics. Stuff Dylan was too old for. Even so, he opened a copy of *Through the Looking-Glass, and What Alice Found There* and studied the illustrations. He made himself do this from time to time. He was trying to convince himself that the girl who haunted him wasn't real.

Her face floated to mind more and more often lately, bright with wonder or squinting in concentration. And now he was seeing her even in Hevlen's gym, like his brain didn't know when to quit. He couldn't say how he had met her, or where, or when. Couldn't remember anything else about her.

Except for one thing.

He had the distinct idea that she was a queen.

Obviously impossible. How does a kid in Seattle meet a queen? That was how he knew he was only remembering a character from a story. A picture from a book, maybe.

He flipped a page and found a drawing of Alice with a crown and scepter. But her inkblot eyes held nothing familiar.

The bell on the shop door jingled, and a customer walked in. Dylan poked his head around a shelf. Not a customer. Hunter, lumbering around like he owned the place.

"What are you doing here?" Dylan called. "I told Mom I'd work today."

"Good for you," Hunter said, heading toward the back room.

Dylan shoved the book back in with the others on the shelf and wandered toward the counter. "What's the movie we used to watch when we were kids?" he called to Hunter. "The one with the girl who's a queen?" Could be that's where Dylan remembered her from—a movie.

No answer from the back room. Hunter had a terrible memory for movies. He never watched one twice unless it included an exponential number of explosions.

"*The NeverEnding Story*?" Dylan wondered aloud. The girl in that movie was technically an empress. Close enough?

Dylan thought he heard someone rummaging through the bins near the door. A customer after all. He closed his eyes and tried to guess exactly where the customer was standing. *The bin on the far left—DVDs.* He didn't have to guess. He could feel it in the way the air moved—could sense it with his vorpal. He checked the mirror in the corner of the ceiling and saw that he'd been right: a girl in a canvas jacket stood at the DVD bin. Dylan slid behind the counter and propped himself against a stool to wait.

Hunter emerged from the back room carrying the cash box. "We watched too many weird movies when we were kids," he told Dylan. "How am I supposed to remember a..."

"Girl queen. She had these eyes like"—Dylan pictured them in his mind—"like cracked ice." He waited for some hint that Hunter knew what he was talking about. He could swear he heard a clicking sound coming from Hunter's brain, thoughts shuffling and reshuffling.

"I'm not really sure she was from a movie," Dylan admitted finally. *Or a book,* he added to himself. "I might have met her somewhere."

It was always dangerous to say something like that to Hunter, that he'd met a real queen in person. Like he'd stumbled across her in a coffee shop or maybe over in snooty Bellevue, ha-ha. Those kinds of admissions made Hunter deeply unhappy. A *Huskies losing to Oregon* level of unhappy.

"It doesn't matter," Hunter said. "Stop worrying about it, okay?"

Can't, Dylan thought, and pictured her eyes again: cracked ice, sunlight reflecting off every facet. *Why do I remember someone who isn't real?* Add it to the list of Impossible Questions.

Hunter pulled a cloth from his back pocket and handed it to Dylan. "Dust instead."

The girl in the canvas jacket popped out from behind a shelf of junk, a shiny mask strapped over her face. "Hey, Hunter, what do you think?"

Hunter chuckled. "C-3PO."

"It's not," the mask-girl said. "It's from—"

"*Metropolis,*" Dylan said. "That robot girl."

She shoved the mask up over her dark hair. "Have you seen it? The movie—*Metropolis*?"

"Sure," Dylan said. "Who hasn't?"

She smiled, her brown eyes reflecting the gold of the mask. Her hair was like polished wood, like the black walnut trees behind his house when they were wet with rain.

Hunter set the cash box on the counter, a little too hard.

"Grab whichever DVDs you want, Chess," Hunter said to the girl. "I'm just gonna put a twenty in here and that'll cover it."

"There's another bin of them you didn't go through yet," Dylan told her, pointing.

The girl—Chess—gave him a brief look (curious? interested?) and then disappeared down an aisle. Dylan swiped dust from the glass counter with the cloth, thinking about that look, until he noticed something under the glass: a wide band of gold etched with vines.

He clamped a hand on the counter, dizzy with confusion.

"Where'd this come from?" he asked Hunter.

Hunter shrugged. "A guy came in yesterday."

It's a bracelet, just a bracelet, Dylan told himself.

But in his mind he could see the Girl Queen sliding it onto his arm.

"Dylan?" Hunter said.

"This is mine," Dylan said.

Hunter snorted. "It's yours if you have three hundred dollars."

"It's mine. I got it from . . . from . . ." *Where?* He reached for it with a shaking hand and touched cool metal. Instantly, the smell of moldering leaves came back to him, along with a barrage of images: the damp fallen trees in a shaded forest, a girl's porcelain face. A gilded rooftop glimpsed through a puzzle of branches. *She put her hand in mine, her fingers were so cold. Mud all along her hem and spattered on her bare feet. "Where are we going?" She looked at me over her shoulder and then the light was in the branches and in her hair . . .*

He remembered. Not only the Girl Queen but . . .

. . . a forest.

Where?

He slid the band onto his wrist. *The cold metal sliding up my arm. Her voice uncertain: "Remember me."*

A prickle went down his neck. He remembered Dad reading from *The Blue Fairy Book,* remembered listening so intently that everything around seemed to vanish.

He remembered the world parting to reveal enchanted trees, water churning over rocks.

Things no one else could see.

Hunter snatched the gold band off Dylan's wrist. "You got it from the display. And that's where you're going to leave it unless you can pay for it."

Dylan's hands trembled. He looked again at the gold band. *Was* it just a bracelet?

Of course it was.

And those memories? That place?

A dream, he told himself. *An image from a storybook. A childhood fantasy only a sad loser would still believe in.*

Chess returned with a stack of DVDs. "Wow," she said, coming closer to peer at the gold band Hunter still held. "Looks like something from *Lord of the Rings*."

"Here, try it on." Hunter held it out, and she slid the band onto her wrist before Dylan could object.

"Looks good on you," Hunter told her, spearing Dylan with a glare.

"Yeah, it's cool." The girl turned her wrist to admire the band some more.

"So keep it for a few days," Hunter said.

"What? You can't take stuff from the store," Dylan said to Hunter, his voice sharp with desperation.

"She's borrowing it," Hunter said. He passed the DVDs back to Chess. "This all you want?"

Chess nodded. She looked between him and Dylan. "Are you sure it's okay for me to—"

Hunter grabbed her hand and steered her toward the door. "You want bagels?"

The bell over the door chimed again and they were gone.

= ≠ =

Dylan heaved plastic file boxes out of Mom's closet and disemboweled them. Papers spilled over the carpet: Dylan's childhood artwork. Paintings of green fish and bulbous insects, of uneven spirals like whorled snail shells.

Shaky drawings of a girl's face.

Another memory rushed to mind: *swimming through dark, frigid water. Around him, tiny fish, drifting insects, crustaceans felt their way along gravel and silt. The water brightened, and Dylan surfaced in a sunlit cave.*

A girl with ice-bright eyes pulled him by the hand up a rocky crawl that bit into his bare toes. He felt he was moving through a spell: the clinging mist, the chime of water dripping into shallow pools. The walls of the cave were dimpled with nooks where odd treasures lay like catalogued talismans. The girl picked them up one by one: a pearly snail shell the size of her fist, a yellow-green mushroom gone brown under the cap, a clump of water-logged feathers, a smooth river rock veined with blue and red. Her collection.

Footsteps and then Mom's voice interrupted Dylan's thoughts. "What are you doing?"

Dylan shoved the papers into a folder. "Looking through some old stuff." He didn't know why he felt embarrassed about it. But it was like being caught sleepwalking, like explaining a dream to someone only to have it come out sounding absurd. Plus, he never went into Mom's closet, not even just to look at old papers. "Did you see that gold bracelet that came into the shop yesterday?"

In the doorway, Mom held her half-open laptop in one

hand and squinted at Dylan. "No, and I wish you boys wouldn't offer loans on stuff like that without calling me in to do the appraisal."

"I think Hunter brought it in. He found it somewhere."

Mom set the laptop down on her desk and flipped through a stack of bills. "Where would Hunter get something like that?"

"I don't know."

Mom frowned at Dylan.

"Well, make sure you hold that stuff and wait for me in the future."

She straightened a framed photo she had knocked over: Hunter and Dylan standing knee-deep in lake water, smiling with the sun behind them. She glanced from the photo to Dylan, then bent to ruffle his hair affectionately.

"Do you remember a girl at the lake?" he asked. "When you took me and Hunter there for Fourth of July? She showed me a cave."

The lines around Mom's mouth deepened. "I don't know, Dylan. Maybe." She glanced at Dylan's folder of artwork. "How about spending a little more time in the here and now? When am I going to see a progress report from school?"

Dylan pushed the box back into the closet, but stuck the folder under his shirt. "When's Hunter getting home?" Maybe Hunter remembered the girl, the cave.

Mom's attention was back on her laptop and the bills. "Late."

"How come when I take the car I have to be home by ten?"

"He didn't take the car, his girlfriend picked him up," Mom said. "And from now on you're *here* every night doing homework. Until I see a progress report, you won't be so much as *looking* at the car."

"Mom—"

She waved off his protest. "Enjoy the view from your room, sir."

"The view from my room is of your car." Dylan waited to see if she would crack a smile, and she did.

He stole away to his bedroom with the folder of drawings. The pine needles scrabbling against his bedroom window brought back another memory: searching in the yard for his pet rabbit, which had slipped the latch on its cage again. Worrying, absurdly, that it had crossed over into one of the magical lands in the books Dad read aloud to him and Hunter. And then yearning to be there, in that magical land, away from the sound of his parents arguing in the kitchen.

Dylan closed his eyes now, listening to the wind, and imagined himself in a forest. He smelled damp wood, heard a stream rolling over rocks. One step to the side, maybe, and he'd be there again, in the imaginary land he used to call the Other Place.

He opened his eyes to pine needles splayed across ordinary glass.

He'd ask Hunter about the girl and the cave.

He waited in the den, hoping to catch Hunter when he came home, but later he woke up on the couch with the TV still on, not knowing if he'd only dreamed about the Other Place in the night or if he'd actually gone there. He vaguely remembered chasing his pet rabbit, hearing his parents arguing in the kitchen. So, dream.

Spread across the coffee table were the childhood drawings he'd taken from his mom's closet: lopsided toads and spotted trees and a girl with overlarge eyes. *Does the Girl Queen still wait for me? Does she think I've forgotten?*

He gathered the papers up and stumbled into the kitchen.

Hunter came down while Dylan was still eating breakfast. Dylan was wearing one of Hunter's school blazers—it looked good with the Battle of the Bands T-shirt he'd picked out from the pawnshop a couple of weeks ago. Sort of preppy punk. He hunched over his cereal bowl and hoped his brother wouldn't notice.

Hunter stopped short in the middle of the kitchen and narrowed his eyes at Dylan. Annoyed? Dylan tried to use his vorpal to control what Hunter was seeing. It *snicked* and *pinged* all over the place, like some kind of crazy radar—a sound only Dylan could hear. Hunter glared at his own blazer on Dylan's back. He opened his mouth to say something. Dylan kept his vorpal bouncing off the fridge, off his back, off the fridge.

"You got milk on your shirt," was all Hunter said, and then he went to the fridge.

Dylan smiled. He had pulled it off.

He had a theory about why he could do things like that: He knew everyone had a vorpal, because he could sense them, but most people's vorpals were weak. Dylan's was strong enough to overpower anyone else's. His vorpal could trick theirs into seeing what he wanted them to—when Dylan could control it.

"Does your girlfriend still have that bracelet?" Dylan asked. Got straight to the point; might as well.

Hunter swigged orange juice from the carton with a disinterested air. "It's not yours. I don't know why you think it is."

"Where did you get it?" Dylan asked. "Will you just tell me?" *Tell me where you* really *got it.*

Hunter fumbled with the carton. "I found it," he admitted. Dylan tensed.

"Out in the shed. It must be—" Hunter almost dropped the juice, finally wrestled it back into the overfull fridge. "Something Mom put out there after Dad left, or . . ."

Or I put there myself years ago. "I think it's mine," Dylan said, his skin going hot. "I think it came from . . ." The words whooshed out before he could stop them: "The Other Place."

A sound came from Hunter's brain like *whirrrr-crack!* He turned away; Dylan couldn't see his face. "I thought you would give up on that kind of thing after Dad left." He turned back, smirking. "He used to love that stupid crap."

Heat spread up into Dylan's head, settled behind his eyes. "Is that why you took it—you're still mad about all that? Because he listened to my stories about the Other Place?"

Hunter scowled. "I don't care about Dad."

"You won't even talk to him on the phone."

"Because I don't care."

"He knew the Other Place was real. He knew I could see things."

"That's a nice story." Hunter smirked again. "Just like that story you told me about how Dad asked you to come live with him."

The heat behind Dylan's eyes exploded. "He *did*. It's not like he'd admit it to you. He didn't want you to feel bad. He only had room for one of us on the houseboat."

Hunter glowered at him. "Then why didn't you go?"

"I . . . I didn't want Mom to be sad. You know that."

"Is that also why you got yourself kicked out of Hevlen? You didn't want Mom to be sad? Yeah, you're making life real easy for all of us."

Mom strode into the kitchen, car keys jangling. "What are you two arguing about this time?"

Dylan kept silent. He couldn't win with Mom against Hunter.

Why can't she see what a jerk Hunter is? Another Impossible Question.

Mom eyed the rumpled pillows on the couch in the living room. "Dylan, did you fall asleep doing homework last night? How are you going to keep your grades up if you watch TV while you study?"

"Mom—"

"I'm serious about what I told you last week," she broke in. "If anything goes wrong this semester . . ."

Dylan swallowed. "My homework's right here." He

nodded at the folder full of drawings on the table and hoped she wouldn't look too closely.

Hunter snatched it up.

"Hey!" Dylan grabbed for it, but Hunter's reach was famous.

"This what they teach in public school?" Hunter held up a wobbly drawing of a bird. "They give you the option to write your essays in pictures?"

Dylan stood and tore the paper from Hunter's hand.

"What is all of that?" Mom asked.

"Should we get a first grader to tutor you?" Hunter asked Dylan, snickering.

"Hunter," Mom said in a low warning tone.

"What?" Hunter said. "He had his chance at Hevlen. He blew it."

"Shut up!" Dylan said, hands shaking with anger as he shoved the drawing back into the folder.

"And now you're screwing up public school too. Just like you screw up everything."

Dylan's gut dropped. Nobody thought he'd ever live up to his older brother.

Not even Hunter.

His mom held out her palms. "Stop already. Once upon a time, you two were friends."

"Until Hunter's head got too big for his body," Dylan said. *Until he made varsity. Until he started acting like he wouldn't be caught dead reading any of the books we used to love reading with Dad. Just because he wants to prove that he doesn't care that Dad left, that he never needed Dad anyway.*

Mom put a hand on Hunter's shoulder. "Leave Dylan alone about school."

"You know he cuts all the time," Hunter said.

"You would too if you had to spend your lunch hour hiding from punks," Dylan muttered.

Hunter smirked. "I wouldn't have to." He hooked an arm over the top of the fridge. "Neither would you if you didn't read kids' books in the cafeteria."

Dylan pushed away an ancient memory of Hunter reading to him from a book of fairy tales in the car on the way to the lake house: *"I cannot return home," said the girl as she moved in the water. "I belong here now." And they saw that in place of legs she had a long, glimmering fishtail.*

How could Hunter forget how much we both loved those stories?

"Grab your lunch, Hunter," Mom said, heading for the front door. "And Dylan—no more cutting school." She gave him a hard look and went out.

Hunter slung his backpack over his shoulder and reached into the fridge. "Mom doesn't need any more trouble from you."

Dylan's throat tightened. The memory came again: the fairy-tale book, trees rushing past the car window. And then another flash: the two of them slipping into the Other Place, where a palace waited.

"You remember, don't you?" he asked Hunter. "You remember going there?" He felt his vorpal reaching out even as he said it, searching, searching.

Hunter stood staring at a shelf of produce, his faraway

gaze lit by the fridge's glow. "You think that bracelet's going to help you get back to some magical land?" He slammed the fridge shut. "Trust me, it's not." He turned toward the front door. "Just forget about it, Dylan. Life's better in the real world."

"For some people," Dylan mumbled as Hunter pulled the front door shut behind him.

Dylan left his half-eaten cereal and went out to the city bus stop on the corner. He was supposed to walk to school. Drury High. But he wasn't going to Drury. Everyone mistook him for Hunter; he might as well make the most of it.

He got on the bus thinking of that gold cuff. *Remember me.*

The bus dropped him off at Hevlen late. *Can a person be late if he isn't enrolled?*

He went to philosophy, which was the only class worth going to school for, and wasn't offered at Drury. He had to do stuff like this when his brain went numb from boredom.

Mr. Conrad looked up, brow furrowed, when Dylan walked in. Dylan could sense the man's vorpal whirring weakly like a run-down clock. Dylan stood rooted to the spot and tried to figure out if Conrad recognized him this time. Or if he remembered that Hunter didn't take philosophy this period. "I, uh, have to switch to first period for today, because . . ." Dylan's voice trailed off.

Conrad spoke to the class: "Mr. Yates here is demonstrating the principle of sufficient reason: There must be a reason he has walked in during the middle of my class."

Dylan's face burned.

"But that does not mean his tardiness happened for any

end," Conrad went on. "A reason but not a reason. Have a seat, Mr. Yates."

Dylan hesitated. It took him a moment to figure it out: *He thinks I'm Hunter after all.* He dropped into an empty chair.

Conrad turned back to the board, paused. His vorpal grated against Dylan's bones, searching, and then retreated from Dylan's reach. "Is it you who plays basketball?" he asked Dylan. "I'm told we won the game Saturday." He didn't wait for an answer, just went back to scribbling on the board.

Everyone else in the room still had their gazes trained on Dylan. He could almost hear their thoughts. *Great game. Nice job.*

It wasn't so bad sometimes, being mistaken for Hunter.

In fact, Dylan had to admit to himself the real reason it happened so often: He wanted it to.

During morning break, Dylan found a bench in the quad and started scribbling in his notebook the things he remembered about the Other Place: the drum of bird wings under the tower roof, the whir of wind-up clocks in the hall.

He remembered discovering a carved tree in the palace garden whose branches were really handles that rang hidden bells.

He remembered the maze of boardwalks over marshland, and crouching to rescue a tiny creature all covered in spines, only to have it pierce his hand.

He remembered floating in ocean water so buoyant

he'd half expected to look down and find he'd grown a fish tail, and then wishing he *had* grown a tail, because it would mean he would never leave, that he belonged there.

Something tugged at Dylan's attention. He sensed Chess even before he saw her sitting under the trees at a table, sharing a pair of earbuds with another girl.

He stood up and walked across the quad, feeling drawn to the gold bracelet glinting on her wrist. Could he get it back from her? Probably not, but Hunter could.

That was another thing about Dylan's vorpal—usually he could use it to convince someone who *wanted* to be convinced. And who at Hevlen wouldn't rather be around Hunter than around Dylan? Especially Hunter's girlfriend.

She turned to flash him a knee-weakening smile. Then she froze, yanked the earbud away. The buzz of some pop song with an urgent beat accompanied her sudden confusion.

"Movie tonight, huh?" he blurted, scanning the science fiction film club flyer she held in her hands, hoping to distract her from whatever was making her look at him like that. Kate Chesterfield was listed as the film club's president. Chess? Had to be her.

Chess's gaze narrowed. "*The Day the Earth Stood Still.*"

Dylan's gaze went to the gold band that had slid down her arm. "You're wearing the bracelet."

She put a protective hand over it, scrutinized Dylan. He could hear her vorpal, undeveloped as it was, *snick-snick-snick*. Why were everyone else's vorpals so much weaker than Dylan's? Impossible to say. Maybe it ran in families—

his brother's was stronger than most, but he never used it, didn't really know how.

"You're Hunter's brother." She tilted her head to one side. "From the pawnshop."

"Dylan," he said, a bit deflated.

"Took me a minute to recognize you."

Dylan shifted his stance. Well, it had *almost* worked. He looked at the bracelet. He could still ask for it back—she'd been nervous about taking it from the shop.

An image popped into Dylan's head: Chess smiling at him, the gold robot mask pushed up over her dark hair. Like a matching set, mask and bracelet.

He tore his gaze away from her and pointed to the flyer. "Which appendage will it cost me to get into your club?"

"What?"

"Arm? Leg? I'm prepared to give both."

She looked him over.

"You're appraising them," he said, shifting nervously under her gaze.

"No, it's just . . ." She gave him that same curious look she'd given him in the pawnshop. Same glint in her eyes. His legs wobbled. "I thought you didn't go to Hevlen anymore."

Dylan's stomach tightened. He looked down at his uniform—his brother's uniform, pants and blazer, rolled at the hems and cuffs. Plus the Battle of the Bands shirt from the pawnshop, definitely a violation of the dress code. Was it the shirt that had given him away? Hunter never wore anything from the shop—he couldn't be sure it hadn't been pawned by someone from school. He was careful about that kind of thing.

Chess was still looking at him, waiting for him to say something. At any minute he might offer her a shop discount on obscure movie paraphernalia out of sheer awkwardness. He might start quoting *Metropolis*. Now that he thought about it, he already was. It was a silent movie.

He cleared his throat and studied the flyer for *The Day the Earth Stood Still*. "Are you showing the original or the one with Keanu Reeves?"

"Do you have to ask?"

Dylan laughed. "Maybe they should have cast him as the robot." He tweaked his neck and made his face into a blank mask, Keanu-style. "*The Day Keanu Reeves Stood Still.*"

Chess smiled, a slow smile that had Dylan holding his breath to see how it would end. She tilted her head to the side. "Seven o'clock. In the auditorium."

She turned back to her friend. Dylan eyed the bracelet still glinting on her wrist. Later, maybe.

His stomach rumbled. He shivered against the chill coming off the gurgling fountain—

Since when had there been a fountain around here? He turned toward the cafeteria.

The building was gone.

And the crowds of students.

The burble of water was a stream and he was in a wood.

But only for one more step, and then the buildings returned, with the deafening noise from the crowd. Dylan jerked to a stop, as if doused with a bucket of water. The mineral smell of cold dirt lingered. But the wood was gone.

He gasped for air, then doubled over with his hands on his knees. His heart was a skittering rabbit.

The Other Place. He'd stepped in for a moment, and then stepped right out again. Was that what had happened?

His skin prickled in the cold.

Rain drummed on the city bus window later that afternoon on his way home from the public library. Dylan sat in the back, whipping through the pages of a tattered book, desperately looking for the Girl Queen. He found a woodcut illustration called "The Fish-Girl." *How do I get back there?* he asked her. As though a picture could answer.

Why is it so hard? he wondered. *What's keeping me locked out?*

In *The Blue Fairy Book,* rewards always went to the virtuous, to the pure of heart. *Maybe that's my trouble.* He hadn't exactly been virtuous these past months: lying, cheating, pretending.

He'd been looking for his rabbit the first time he'd found the Other Place, so maybe *that* was the key: You had to look for something lost. But it wasn't *only* that he'd been looking for something lost.

He'd also desperately needed to get away.

His parents had been arguing. Mom was angry at Dad for disappearing again, instead of being happy to have him home. Whenever they shouted at each other, Dylan would wish for someplace nicer. And then it would appear: the Other Place.

Like a dream.

Or a hallucination.

Am I going crazy?

He could see the Girl Queen so clearly in his mind: a half elf, winter-pale. Not perched on a throne, but out in the trees, climbing just as well as his brother could climb the trees behind their house. Scolding Dylan in a language he didn't know but a tone he could understand—*Higher, higher!* Swinging by her knees, teasing him for being afraid. Her hair hanging down, a shivering flame inverted.

Someone leaned over his seat. "Fast reader."

Dylan looked up. He recognized a girl he'd gone to elementary school with. The hood of her dingy anorak framed her face so that she looked as little like a queen as possible. The effect was so jarring that Dylan only stared dumbly.

"I heard a rumor you were going to Drury this year," she said.

Dylan's brain finally started working again. "True story," he said.

"How come I never see you around?" Her cheeks were pink with the cold. Dylan remembered a brief crush, fourth grade. Some incident involving his sticking an eraser into her ear. He prayed she didn't remember. "Are you on work release?"

"Something like that," Dylan said. Better than telling her he'd cut school to go to philosophy class at Hevlen in the morning and hang out at the public library all afternoon.

"Me too." She waved a hand at her black pants, which Dylan supposed was part of some work uniform. "What book is that? Looks ancient."

Dylan clapped it shut. "They've got this whole collection of rare books at Washington State that they'll mail to the local branch."

She blinked. "Cool. Is that where you work—the library?"

"I, uh . . . I spend a lot of time there."

"I work at the pet store downtown. The one with the weird snakes and exotic birds? I basically just clean up all kinds of abnormal animal crap. You should come by and see these really freaky giant lizards we've got. Monitors."

"Yeah, I've seen them." Dylan gazed out past the raindrops at shining sidewalks sliding past. "I used to go in that shop as a kid and try to draw them. All my old school artwork looks like it was copied from cave paintings of dinosaurs."

He turned back to find her confused expression.

"That place used to be a comic shop when we were kids," she said. "The pet store moved in only a few years ago."

Dylan gripped the rail, suddenly unsteady. "You sure?" His heart pounded. Did that mean he'd seen those animals in the Other Place? He reached up and yanked the cord. "Uh, this is my stop." The cord was wet. No, his palms were sweating.

The girl moved aside to let Dylan stand. "Hey, you want to go to a party Friday?" she asked. "Bunch of Drury kids, no tie needed." She flashed a smile.

Dylan turned toward the door as the bus lurched to a stop.

"Or do you have plans with your Hevlen friends?" the girl asked.

"No, no plans." He imagined calling them up: *Hey, guys, remember me? The guy who got kicked out?* Then he imagined himself at a basement party with Drury kids. *Yeah, I left Hevlen. I guess they got sick of me—must have been all those math awards.*

"It's at that puke-green house behind the high school," the girl said. "You know the one?"

Dylan just nodded, waited for the door to *whoosh* open, and then barreled down the steps. He crossed the street toward his house, then froze. His mom had just stepped out onto the porch. "What are you doing home so early?" she asked.

Dylan tucked the fish-girl book behind his back so his mom wouldn't see it. He definitely couldn't tell her he'd gone to the library instead of to Drury. "Fast learner?" he tried.

His mom glowered at him. Clearly not in a joking mood.

"Early release day," Dylan said quickly. He reached tentatively with his vorpal and tried to gauge whether she believed him. Maybe they could go for fish and chips, just the two of them. It'd been ages since they'd done anything like that. *Here's an Impossible Question: How does a mom forget she has* two *sons?*

"If I find out you're still cutting classes—"

"I know, Mom."

"—you're off to your dad's, I don't care at which end of Puget Sound he's got that houseboat parked."

"Okay." Dylan rubbed a hand over his eyes. They'd had this conversation one too many times.

His mom studied him in silence for a moment. Her vorpal ticked back and forth like a metronome. "I just came home to take Hunter to the doctor," she said. "And now I'm heading back to the pawnshop."

No fish and chips, then. "They find a way to stop his ego from swelling?"

"Very funny. Jumper's knee. And he's fine," she added in a way that said Dylan should have asked. She walked past him toward the car Dylan hadn't noticed. But then she stopped, turned to look at the book in Dylan's hand.

Dylan felt a surge of panic—she'd freak if she found out where he'd been all afternoon. He imagined the novel as a chemistry textbook and tried to send the same thought out to her.

"You know what?" she said, moving her eyes to Dylan's face. She chewed her lip. "You get a good report card this semester, maybe we'll go to the lake for Thanksgiving."

The book felt heavy as lead now. Dylan squashed his rising guilt. He nodded, and then she headed to the car.

As he stepped into his living room, he squeezed his eyes shut like he sometimes did when he walked into a room, and prayed he would step into a different world.

He opened his eyes to find darkness.

The air was close and warm and stale. This wasn't his

living room—where was he? He reached out and knocked his elbow against wood, brushed his hands over linen and soft velvet. A crack of light showed between double doors. He was trapped in a wardrobe.

He breathed in. He knew that smell—*her,* the Girl Queen. These were her clothes, her wardrobe. He was in the palace. In the Other Place.

"Hello?" he called, and pushed at the doors. Locked. He pounded his fists on the wood. "Let me out!" He was like a maniac. "I'm here! I'm here! Let me out!" She would be there any moment, her face glowing with surprise at seeing him. "Let me out!"

Finally—footsteps. Rushing to meet him. It was her. The doors shuddered.

Dylan blinked in the yellow light of the living room. The wardrobe was gone. He was only scrabbling at the inside of his own front door.

Hunter eyed him from a doorway upstairs. "Where'd *you* come from?"

Dylan collapsed against the wall and clenched his eyes shut again. He reached out with his vorpal. He flung out his hand in search of a wardrobe door, hanging clothes. Nothing.

"Are you drunk?" Hunter asked. "It's two o'clock. And shouldn't you be at school?"

"Leave me alone."

"I want my blazer back."

Dylan shrugged it off and hurled it up over the banister.

Hunter snatched it from the railing, held it out in his fist.

"Stop doing that. Stop pretending to be me." He went back into his bedroom.

Dylan's mouth went dry. Hunter knew? He wiped his sweaty palms on his pants—Hunter's pants—and then realized he had lost the library book, the one with the fish-girl illustration. Dropped it outside or left it in the Other Place? He checked the porch—wasn't there. His head felt muffled, confused. *How did Hunter know?* He went up to his brother's room.

It was cluttered with half-disassembled junk from the shop—DVD players and microwaves waiting to be repaired. Hunter sat at his desk, fiddling with a dinosaur of a radio that looked like it had time-traveled there from some unchronicled era. At his elbow was a framed photo of Chess squinting against the sunlight. A UW Huskies poster overhead was stuck with so many thumbtacks that Dylan wondered if Hunter was afraid it'd be stolen. Then again, he'd caught on to the fact that Dylan had borrowed his clothes, so maybe that wasn't such a crazy idea.

Hunter jerked on some hazardous-looking wiring. "What do you want?"

"Did Chess tell you I was at Hevlen today?" Dylan asked.

"Chess?" Hunter looked up, his screwdriver clutched like a dagger.

"That I was wearing your blazer and . . ." Dylan looked down at the pants he was wearing.

Hunter seemed to notice them for the first time. His gaze darkened. "Did you think I wouldn't hear about Conrad's class?"

Dylan's stomach dropped.

"Why do you do that?" Hunter went on. "Everyone thinks you're crazy."

A wave of dizziness hit Dylan. They knew? They had all noticed he wasn't Hunter? He put a hand against the door frame to steady himself. "Sometimes . . . sometimes people think I'm you. Because of—"

Hunter stood, grabbed the blazer he'd discarded on the bed. "Because you wear my clothes? Funny how that works."

Dylan shook his head. "It's more than that. You know it's more."

The silence was thick with Hunter's contempt. "Your vorpal." He crossed his arms.

It sounded so stupid coming out of Hunter's mouth. *It always sounds stupid.* Vorpals, a girl queen waiting for him in a palace—it sounded crazy.

"You've got to stop, Dylan." Hunter jostled his arm. "Come back to reality."

Dylan jerked away. "I'm not crazy."

"Dad really screwed you up, didn't he? Letting you believe all that stuff was real."

Dylan felt the cold sting of windy Alki Beach, remembered the day he'd asked Dad the Last Impossible Question. The Impossible Question that had changed everything between them. And then right afterward, when Dylan had gone to the shed, hidden the bracelet . . .

He pushed the memory away. "It *is* real. Even Conrad—"

"Conrad is a thousand years old," Hunter said with a

snort. "He doesn't know who's supposed to be in the class and who got kicked out of school for *cheating on a stats final.*"

Dylan winced.

"Why *did* you cheat, Dylan?" Hunter sounded plaintive, almost angry. "You're smarter than most of the kids in that school. Dad was so proud of you—came to all of your math competitions before you left Hevlen," Hunter said. "He's never even come to any of my basketball games."

Wrong, Dylan thought.

At Alki Beach five years ago, Dylan had watched the boats and told Dad about the sails he'd seen along the river in the Other Place: shimmering membranes made from dragon wings. *Mom doesn't like to hear about those things,* he'd told Dad. *Can't I come live with you instead?*

The Last Impossible Question.

Dad's whole face had changed, shifted like sand trickling down a steep bank. *Not everyone's fit to take care of a kid, Dylan. You're better off with Mom.* Dad's voice was like water flooding his eardrums, like a wave crashing over his head.

It's time to give up those stories anyway. None of it's real. You know that, right?

"I hated those math competitions," Dylan said, his throat raw. "They were all Mom's idea. I never wanted Dad to come."

Hunter shook his head. "What *do* you want, Dylan?" The air hummed, full of Hunter's exasperation. Maybe it was just the radio. "What will make you stop this? *Tell* me, I'll *give* it to you."

Dylan's gaze went to the photo of Chess.

Hunter noticed. He pushed Dylan against the door frame. "You're living in a fantasy world."

Dylan caught a metallic glint of fear in Hunter's eyes, even though Dylan was the one with a doorjamb pressed against his backbone. *Because he knows my vorpal is stronger than his.*

Unless they were right, Dad and Hunter. Unless it was all in his head.

Dylan suddenly couldn't catch his breath. He thought he could feel his vorpal like an extra organ, churning next to other worthless organs—appendix, gall bladder. But he was afraid to use it, afraid that if he tried, it wouldn't be there, that he was fooling himself after all.

Hunter still loomed over him. "All of this crap you're pulling—getting kicked out of school—can't you see what you're doing to yourself?"

"Can't you," Dylan pleaded, "can't you just admit that you remember where we went when we were kids?"

Hunter's jaw tightened. His vorpal ground like stuck machinery. "You know what I remember?"

Just say it. Tell me you remember. I didn't make it all up. Please.

"I remember you pretending."

Dylan thought his lungs might be going flat. He searched Hunter's face, trying to figure out whether to believe him. He couldn't decide.

He turned toward the stairs.

"Dylan?" Hunter said. "Stay away from Chess."

= ≠ =

Dylan couldn't help himself—he sneaked out of the house and went to the film club that night.

"Klaatu barada nikto," he said to Chess at the door to the auditorium, just like in the movie. He jammed his hands into his jacket pockets. Why did he always have to be so weird?

"Aren't you clever—a line from *The Day the Earth Stood Still.*" Chess still wore her uniform, plus a fleece cap that made her eyes seem bigger and brighter, even in the low light. The bracelet peeked out from under her jacket sleeve, but Dylan hardly thought about it: Her vorpal was pulsing candy colors, making halos tremble at the edge of his vision.

He knew he was ridiculous for thinking about vorpals at all. But he couldn't help it. He could swear her vorpal was radiating happiness, reaching out to him with fingers of heat.

"You do this every week?" he asked.

"Yeah, it's fun. Let's grab seats."

She led him to the front row.

After they sat down, she leaned close. "Besides, Tuesdays are the nights my parents always render due benevolence, so I'd rather not be at home to see them flirting." She rolled her eyes.

He turned the phrase over in his mind, then shoved his hands in his pockets, embarrassed. "What's that from, Shakespeare?"

"King James."

"Right, that's a Shakespeare play."

She laughed. "You're funny."

He realized his mistake—*the King James Bible, dummy.* But she thought he was funny. Someone passed him a bowl of M&M's. "Does Hunter ever come to these things?"

"Robots don't appeal to him."

"Not even *Blade Runner*? Acid rain, shady corporations?"

"He thinks it's weird that Harrison Ford falls in love with a girl who's not real." She elbowed him. "He's *your* brother. Shouldn't you know?"

Dylan cracked an M&M between his teeth.

"I think *Blade Runner*'s romantic," Chess went on. But she was giving him that slow smile, so he didn't know if she was being serious.

Someone started up the projector.

"What would you want with a guy who can't appreciate *Blade Runner*?" Dylan asked.

"I don't date him for his taste in movies," Chess said.

"So why do you date him?" Dumb question—Dylan had seen how all the cheerleaders crowded Hunter after a game, how girls fawned when Hunter did something as mundane as order a cheeseburger.

But Chess took a second to think about it. She looked up at the ceiling. "In the movies, the best guys to fall in love with are always a little sad."

Dylan snorted. "What does Hunter have to be sad about?"

"Don't know. But he always seems like he's trying to make up for something, you know?"

An image came to Dylan's mind of Hunter jabbing at the old radio, sweating over something that would never work again. "No, I don't know."

Chess shrugged. "Like he lost something."

Dylan got a weird feeling in his stomach.

"Speaking of—what happened to your uniform?" Chess gave him a playful smirk.

Dylan ducked his head. He still hadn't explained to her why he'd been at Hevlen today. "I realized they can't actually dock me points if I'm not enrolled here, so I figured it was safe to stop wearing it."

She looked at him sidelong. "Why did you come tonight? If you're not enrolled here?"

"You bought all the good movies from the shop, so now I have to come here to watch them," he joked.

Her smile went crooked.

She thinks you're weird, Dylan told himself. *She probably heard about you sneaking into philosophy class.*

The movie started. Dylan trained his eyes on the screen.

Chess's gaze lingered on him a moment longer, her vorpal glowing bright in the dark room. Like the Girl Queen in the forest, standing in a shaft of sunlight that lent her an otherworldly glow.

Dylan tried to concentrate on the movie, but Chess glimmered in the corner of his vision the whole time. He brushed his shoulder against hers and she leaned closer. Solid, warm. He slid his hand into hers, thinking, *I'm Hunter, I'm just Hunter.*

She smiled and leaned farther into him. "My mom

knows I'm going to hang out at your shop tomorrow—she wants to come by and pretend to look at the jewelry so she can spy," Chess said, squeezing his hand.

Dylan stiffened. It had worked. He pulled his hand away, disgust curling his stomach.

Chess glanced at him. "What?"

"Nothing."

A flush crept over her face that he could see even in the dim light. She must have realized he wasn't Hunter. She leaned away, probably telling herself that the movie had made her forget who was sitting next to her.

Dylan shoved his shaking hands under his legs. *Why did I do that?* He hadn't thought it would really work. He'd only wanted to hold her hand.

He glanced at her again, but her gaze was glued to the screen.

After the movie was over and Chess had lifted the pull-down screen, Dylan carried the crate of leftover root beers to Chess's Subaru. They were pretending nothing had happened. Chess argued with herself about sentient robots as if Dylan were only an audience.

He interrupted her. "Do you think another world could exist right next to ours?"

Chess unlocked the car. "Are we talking *The Matrix*—our world is just a dream, there's another world beyond it?"

"More like different realities, but each one is real." He set the crate in the backseat. "Or maybe there's another world and it's not real but you can still go there. Does that even make sense?"

She nodded. *"Inception."*

"But in *Inception,* they weren't physically going anywhere. Everything that happened was just in someone's head." He watched his breath come out in streams of vapor. He was freezing cold.

She reached for the door handle. "Get in."

He hesitated. They both shuffled awkwardly.

"Go ahead—it's like an alternate world in there when you blast the heat," Chess said with a smirk.

He slid into the passenger seat. "Did you ever read the Narnia books? Or Harry Potter?"

"Sure." She turned on the engine but didn't put the car into gear.

"Well, that's what I mean about other worlds."

"I hadn't thought of Narnia as an alternate universe. More like . . . a fairy-tale land."

Dylan tried to look at the world as someone from the past would, as if he were in some futuristic movie. The half-frosted windshield. The dashboard display, all lit-up dials and slide-down switches. They could be wonders if you considered them with the right frame of mind. This could be a fairy-tale land, to someone.

"Do you think we're too old for Narnia?" he asked. "Or anyplace like that? Fairy-tale lands?"

"Reading about magic's not much different from watching movies about robots and replicants, I guess."

"No, I mean do you think we're too old to be allowed to go there? In stories like that—in fairy tales—you have be *pure of heart.*"

She narrowed her eyes at him, smiling. "Are you trying to tell me something about your intentions with me?"

Dylan felt a flush creeping up his neck. "I just meant . . ."

She brushed a hand over his arm. "I heard why you had to leave Hevlen."

He tensed. "About how I stole the answer key for the final exam." He turned toward the window, saw only his dark reflection. "That was dumb. I've been doing a lot of dumb stuff ever since . . ."

"Like what?"

"Like . . . taking my brother's stuff." *And hanging out with my brother's girlfriend.* His arm still tingled where she had touched him. "Not exactly pure of heart." He turned back to find her staring at him.

She pulled up her sleeve to show the gold bracelet. "Is this why you came tonight? You wanted the bracelet?"

Dylan still couldn't make up his mind—was it only someone's lost bracelet or was it a relic from another land? A land no one else could see. A land that couldn't possibly exist.

He ran his fingers over the gold, almost touched her skin. His whole hand was tingling. Was it really so bad, to be here in the real world? With a girl he knew wasn't imaginary? "No, I didn't come for this," he said to Chess.

"Something else of Hunter's, then." Her gaze was piercing.

Dylan briefly considered the possibility that she could see straight through his skull to his thoughts.

She moved her hand closer to his on the seat. Inviting him to hold it? That seemed like a crazy idea.

How do you know if a girl likes you? The most Impossible Question of all.

"Why *did* you come?" she went on. "Are you here from the future to warn me of impending doom?"

Her smiled reeled him in. Their fingers touched. He finally put his hand on hers. "I've been looking for something," he said. "But like an idiot I don't know what it is." He leaned over and kissed her.

She pressed the front of her shoulder into his and kissed him back. Hot air roared in his ear. It was the sound of a storm or a spell, even though it was just the heating vent. The warmth crept down to his toes, into his numb fingers.

"I don't want a girl who's not real," he said, as if that were a good explanation for kissing someone else's girlfriend. *I don't want the Girl Queen, I want you.*

She looked puzzled, then smiled anyway. "It worked for Harrison Ford."

"Not in the director's cut."

Her smile faded. She put the car into gear. "In that version, he wasn't real either."

The next evening, the wind rattled the windows in Dylan's house as though calling to him, but he shut out thoughts of other worlds. Chess would be at the pawnshop. She'd said so last night at the film club. Dylan grabbed a Narnia book, thinking she might like to borrow it, and tucked his earnings into his pocket; he had enough to finally buy those boots he'd been eyeing. He jogged downstairs, wondering if Chess was at the shop already.

Mom was in the kitchen. He thought she was supposed to be at a PTA thing while Hunter ran the shop. She turned as he came in, one hand plastered over her forehead.

"Where have you been all day?" Her voice trembled.

Dylan sensed trouble. He shrank against the counter. "School."

"Really? Which school? Because I called Drury today to find out how many absences you have."

Dylan's skin went cold with dread.

"They told me they don't have any record of a Dylan Yates enrolled there."

The book in Dylan's hand almost slipped free. He tucked it under his trembling arm.

"Which is funny because I remember filling out the paperwork. What did you do, pull yourself out somehow?" Her gaze drilled into him. "What have you been doing the past two months?"

Dylan looked down at the floor. *Studying on my own, in the library. Sneaking into Hevlen.*

"I told you, Dylan, I warned you that if you couldn't make it work at Drury—"

"I'm sorry," he said quietly.

She crossed her arms. "Too late. I called your dad."

Dylan's heart jerked sideways. "He doesn't have room for me on the houseboat."

"He'll *make* room."

Dylan gave her a pleading look he knew wouldn't work. To his surprise, Mom's face softened. She brushed her thumb over Dylan's brow. "Is that what this is all about?"

she asked. "You just wanted to live with your dad?"

Dylan turned to stone. Once he had wanted to live with Dad, a long time ago. But now . . .

Mom sighed. "You remind me a lot of him."

Because we're both screwups?

"He has a restless mind, like you," Mom said. "I thought the math team would be good for you, would help ground you."

Dylan turned from stone to lead. "Then why didn't you ever come to any of my competitions?"

Mom twitched back in surprise. "That was your dad's thing. He was so proud of how much you'd grown up—"

"But I hated math team! You're the one who made me join. I knew you'd never let me quit unless . . ." *Unless I cheated on my stats final and got kicked off the team. But then I got kicked out of school instead.*

He could hear the whir of Mom's thoughts behind her eyes, the buzz of her consternation. "Everything's going to be fine," she said, her voice strained. "This will be your chance to start over."

"I *can't* go to Dad's," he said. "Please, Mom."

Don't you want me to be your son anymore? Why don't you love me like you love Hunter?

"Dad's expecting you at the bus—"

Dylan was out the door before she finished. Down the walk in eight quick steps. What had he done? He'd been so stupid.

No, crazy. He was losing it, had lost it. Sneaking into Hevlen, searching for a fantasy land.

But he'd tried before to prove to Mom that he wasn't a screwup, and she'd never even come to his competitions. He'd tried to forget about the Other Place like Dad wanted him to, but that only meant he was left with nothing.

Even Hunter thought he was a loser. Hunter knew, somehow, that Dad had never wanted Dylan to come live on the houseboat. And he knew Dylan was hurt enough to lie about it.

The wind chilled his cheeks, his bare arms. The trees along the street groaned. He rubbed his hands over his face. He didn't want to live on a boat, and he definitely didn't want to live with Dad. Not after that day at Alki Beach, the way Dad had made him feel. *It's time to give up those stories anyway. None of it's real. You know that, right? You're not a hero rescuing some girl queen.*

Dylan shut out Dad's voice. He could go to the lake, maybe. He and Hunter had always said they'd go live there someday. That they'd sleep right in the sand, on the man-made beach. *Some people do that,* his brother had once told him, *sleep wherever they get tired at the end of the day, in places where it's really warm.* Just like in fantasy novels, where there always seemed be a pile of hay or some springy grass and a sky full of stars overhead.

He still had the boot money in his pocket. Forget the boots, he'd have to spend it on a bus ticket now. Dylan could go to the lake, try to get his head straightened out for a little while.

He could even get a job at the sandwich place they always ate at.

He realized he was heading for the pawnshop, to where he knew Chess would be tonight. He let his feet take him there.

Through the glass front he saw her inside, rummaging through a cardboard box that had left a wide trail through the dust on the floor. His heart went brittle at the sight of her. He reached for the door handle.

"Forget the cash?" Chess said without looking up. "That bagel place should keep a tab for you. You probably account for about half their business."

She thought he was Hunter again.

"Hey, don't forget my mom's stopping by later," she said. "Best behavior, okay?"

She walked over to him, and Dylan didn't know if she realized her mistake or not. He didn't want her to. "I don't have bagels," he said weakly.

"Don't sound so sad about it." She wrapped an arm around his waist.

Dylan's heart sped up.

"Hey, you brought one of the books I asked about," Chess said.

She'd asked about it? "Yeah," Dylan said absently, setting the Narnia book on the counter. He could think of little else than her hand on his hip. He prayed she wouldn't realize her mistake.

Chess gestured at the cardboard box. "I picked this up at a garage sale. Serious bargain. It's all stuff you could make a profit on, I swear."

She held out a battered fedora. "For your brother."

"My brother?"

"Trust me, it's perfect for Dylan. Straight out of Indiana Jones." She stuck it on her head, tilted it over one eye. "He's got to be into that."

Dylan felt weak all over. All he could manage to say was "Not the Crystal Skull one."

"That one's crap compared to *Temple of Doom*."

Dylan got a sudden flash of Hunter sprawled next to him on the corduroy couch in their living room, humming along to the theme that would stick in Dylan's head for the rest of the day. Back when Hunter would still watch movies like that with him.

"Shit, what a title." Dylan let out a strangled laugh. Chess laughed with him.

"Don't start," she said. "You have no taste in movies."

Dylan spotted Hunter coming up the sidewalk with a paper bag in hand. The bus at the curb flashed *Greyhound Station*. Dylan reached for the money in his pocket, his saved-up earnings. He could give it to Hunter, use his vorpal to convince *him* to go to the lake, just for a little while.

He imagined going to philosophy every morning in Hunter's place, blowing off basketball practice to hang out with Chess. Just for a few days, a week. His vorpal could handle it if he tried a little harder.

Outside on the sidewalk, Hunter paused and gave the bus a wistful look.

Dylan's mouth went dry. Had *he* made Hunter do that?

He backed off, backed right into a shelf, scuttled along the length of it until he was hidden from the window.

"Hunter?" Chess called from the front of the shop.

The door *whooshed* shut. Hunter clutched the bag of bagels. Dylan used his vorpal to make Hunter forget them, to make Chess not see them so she wouldn't get confused.

"You didn't pay money for that, did you?" Hunter asked, grimacing at the hat on the counter. "I don't think anyone will buy it."

"It's not to sell," Chess said. "And yes, some people would buy it."

Hunter shrugged. "I'll pretend you're making sense."

"Is your brother coming by today?" Chess asked as Hunter moved to put the hat on a stand.

"Probably not. I heard my mom saying something about making him go live with my dad." He walked back over to her. "Don't look so shocked. I told you he's been cutting school like every day."

Hunter slid his hand over her arm. Chess stepped back, her mouth twisting.

"Were you wearing a different shirt earlier?" she asked.

Hunter looked down, as though he needed to check. "No."

Dylan glanced down at his own shirt, the one Chess must have been remembering.

Chess chewed her fingernails. Her eyes were cobwebbed with confusion.

"What's wrong?" Hunter asked.

"A minute ago you were…" Chess studied Hunter's face. She looked for a moment as though she didn't recognize him. As though she'd forgotten the difference between him and Dylan. "You seem different. Something's missing."

Hunter's gaze went to the display under the counter, as if Chess were talking about the inventory.

In between shelves of hat boxes and bicycle parts, Dylan felt a hopeful stir. It was him Chess was missing. He looked at the Narnia book on the counter. A book Chess had asked for because Dylan had mentioned it.

"Do you think Dylan will be okay?" Chess asked Hunter. "Couldn't you talk to your mom, see if she'll let him stay and try again at school?"

Blood roared in Dylan's ears. He thought of the frosted windshield of Chess's car, the heater thawing his cold hands. He had kissed her. She hadn't stopped him. She'd made a joke after he'd made that *Blade Runner* reference, as though kissing were a normal part of any conversation. She seemed to like it. To like *him,* not him-pretending-to-be-Hunter.

Hunter turned away from Chess with a glower. "Doubt I could change my mom's mind," he grunted. He shoved boxes out of the way and sent others zooming toward the back room with superhuman strength. Dylan realized the boxes were empty.

"Where did these bagels come from?" Hunter asked, glaring at the bag on the counter. Dylan had made Hunter forget all about them.

Dylan's vorpal was strong today. He really could make Hunter walk to the bus station. He could make Chess forget about him, at least for a little while. Dylan might never get back to the Other Place, but he could still use his vorpal.

He could use it to get what he wanted here in the real world.

The wind-chime voice of the Girl Queen came back to him, speaking words he didn't understand. He would never see her again. Chess was all he had of happiness.

Dylan maneuvered through the shelves toward the front of the store. He stopped as Chess spoke again to Hunter: "Here, I've borrowed this way longer than I meant to," she said.

From behind a stack of DVD players, Dylan saw Chess tug up her jacket sleeve and pull the gold bracelet off her wrist.

Hunter took it from her, turned it over in his hands.

"What's wrong?" Chess asked. "Is it scratched?"

"No, it's just . . ." Hunter shook his head, cleared the foggy look from his eyes. "It reminds me of this place Dylan and I used to visit when we were kids."

Some invisible hand wrenched the wiring in Dylan's chest.

Chess looked confused. "Not the lake?"

"Somewhere else." Hunter seemed a million miles away. "It doesn't matter. We haven't been there in a long time."

Dylan's muscles all went rigid.

"I keep thinking I'll get back there someday, but . . ."

It's real, Dylan thought. *I was right.*

Hunter slid the bracelet onto his wrist. He did it so easily, it was clear he'd done it a million times before.

You found that bracelet ages ago and hid it from me, Dylan realized. *You thought it could get you back to the Other Place.*

But it would never work. Hunter's vorpal wasn't strong

enough. It wasn't anywhere near as strong as Dylan's. Dylan could feel Hunter's vorpal even now and it was weak as water.

He'll never get back there.

How often had Hunter gone there when they were kids? Two, three times? Dylan's stomach was a steel clamp. He couldn't count the times he himself had gone.

And every time, he'd come back with a million stories for Dad. Dad would eat it up, would tell him he had a special gift. Hunter could never compete with that, didn't even try.

It seemed so obvious now. All these years Hunter had been trying to make up for what he had missed out on. With basketball, with girls.

With Chess.

Dylan bumped against the tower of DVD players. Chess whirled at the sound, spotted him.

Dylan wielded his vorpal, strong as a sword. *You don't know me.*

"Oh, I didn't hear anyone come in," Chess said. "What are you looking for?" Her gaze was bland, disinterested. She didn't know him.

Dylan opened his mouth, but nothing came out. Hunter had taken off the bracelet and was shoving it into the display. Dylan pointed to it. "How much is that?"

Hunter's gaze slid over Dylan. "I could negotiate. Someone else wanted me to hold it, but—" The smallest line of confusion appeared between his brows.

Dylan's gone, Dylan thought at Chess. *He's not coming*

back. You've got Hunter and he's got you and Dylan's long gone. He thought it with his vorpal—*snick-snick-snick.*

"He left, didn't he?" Chess said. "Went out on the bus. I don't think he's coming back."

"You can buy it if you want," Hunter said. "He's not coming back for it."

Dylan reached for the money in his pocket. He should use it for a bus ticket. He should forget about the bracelet, forget the Other Place. He would go live with Dad, start over. No more fairy tales, no more screwing up.

Hunter was frowning at him. Figuring out who he was? No, just waiting for an answer.

I should tell him about the basketball game, Dylan thought. *Tell him Dad was there.* But how could he? *Hunter thinks I'm a stranger right now.*

He opened his mouth, trying to figure out what to say. But all that came out was "Yeah, I'll buy it." He put his cash on the counter.

"You want to look at it first?" Hunter said, holding out the bracelet.

Dylan took it and turned toward the door. He wasn't going to his dad's. He couldn't. The most he could do was take the bracelet away and help Hunter forget about the Other Place. Help him be happy in the real world like Dylan had never managed to be.

"Hey, wait!" Hunter called.

Dylan held his breath as he walked out of the shop. The bell on the door tinkled.

It went on tinkling, like water over rocks.

And on and on—

Dylan looked up. A stream cut across his path, trickling over mossy rocks. A canopy of sun-lit leaves shuffled overhead. His breath whooshed out.

The lattice of branches all but hid a gold-roofed palace. Through a tunnel in the trees—some engineered walkway—Dylan glimpsed a distant city of glass like a gathering of soap bubbles. The cold air pricked his lungs, his eyes.

The Other Place.

"Hello?" came a voice.

Dylan spun. It was her. A bolt of electricity shot through him. She was taller and full of new angles, but with the same pale-water hair and glass-smooth skin. She'd come to meet him. She hadn't forgotten.

"You came through yesterday, didn't you?" she said. "And before that, of course—a long time ago. I remember you."

The air seemed to bend around her as though she accepted obeisance even from molecules. Her eyes were blue as ice. Dylan wondered briefly if they changed color when she was warm, if there was as much magic to her as he remembered.

She crept closer, as though afraid to scare a skittish animal. "Do you know where you are?"

It was cold out in the wood. Frigid mud seeped into his sneakers. There wasn't the rain-and-salt smell of Seattle. "The Other Place." *How can it be true? How did I get here?* He had about a million more Impossible Questions, too many to ask.

Her vorpal was all shifting puzzle pieces. "The . . . ?"

"I'm too old," Dylan blurted. "I shouldn't have been able to come back. I'm too . . ."

He'd forgiven Hunter. In his own way—by taking the bracelet. That was why he'd been able to come. Some rotten core had lifted out of his heart.

"Will they let me stay?" His voice was plaintive, like a child's. *Can't I come live with you?* An Impossible Question, but she didn't seem to mind.

"No one can make you leave," she said, and gripped his hand as if to anchor him. Her vorpal was strong, and he felt a ripple of sadness pass from it into his skin when she spoke again: "Do you remember me?"

She thought he'd forgotten. "I've been looking for you, trying to get back here," he said.

She threw her arms around his shoulders. "And I've looked for you. The same way we once looked for gold in river gravel, for something we never expected to find. But now you've finally come again."

She'd learned so many new words since he'd last seen her, when he'd taught her his language in bits and pieces. *How did she learn to say all of that?*

She stepped back and her vorpal was a wave of brightening air. "Others from here have gone to your world, but they never saw you. I would have gone if I could have. They've been to your world many times."

"When? I didn't know it worked that way."

"Before you ever came here," she explained. "Years before. We discovered . . . a leak. Where our two worlds press together, energy flows from your world into ours. It led us to you."

He shook his head, unable to take it all in. "But why would you want to leave a magical kingdom for sidewalks and trash cans?"

She laughed and pulled him by the hand through the trees. "Because we are curious about your world. Like you were about ours when you were a boy."

She led him along the bank of the stream. A map unfurled in his mind: The stream led to a river, to a sunlit cave where he'd seen treasures stored. It fed other streams that ribboned through the forest, through secret glades where he'd once built forts out of fallen logs. Farther along were the marshes covered with boardwalk mazes intricate enough to leave any adventurer as dizzy as Dylan felt now.

"Do you remember *everything*?" she asked him. "The den we carved in the bank of the stream? Eating berries there until the rain brought our mud ceiling down around us?"

She laughed again, then stopped and turned to him. "You're the first from your world to come here. You're the first to learn how to use such an ability."

"Ability?"

"That allows you to find another universe."

"Universe?"

She frowned. "Is it the right word?"

"I—I don't know." He thought of his conversation with Chess the night before—alternate universes and fairy-tale lands.

The Girl Queen had brought him to where he could get a better look at the palace through the trees. It wasn't as big as he remembered. Just a house, really. Tall flashing windows, a rooftop gilded with yellow-gold leaves. A palace to a young boy desperate for fairy tales, but not actually a palace.

Are they real, the things I see?

He turned back to her. "You're . . . real." A real girl, in a real place. It wasn't his own world. It was some alternate universe.

Her arms were slim and strong around his shoulders again. "I'm as real as you are."

Dylan's shoes sunk into the muddy bank of the stream. The silt on his sneakers shone like copper. His vorpal glinted like scales on a fish tail. He could see it.

Like a halo of light around him.

2.

WHEN WE WERE TV

(ten years from now)

BRIXNEY

My training at Flavor Foam went something like this: "First you punch the proper button on the machine, which releases the mold—maybe of Robert Pattinson In His Heyday or Cartoon Princess Number Five." That was my manager speaking. One of two managers, so I tend to think of him as Mr. One. I think of the other as the Other One. Mr. One is skinny as a mendicant and always has his palms pressed together as if he's begging me to do these things. Please, *please* press the button next to the corresponding image. Please don't break the mold, or if you do, please try to land safely on your ass when I give you the boot.

"The mold goes on the souvenir plastic plate," Mr. One begged, extending his palms toward me and the mold in turn, "and then the nozzle of the injector goes into the top, and then the edible foam goes into the mold. Does the customer want a flavor gel? Most likely the customer does. Use the gel gun to shoot that in too."

He gave a very long pause here and squinted at me with concern, like he wasn't sure I could handle all of the instructions at once. The gel gun dripped purple goo on the counter. "It'll be your job to clean this up, by the way," he whispered to me.

I nodded and wondered if he meant right then. But he plowed on.

"The mold gets removed in *two* pieces," he said, breaking it apart and tossing said pieces into the return bin, "and then you've got Boisterous-Berry Action Star Turned Family Film Dad or whatever."

We stood back to admire the Flavor Foam Head's paternal grin. The purple gel glistened in the overhead lights. I secretly think Flavor Foam Heads are the weirdest snack ever invented. They're supposedly made of "plant proteins" and "stabilizing agents," whatever that means. I suspect they might actually be made of injectable wall insulation, but they're somehow delicious, especially with Fudgsicle flavor gel. Plus, they're low-fat.

And the foam looks good onscreen—shiny and colorful and weird enough to make you look twice. Flavor Foam has cameras jutting from every corner and TV screens mounted on the walls so customers and employees can enjoy a few minutes of manufactured fame. The thought that Flavor Foam's customers can watch me screw up onscreen used to horrify me. But now I'm used to it.

"We have all the FeedBin molds over here." Mr. One indicated a new machine on the counter. "These are a big hit with kids obsessed with the videos on FeedBin that've gone viral. They want to eat Flavor Foam Heads of ordinary people who become overnight Internet sensations, like Grumpy Boy Swearing He'll Never Sneeze Again. But don't make the mistake of thinking it's only kids who want this. Adults want it too. They want to get Man Who Makes Millions Selling Comic-Con Costumes Out Of His Basement so they can smash in his Flavor Foam Head as punishment for his undue success."

And for his weird haircut, I wanted to add.

I'd actually watched some of that guy's online feed once. He'd installed a camera in his basement so you could see how he carved up styrene sheets for costume armor. But the camera was attached to the ceiling, so mostly you got to see the back of his head as he leaned over his worktable.

People will watch anything halfway interesting on Feed-Bin, even a video of someone eating weird food like flavor foam. All they want is to get lost in Random Internet Weirdness Land.

These days I'm pretty much stuck in Crippled By Debt Since Sudden Death Of Parents Land. Hence the new job.

"And Brixney?" Mr. One pleaded, palms pressed to his heart. "We like to be camera-ready at all times here. So, the Woe Is Me face? That's not going to work."

I gave him a sudden, startled smile that probably made me look like Toddler Confronted By Hungry Water Fowl.

"Exactly," Mr. One said, bowing his head in reverent approval. "That really rounds out the customer-slash-viewer experience."

= ≠ =

I spend my breaks poking around on my handheld e-frame—a sadly outdated, brick-like model that I rent from the debtors' colony where my older brother and I live because he's so far in debt. For work, I use its recognition software to identify appetizers so that I don't accidentally serve gravy fries to a kid who's ordered cheese fries (trust me, our gravy and our cheese look identical). But during my breaks, I use it to browse FeedBin for top-rated feeds.

I like to watch the feeds from cameras planted in stores and offices and restaurants. Even a lot of security cameras are connected to the Internet these days, although I don't really care to watch someone standing in an elevator. Sometimes I find a real gem of a feed coming in through the built-in camera in someone else's e-frame. People will whip out their e-frames to film just about anything happening around them and they're not shy about sharing it on the Internet. A lot of times that's the best way to catch the weirdest or coolest or most embarrassing stuff. Not everyone likes to be on camera—I get that. But if a big corporation decides your feed is popular enough to advertise on, it means you get a cut of their ad revenue, so at least you get paid for your humiliation.

Lately I prefer to watch streaming video of People Having The Worst Day Ever so I can add sympathetic emoji in the comments section (except my e-frame doesn't support emoji, so I have to transcribe them): Jaycub of Mill Creek gets dumped for a guy wearing a shirt that says *Llamas Love Me* (Teary Face). Middle-aged Darren goes on a series of soul-crushing interviews, during which he realizes his computer skills are hopelessly outdated for today's job market (**Dismayed Face**). Overlarge Allasin weeps on the pioneer costume of a Little-Bitty Prairie ride-operator because her overlarge son can't fit in the safety harness for Wagon Train Chase (**Dismay with Inverted Eyebrows**).

Sometimes I use my e-frame to call up their locations, the Jaycubs and Darrens and Allasins. I think about heading out to Mill Creek Mall or Technology Is Supreme Office Park to watch the events unfold before my own eyes, or even stick out my e-frame to add another feed to the Bin. But then I think of Griffin.

I met Griffin at the MyFuture debtors' colony when my older brother (and legal guardian) was sent there with me in tow. Griffin had been in with his dad for three years already because of a massive amount of credit card debt that had been bought out by a ruthless collection agency. My brother had a messy mortgage that he'd tried to take on after our parents' death, plus medical bills from our parents' last few comatose weeks of life. In hindsight, we should have sold the house right after our parents' car accident and used the money to pay the hospital. But how can you sell the rickety porch your dad built, or your parents' bedroom, or the marks your mom's favorite swivel chair left on the wall? You can't. So you end up giving it to the bank when your mortgage falls into default.

Griffin got me the job at Flavor Foam so I could help my brother chip away at his debt and get out of MyFuture. As a minor, I can't have any debt attached to me and can come and go as I please. But Brandon's stuck there, can't even go around the corner to get a burger or take a swim in the lake or anything. Not even to, say, get a job with which to pay off his debt. What he *can* do is try to come up with some clever activity that will make his feed popular and attract advertisers. But nothing that involves nudity, or suggesting nudity, or suggesting anything else that typically goes on in a motel, because then the government comes in and confiscates all of MyFuture's cameras and e-frames, and no one makes money, least of all Visa. The government doesn't mind what your average person does with a camera and an Internet connection, but it's pretty intent on preventing debtors' colonies from becoming porn plantations.

Residents in MyFuture are great at pulling together to attract hits on their feeds. Once we did a reinterpretation of *Les Misérables*, with Javert as an obsessive collection agent and Jean Valjean doing everything he could to avoid having his adopted daughter grow up in a debtors' colony. Small-time review sites called it "poignant" and "relevant," but Rotten Tomatoes never mentioned it, and it didn't catch on at FeedBin.

We also had a good gig going where we charged local schools to bring in kids so they could see firsthand the dangers of high interest rate credit cards. But a couple of credit companies shut that down real fast with some bad press about children being exposed to former addicts and dropouts.

Brandon did everything he could to play up our own

hardships for the camera—Isn't It Sad That A Couple Of Orphans Are Stuck In A Mold-Infested Motel With Former Gamblers And Alcoholics? We got a week's worth of advertising by drawing out an argument about me quitting school to get a job.

And people really tuned in to see my relationship with Griffin build.

The first time Griffin saw me, I was crying in the stairwell at MyFuture. It was my first day there and I'd just found out Brandon and I had to share a room with another person and discretion dictated that I sleep on a cot in the bathroom.

Griffin tried to cheer me up by telling me that at least the place had a pool.

But there's no water in it, I said.

You have to bring your own, Griffin said.

I wiped my eyes on my sleeve and peered up at him from the dingy carpet of the stairwell landing. I figured this was the best he could do at being funny, so I played along. *No one told me,* I said.

He considered for a moment and then said, *I could let you borrow mine.* He took my hand and pulled me up while I was still trying to figure out if he was joking. Then he led me outside and down into the empty pool, where an entire sloping wall was covered with 3-D chalk art of a whale swimming in sun-lit water. It was so beautiful that the only thing I could think of to say was, *This is better than the water I would have brought from home.* And Griffin shrugged and said, *It's the only water you can't get wet.*

He had tons of ideas, all the time. Once he used his chalk to add a footnote to the slogan MyFuture had painted on a giant sign on the roof:

MyFuture

where my future belongs to me*

once I obtain a release of lien

He always told me not to take it all so seriously. *Stop staring at the sidewalk,* he would say at the plaza. *It's not like you're in debt to these specific people.* And I'd try to shake the feeling that tourists were going to walk up to me and demand that I pay them for the toothpaste I'd used that morning.

With Griffin, it was easier not to wallow in self-pity. So I spent all my time with him, at work and at MyFuture. In the mornings when the food truck delivered breakfast, the cost of which was added to our debts, we'd peel the foil off our plates and fashion it into ninja stars. In the evenings, we'd browse FeedBin, watching families watch TV together, and spying on old friends from schools we'd never again attend. On clear nights, when the stars were white on black instead of smoggy gray, we'd lie on the roof together and say cheesy things like, *At least they can't charge us for moonlight.* Although later they did, by way of imposing a curfew and fining those of us who broke it.

Then Griffin started talking about us leaving the colony together and sorry if that meant not helping alleviate our families' debts but didn't I want a future? A real future without a lien on it? Our sobby love story got decent ratings, enough to pull in ad revenue, even. Customers came into Flavor Foam to watch me argue with Griffin in person. Mr. One had our supplier make a mold in the shape of Griffin's head. You can still order Lover Boy With Big Plans To Get Out Of This Town, although nobody does. Nobody except me.

The day Griffin turned eighteen, he took his share of the revenue we'd gotten from companies who had advertised on our feeds and he bought us Tickets To The Big City. But I wouldn't leave Brandon alone in a debtors' colony with no way to get out. So Griffin left and I had to do (terrible, disproportionate) chalk art on my own. And I stopped going on the roof to look at stars. And I stopped watching feeds of happy families in real living rooms. And foil was just foil.

My Tuesday afternoon regular is a guy I think of as Saint Professor, a brand-new English teacher who comes in after school. His cheap suit and cartoon character tie prove he's straddling the line between determined and defeated. He must be finding it hard to meet his classroom objectives, because he likes to lecture me on how to do my job.

"What have you got in the way of historical heroes in government?" he asks.

I use my e-frame to scan his tie. An old *Bad Dad* cartoon episode pops up. "Honestly, I wouldn't count on that being a demand we cater to." *Bad Dad* always reminds me of junior high—watching episodes after school with Brandon while we ate maple syrup straight from the bottle. We would have *inhaled* flavor foam if it had existed back then. Sometimes I bring it to him from the restaurant, but I can tell he only eats it to humor me.

He's obsessed with staying healthy now that he's all I've got.

Saint Professor gives his patient sigh and slowly unfolds a menu. "When I ask for a certain type of mold, you hold open the menu like this." He spreads it in front of me and pushes my e-frame out of my eye-line. "See here where the categories are listed? See how they're color-coded?"

I try to decide which pointy objects I'd most like to hide in his flavor foam.

"Want to guess what color historical figures get, or do you already know?" Saint Professor says in his slow, deliberate voice. "Hmm?"

The color of your blood when I stick you in the eye with that *Bad Dad* tie pin?

"It's green," he says. "Historical figures and aging athletes both get green. Now, if I scan the menu for green stars, I'll find—look here—that's Oprah. She also gets a light blue star for being a religious figure. That's not political, which is what I was looking for, but you know what? Close enough, because actually I believe they made her honorary mayor of a couple towns during that year she was battling colon cancer. So I'll take Oprah Bellowing Her Generosity."

"How ironic," I say, thinking back to Oprah's online tirade against Bad Dad's parenting methods.

"Pardon?"

"Nothing." I whisk the menu out of Saint Professor's hand.

He glares at me over the top of his glasses. "I'll have Blueberry Muffin flavor gel, young lady."

I plod to the mold machine. My other manager, the one I call the Other One, is lounging behind the counter, nibbling melted cheese off an order of cheese fries. "Fries are fattening," he explains when I give him a look. "Which mold you need?"

"Oprah."

"Eyes Shining With Empowerment?"

"The other one, Other One." I chuckle at my joke.

"Why do you call me that? You never call Jeffrey Mr. One to his face." He uses a clicky pen to separate the cheese fries from those that have already been de-cheesed. He's the only one who still uses pens to write down orders instead of tapping pictures on a Flavor Foam app. "Why can't I at least be Mr. Two?"

"You don't really want to be that closely associated with Mr. One."

He stops sorting cheese fries to use his pen to whisk hair back over his bald spot. "What if I told you the walk-in freezer is on the fritz again and the ice-cream nuggets are in mortal peril? Then can I be Mr. Two?"

I pause. I could indeed use a good handful of half-melted ice-cream nuggets. And Mr. One would never miss them.

We're not allowed to serve them to customers because even frozen solid they make the Flavor Foam Heads melt, which ruins the customer experience. We're also not allowed to throw them out because company policy dictates that any food thrown out before the expiration date be donated to a local nonprofit, but it also dictates that we not donate high-caloric food to people of insufficient means because, as Mr. One says, "That's the way to a slow genocide, a genocide of the lower class."

"Better hurry," chimes in my coworker Lola. "I already sold off two boxes of those ice-cream nuggets at a premium to table seven."

"Uh, you're not really supposed to do that," the Other One says, pointing his pen at her.

"*Uh,* too late." Lola rolls her eyes.

Lola's what you'd call enterprising. She spends her entire shift orchestrating complicated lovers' quarrels with customers for the sake of Flavor Foam's cameras. Then she goes home and spends all her free time orchestrating complicated lovers' quarrels with her friends for whatever cameras might be mounted in shop windows or soda machines or her dining room ceiling fan. You'd think she'd be making enough in ad revenue now to quit working at Flavor Foam, but her ratings are all over the place. I think people sense that all those shrill fights with brooding boys are staged.

Right now she's using her e-frame to search the tables of college boys, looking for ones on scholarship who might be willing to do desperate things for a cut of ad revenue.

"Darn, full ride," she mutters. "That hardly helps me."

She gives up to watch a feed of a guy trying to convince his girlfriend he's not cheating on her. "What girl would actually be attracted to me?" he says. "I mean besides you?" The feed is coming from one of our own cameras.

"Lola, they're right there at table twelve," I say. "Why are you watching them on your e-frame?"

The big screen over our heads switches to the same feed she's watching. Now all of our customers can watch the guy ask the girls at the next table if they're attracted to him. "Like, would you ever ask me to take off my shirt or anything like that?" he asks. His girlfriend plunges his e-frame into a Flavor Foam Head. Some bot picks up on the fact that the ratings are soaring and plants an American Eagle Outfitters logo in the corner of the screen.

"Love 'em and leave 'em to keep the ratings high," I mumble as I pour myself a pilfered soda, "to keep the ad revenue coming in, right?"

"Add a Cake Batter flavor gel into that Coke," Lola tells me. "Sweeten it up. Your bitterness is poisoning the air for the rest of us."

I take a swig of soda and eye the mold dispenser. I'm in a bit of a self-pitying mood. "Other One, give me Lover Boy With Big Plans To Get Out Of This Town."

"Not again," Lola says.

But I'm already full speed ahead into moody territory. "Push the button, Other One."

"Stop calling me that," he says, but he pushes the button.

I inject flavor foam into Lover Boy With Big Plans. The

giant TV screen quickly cuts to my feed. Mr. One always likes to get this on camera.

I ignore the screen and consider Lover Boy's sad smile. It's been two months since Griffin left. He joined this street art movement in L.A. We still talk some. In fact, we talked just last week. He said he misses me; I asked him why he never calls. There was this long pause during which he was either breathing really loudly or the wind was hitting the mic on his e-frame, and then he said, *I always answer when* you *call* me, like that makes up for it. Then he told me I should come out to Santa Monica, and I told him he should ask his dad to. I admit that was a mean thing to say. We both know his dad can't leave MyFuture until he pays off his debt. But I also think it's mean to abandon your own dad when his only wrongdoing was that he lived off his credit card too long when his unemployment ran out.

I can still hear Griffin's voice, low and sad and mixed in with the sound of the ocean: *Brix . . . It's hard here. It's hard without you.*

It always kills me, that voice.

Then come back, I told him.

I lean down close to Flavor Foam's counter. I return Lover Boy's sad smile, and for a moment it's almost like we're apologizing to each other for everything that's happened. Then I pour my Coke on top of Lover Boy's foam head. It eats through his face and comes bubbling back out of the mold. Fun fact: There's a little bit of baking soda mixed in with the flavor foam. Keeps it foamy. Also turns molds into mini-volcanoes.

A caption on the screen lets our customers—and any viewers—know that they can order Lover Boy With Big Plans To Get Out Of This Town plus a third-tier flavor gel for $12.99. And that Brixney herself will bring it to your table and would probably even pour her soda on it if you asked her real nice. Mr. One must be typing furiously up in the control booth.

Then the old replay starts. Even though I've specifically asked Mr. One not to play it ever. It's me and Griffin in our Flavor Foam uniforms, the old ones without the slimming panels we have now and you can really tell the difference. We're making our Big Plans To Get Out Of This Town. The old Chevron Gas icon shines in the corner of the screen. I just made ten cents. Thanks a bunch, Mr. One.

I decide to take my break early and head out to the patio overlooking the lake. I find a guy sitting on a marble statue of a soda can, very lifelike and squirting some type of brown liquid. The marble soda can, I mean. The guy isn't lifelike. He's sitting too still and when I hold up my e-frame, it can't identify him. The screen shows a little clock icon and then, instead of displaying his name and online profile, just says, NOT FOR HUMAN CONSUMPTION.

My food scanner app is a little hyper, always jumping in before I ask it to.

So he has no profile. Very interesting. Means he's either a criminal who's found a way to scrub himself from the Internet (except he's too clean for that), an e-free who shuns social media (expect he's also too clean for that), or a richie-rich tourist with some outdated idea of discretion (of which we get plenty around here). His hair is shaggy, skin luminescent. I recognize his clothes from a boutique at the other end of the plaza. Definitely a richie-rich tourist.

He gazes out across the plaza, ignoring the notebook in his hand and curiously watching preteens buzz about the pavilion where a Feed-Con expo is going on. In about an hour, all of those kids will be buzzing over to Flavor Foam for a snack break. Probably sans tip money. My calves ache at the thought.

The truth is, I'm not making nearly enough money at this job to put a dent in Brandon's debt. And contrary to what collection agencies think, no relative is going to take interest in our sad plight and come up with the cash to spring us from MyFuture. All we have left is an uncle who subscribes to the idea that throwing money at a problem never solves it, which usually I would agree with.

Also, with Brandon's interest piling up the way it is, he's on track to be transferred to a colony thirty miles south where they sleep eight to a room and get one bathroom for an entire floor.

So a good-looking, richie-rich tourist is just what I need right now. He can either add some pretty to my feed and get me some ad revenue, or he can give me cash directly once I become his temporary townie girlfriend.

I try again with my e-frame. It still can't get a read on him. It also tells me the plume of brown liquid coming from the marble straw is not for human consumption. Way to advertise a soda, right? I try to think of something to say to him, something Lola might say to lure him into the choppy waters of our shop and moor him in a booth with a good camera angle.

I can get you a flavor foam Girl With Pleasing Anatomy four hours before the evening shift.

Please be advised this is not a public drinking fountain but a flawed attempt at advertising soda with something resembling soda but completely unsafe for consumption.

I'm covered in my own skin!

That last one is a line from a feed that was popular last week, but maybe it's too old to reference? Maybe he's heard it so many times it's not funny anymore? He'll have to force a laugh and then wonder why he wastes his vacation hanging out on the plaza meeting desperate locals.

I get so flustered thinking about it that I finally just say, "The seating is located inside. Where the chairs are." It comes off a little snarky. I'm not having the best of days.

Saint Professor, my Tuesday regular, is not happy that I abandoned him.

"I've been watching your feed on my e-frame here," he says. An image of me through one of Flavor Foam's cameras shows on his clunky, school-prescribed e-frame. "I saw you loitering on the patio. When I place my order, you fill it right away."

I'm guessing he had a particularly bad day at school.

"And you don't shove it onto the table like you just did," he continues. "You approach from right here near my elbow and gracefully slide it in front of me. Like a seal gliding over butter."

As Saint Professor leans over the table, I notice a little notebook in his shirt pocket on which he has scrawled *T. S. Eliot*. I almost grunt in frustration. If you're going to lecture me on something, how about poetry? How about ultra-dense symbolism that I'd never be able to decode on my own?

"I come here every Tuesday," Saint Professor says. "I know how these things are supposed to work."

"I'm also here every Tuesday," I say. "Also, pretty much every other day of the week."

Saint Professor's frustrated scowl turns into a smile of genuine warmth. "Don't worry, you'll catch on," he says, and gives me an encouraging chuck on the shoulder.

I grit my teeth. I make no further delay in searching out those imperiled ice-cream nuggets.

And, goodie, there's still some boxes left. I squat in the frosty air of the walk-in fridge and consider ways to prevent Brandon's transfer to Debtors' House, which I've heard serves only one large meal a day and encourages residents to scour the surrounding neighborhood for cans to recycle in order to make some "snack money." Brandon's skinny enough as it is. He thinks I don't know he sneaks his bacon onto my plate every morning like I'm a little kid.

I could call Griffin and ask him to send us some of the cash he's made apprenticing with a guy who does body art. Something I could split with his dad. I toy with my e-frame, considering the idea. Calling Griffin would mean hearing his voice, hoarse with salt air and sadness, and trying to keep my heart from breaking to pieces all over again: *Remember the times on the roof, under the stars? They don't have stars here, you can hardly see the streetlights for all the smog.* It would mean trying (failing) not to get angry at him for leaving.

How can I ask him for money? I haven't exactly been his biggest supporter lately.

Or I guess the better question is—how much does he really owe me?

"Brixney? You know what, Brixney?"

I turn to find Mr. One red-faced with disapproval, hands pressed together under his chin.

"Did you pay for those ice-cream nuggets?" He's pleading with God that it be true.

"They're melting. They're making a mess of the walk-in." I point at an ice-cream puddle leaking onto the refrigerated floor.

"And you're taking initiative, and that's great." He hunches his shoulders. He's practically bowing to me. "But eating food that belongs to the store and not to you? That's a fast ticket to scraping the seat of your pants on the pavement outside the door. Know what I mean? I mean, when I fire you."

"Okay, well, don't fire me." I go into a hot sweat. My stomach rejects the aesthetics of cold ice cream mixed with fiery panic. "I'm just eating ice-cream nuggets that we're allowed to neither sell nor toss. Basically what I'm eating is trash."

"Except that if you were eating trash?" He winces in an exaggerated way, as if pained on my behalf. "It'd be because you were on the streets without a job. Without *this* job, specifically."

My face muscles spasm a little. I bend down on pretense of examining the leaking box. "I think I can staunch this. I'll staunch this mess and then the nuggets can stay here in the box. Yeah, I'll get on that." I nod vigorously, partly to underscore my initiative and partly to shake out the muscle tics.

"Great." Mr. One turns to go. "And I'll tell Lola to take care of the tourist type who's been sitting in your section for a full five minutes without being greeted."

What? No! Not my tourist! Lola will have used him all up by the time I get out there.

I shove a couple of reams of processed cheese into the leaky box and hurry out to tell Lola that my tourist is not for human consumption.

Saint Professor catches me first. He's come right up to the mold bar to talk to me. "I want ice-cream nuggets added to my order," he says. "You didn't tell me those were available."

"They're not."

"I saw you eating them. I saw on your feed."

He saw me eating them?? Since when is there a camera in the walk-in? Stupid Mr. One and his (apparently rational) fear of inventory pilfering.

"We have ice-cream nuggets," I admit, "but I'm not allowed to serve them."

"You're hoarding them for yourself because they've been discontinued."

"I'm not allowed to give them to you," I tell Saint Professor, "unless you are a nonprofit organization that does *not* serve the economically disadvantaged."

Saint Professor frowns in confusion. He slowly shakes his head. "I don't think you've been properly trained at all."

I break away from him and make for my tourist. Lola's squinting at him from a distance, trying to center his face in her e-frame as if that'll help pull up his nonexistent profile.

"*My* section," I hiss at Lola.

I dart over to the tourist's booth and say in my most alluring voice, "What is it you're looking for?"

He looks up at me with an expression as open as the middle of the ocean.

"I'm waiting for a friend," he says. Then, with his head tilted to one side: "This place was different last time I came here."

I glance at the colorful banners slung everywhere. "Yeah, we're doing a promo for FeedBin. I can get you Confused Teen Can't Find His Car if you want."

He swipes his shaggy hair out of his face, giving me a clear view of eyes the deep green color of murky lake water. "No, I mean this place used to be some kind of sandwich shop." I can't place his accent. He speaks slowly, like he's having trouble getting all the consonants out. "With spicy peppers, I guess, that hurt your mouth if you ate a lot of them."

"Oh. Yeah. Spicy peppers are like that, aren't they?" I glance back at Lola, who's watching our feed on her e-frame. I shoot her a look that says, *What's up with this guy?* "So . . . Teen Doing His Confused Thing—that okay for you?"

"Yes."

"You want a flavor gel?"

"Yes."

I wait for him to tell me which kind. He looks at me blankly for a moment—are his eyes green or brown?—and then hurries to pull something out of his pocket. He hands me a silver coin stamped with what looks like a two-headed elephant.

"We don't accept . . . Cambodian currency here," I tell him.

"You could melt it down," he offers.

I stare at him. He's messing with me. I give him a knowing smirk. "I think I've got just the thing for you."

I come back with what Lola and I have dubbed Banana Split The Check, a mountain of banana-gelled flavor foam topped with crumbled Oreos and graham cracker bits. She and I often make it and split the deduction from our paychecks, hence the name. Clever, right? I usually throw in some ice-cream nuggets too, but looks like that tradition has just gone out alongside privacy in the walk-in.

"I find it disquieting to eat faces," I tell the tourist as I slide into the booth with the Banana Split. Mr. One doesn't mind if we sit with the customers. He encourages it, especially if the customer is good-looking and doesn't mind staging an argument or make-out session—it brings in more customers. I'm not planning on staging either, but Mr. One doesn't need to know that.

The tourist digs in with all the self-consciousness of a five-year-old.

"Do you like it?" I ask.

"So far it's not burning my mouth at all," he reports.

"I'll tell my manager to start printing that on the cups."

He gulps down big puffs of glossy yellow foam.

"So what's your name?" I ask, leaning in like I'm breathless to hear the answer.

He pauses for a suspicious length of time. "Michael." He plows on through more Banana Split.

Hmmm. False name. No profile. I'm guessing he's old money. Probably owns a couple of castles that his parents are trying to hide from gold-diggers like me.

I'll try not to let that discourage me.

"I'm Brix."

I glance at a tattered notebook on the table. A name is inked on the cover: *Dylan*.

"Who's Dylan?" I ask, wondering if that's this guy's real name after all.

"My friend," Michael says. He nods at the notebook. "I brought this to give back to him."

"Oh, right, you're supposed to meet someone. Is he as cute as you?" I give him the obligatory conspiratorial wink.

He actually considers how to answer that. "I'm more attractive." Perfectly earnest.

"No need to waste time with false humility, right?" I hold back a laugh. "So where is this friend?"

"I don't know. I haven't seen him in ages. He once told me he comes to this sandwich shop every summer. Longest day of the year, he comes here with his brother, Hunter, and they eat the spicy peppers until one of them throws up. And it's always him—Dylan—who throws up, so his brother gets to be the one who goes out in the kayak first. But as long as I've been coming, Dylan has never showed."

I pause, trying to take that all in. "Are you serious? You come here every summer hoping to run into him? And now it's not even a sandwich shop."

"In his defense, he has no idea I've been trying to get in touch with him. I just figure he must be missing his notebook. It was important to him." He uses his fingertips to straighten the cover.

"Why don't you look him up on your e-frame?" I pull mine out of my pocket. "I can type in his name and you can send him an instant message."

"I don't know his full name. Just first name. Dylan." His shoulders sink. "I don't know where he lives. I don't know his e-frame ID."

"Sounds like you two are close friends."

His shoulders drop farther. "He was in love with my sister."

"Is that a good thing or a bad thing?" I ask, because he seems a little mopey about it.

"It didn't really work out well, in the end."

"But no hard feelings?"

"I hope not."

I meant for *you,* dork. "Hey, happy endings are overrated. I mean, unless you're in a movie."

He looks at me out of the corner of his eye, like he doesn't agree.

I fidget with my e-frame. "How's the banana foam?"

He points his spoon at what's left. "I really like it. I can see why this place isn't a sandwich shop anymore."

"Sandwiches aren't as photogenic." I point to the little camera mounted on the napkin dispenser. At the same time, the giant screen over the mold bar cuts to a shot of us sitting together. I lean farther into the frame. Gosh, we make a cute couple, what with my endearingly bedraggled appearance and his broad Your Troubles Fit On My Shoulders shoulders.

"I'm on your TV," Michael says, frozen.

"Our TV and everyone else's. Well, anyone who's tuned to my feed."

He's still frozen, his spoon poised like an exclamation mark.

"Don't worry," I say. "Until an ad pops up, you know nobody much is watching. Takes a few thousand viewers for that to happen."

"Hey, Pretty-Face!" calls a boy from a crowded booth. In *my* section, crap. "How about we order now?"

I slide out of the booth. "Don't go anywhere," I tell Michael.

He shovels the last spoonfuls of Oreo crumbs into his mouth. Like he's getting ready to leave. And darn it if I don't want to raid his wallet *and* figure out his story.

"I'll get you another Banana Split," I tell him. "Just don't leave."

The boys in the booth wear varsity jackets from the school I briefly attended when I first moved into MyFuture. I recognize one of them from my old math class. He leans back in the booth to look me over. He has a nice haircut—Brandon would look good with that haircut.

"Didn't you go to our school?" he asks me. "What happened to you?"

"Solving quadratic equations doesn't pay as much as it used to." I smile so the sarcasm will go over easier.

He doesn't match my smile. In fact, he looks genuinely concerned. He scratches his shoulder self-consciously, showing off an unfortunate T-shirt tan—stark white underneath his sleeve. The sight of it makes me relax. Here's a guy who isn't trying for perfection. He probably wouldn't mind if I swam in the lake in cutoffs and a T-shirt instead of the swimsuit I don't own.

Would he care that I live in a debtors' colony?

I train my eyes on the table. "How about ordering?"

His friends have their e-frames out and are browsing feeds.

"Whose pants are on my head?" one boy says.

"Excuse me?" As far as I can see, there are no pants on his head.

"Tell your dog to stop laughing at me!" another boy says, and they all break into guffaws. "Tell him to shut up!"

"They're quoting feeds," the boy from math class

explains, pointing at the sleek, silvery e-frames in their hands. "Seriously, why don't you go to school anymore? Didn't you win that Math Bowl? Yeah, I remember my friends all used your feed to cheat off your algebra homework." He smiles sheepishly. Adorable. But what am I supposed to tell him? I dropped out, I'm a *dropout.*

"I'll give you another minute to decide." I turn away and hurry to the back of the store. In a spot where the kitchen steam makes it hard for Mr. One to spy on me, I pull out my e-frame and find Griffin's feed.

He's grimacing at the sun and the wind streaming into his face while he crouches on the Santa Monica pier. A couple of co-eds stand before him, naked from the waist up but for a thick layer of body paint that has transformed their torsos into suburban landscapes. Painted sparrows perch on their collarbones. Griffin looks cramped from all the crouching but otherwise happy.

Does he ever think about his dad toiling on cleanup crew to shave dollars off his debt? Does he ever think of me, working swing shifts alone?

I remember us at the lake together late at night. Tourists gone, locals calling to each other in the dark like birds. Griffin collecting empty beer bottles to balance on the rocks by the shore, making crazy silhouettes. Because Griffin never thinks of trash as trash. *Sometimes I forget I'm stuck here,* he would say on the roof of MyFuture or down in the empty pool, where we'd hide from our cleaning assignments. *Sometimes I think we're just hanging out.* He'd pull me close, and I would smile, because rooftops and empty pools can be just like living rooms and back porches, depending on who you're with.

My e-frame trills at me. Brandon's calling.

"Hey, Brandon."

His pale face and overlong hair come into view. I can tell he's having a bad day. I mean, an especially bad one. The kind that can't be fixed by hunting down the rec room's missing Ping-Pong balls and bouncing them off the walls until they're missing again—our favorite pastime.

"Hey," he says. "Bad news."

"Toilet's clogged again? Brandon, I can*not* share my bedroom with a bowl full of cess."

"They're moving me today. End of the day."

"What?"

"We're transferring to Debtors' House."

All the blood drains from my head. "That's shit. They said we had until the end of the month."

Brandon shrugs, but his brown eyes are full of despair. "What does it really matter, Brix? End of the month, end of the day. You have a secret inheritance I don't know about?"

I rub a hand over my forehead. The smell of bananas and graham crackers makes me feel sick.

"You don't have to come with me," Brandon says quietly.

"I'm just going to leave you? Just let it get worse and worse for you?" Doesn't he get that I've lost enough family already? Doesn't he know that I look the other way every morning so he can put his stupid bacon on my plate? I don't even like bacon. "You're no heartthrob, Brandon, you'll never be able to use your feed to get out."

"I've got good hair," he says, hurt. "Good when I cut it."

"Your eyes are too close together." *And nobody watches nice guys like you on FeedBin. Nobody cares that you fold my laundry or that you line up all my origami foil on your windowsill.*

"Get a place with Lola, work the night shift, and go back to school," Brandon says. "That would be worth it to me, living in a colony. As long as I know you're getting somewhere."

"And I could come visit you on Thanksgiving so you could update me on your shuffleboard score and introduce me to your seven roommates. Great, Brandon. Great idea." I choke back a sob. "How much do we need to prevent a transfer?"

"Ten thousand."

My head feels as if it's detaching from the rest of my body. It's floating away. I can't feel my teeth. Ten thousand dollars.

"There's nothing we can do, Brix." He's full of sympathy, his brow creased with concern. For me, the idiot. *He's* the one who can't get out.

I think back to the day, the big day at the hospital. That black pit day when we said good-bye to our parents and took them off the machines. Brandon held my hand and I held Mom's limp hand and we told Dad we'd never sell his big-screen or forget to feed the cat, and we said good-bye. Because there was nothing we could do.

Screw that.

"We have until the end of the day," I tell Brandon. "Put some sunglasses over those beady eyes of yours and start playing to the camera." Even as I say it, a Sunglass Shack icon pops up in the corner of my screen. Our drama is increasing the hits on Brandon's feed. But that's not going to last. Pity is entertaining for only so long.

I march out to Saint Professor's table and press my hand over the camera mounted in the napkin dispenser. "You want ice-cream nuggets? You know what *discontinued* means? It means you'll never see those nuggets again. Unless you're willing to pay good."

Saint Professor goes silent with shock. He fidgets with his cartoon tie the same way my dad fidgeted with his own tie when a salesman came to our door and offered to install cameras in our house so we could explore the exciting world of profitable family drama.

I still wonder what would have happened if Dad had said yes—whether Brandon and I could have saved ourselves from this mess by letting people watch us scramble to keep ourselves out of a debtors' colony.

But Dad would never have said yes. "Sincerity facilitates meaningful connection," he always said. No, Dad. Financial solvency facilitates meaningful connection.

Also, being alive so you can care for your children instead of saddling them with your debt. That would facilitate a meaningful connection too.

"I've got seven boxes in the back," I tell Saint Professor. "You think about how much you're willing to pay for those boxes. And it's going to include that notebook in your pocket. I'll be back in a few minutes."

I leave him boggle-eyed and swing by the booth of boys from my school. "You ordering or not? Because if you're not, I'm going to give your table to that business type in the lobby over there who looks like she wouldn't mind getting into a screaming match with me if it meant increasing advertising for her company."

The guy from math class lifts his eyebrows. He seems duly impressed with me. "What're you doing when you get off work?" he asks. "Want to go to the lake?"

I form an image of me dangling my bare feet over the side of a dock, sharing a bag of pretzels with a decent-looking guy who appreciates me less for my taste in tight jeans and more for my ability to win a Math Bowl and chew out obnoxious customers.

But then I come back to reality, assess his scuffed-up sneakers, and decide sharing a nice moment with a middle-class local isn't going to keep Brandon off the bus to Debtors' House.

"Sorry, can't," I say. I'm aware of a sharp pain centering in my solar plexus.

I suck it up. I cover the nearest camera with my hand and convince his friends to give me double tips for sneaking them beer-injected foam.

Then I go back to Michael's table with another Banana Split. A couple of preteen girls have come in from the expo and are huddled a few feet away, recording Michael with their e-frames.

I take a deep breath, plaster on a perky smile, and slide into his booth. "So," I say, "your friend left his notebook behind and your conscience won't let you rest until you return it."

Michael picks dried foam off the table. "He didn't mean to leave it." The croak in his voice tells me he's only hoping it's true.

I flip open the faded cover and find a scrawled line of text: *You will find the Other Place when you look for what is lost.* Underneath that is a title written larger: *Stories of the Girl Queen.*

Michael touches the page, runs a finger over the dents left by the pen. "They're all about my sister. She's not really a queen or anything."

Darn, so he's not foreign royalty. "She's the one your friend Dylan was in love with?" I flip through pages covered in dense handwriting. "How come your sister's not the one trying to return it?" Year after year after year.

"Because I'm the one who wants him to have it back," he says into the plate of Banana Split. "When he left—well, it was my fault. I thought maybe if I give this back to him . . . I don't know. I just feel like I owe it to him." His murky-lake eyes go murkier with some particular brand of sadness. Lamenting A Lost Friendship or, more likely, Guilty About How Things Ended.

I feel like brushing his hair back, patting him on the head, telling him it'll be all right. But then a heavy weight drops into my stomach. Because what are the chances this Dylan guy is going to show up after all these years?

My mind goes to Brandon and this funny thing he does. *I'll be God, you be Adam,* he says. We imitate the figures on the Sistine Chapel—I lounge with my hand barely out-stretched, like lazy Adam on his hill. Brandon plays God, straining forward, reaching for my hand with an eager index finger. I'd like to tell Michael: *You're God, and this Dylan guy is Adam.*

Michael eyes the girls huddled nearby. "They're filming me."

"Don't look so surprised. You're a good-looking guy." I reach across the table and rest my fingertips against his arm.

He looks down at my hand, up at me. His expression darkens. "That's not going to end well," he says in a low voice.

I pull back, flooded with embarrassment. "I was just..." I can't meet his gaze. He's not stupid. He knows when a girl's trying to get into his wallet.

I glance at the girls who are filming us with their e-frames. A few more have joined them. I think of Brandon and his kind, beady eyes that no one wants to see on camera.

"Look, Michael," I say. "We both need something. I need money to keep my brother and me from being transferred from a rat-hole debtors' colony to an even worse rat-hole debtors' colony. And you need to get your friend's attention so he'll come down here and ease whatever's weighing on your conscience."

Michael forgets about the second Banana Split.

"You see those girls over there?" I continue. "They might be able to help us both. The more cameras that are on us, the closer you and I get to what we want."

He thinks it over. His breath goes fluttery with anxiety. "So what do we do?"

What would Lola do in this situation?

No, I don't think I'm up for what Lola would do. I'm not that desperate.

Well, not yet. I'll see what I can come up with on my own first.

"You could start by unraveling the mystery. Why no profile? Are you a young presidential hopeful trying to keep your reputation unsullied? Or maybe a modern-day vampire—you've got a reflection but no camera presence?"

Michael lowers his head and peers up at me. "Try something weirder."

"Weirder?" I get a feeling like soda fizzing up through a flavor foam mold.

He glances at the girls tittering nearby with their e-frames held out. "Touch my arm again," he tells me.

I give him a questioning look but slide my hand over his forearm. His skin has the warm, dry feel of someone who spends his days in the sun and takes his dinner on the veranda.

"No," Michael says. "I mean *touch* it."

"I am." The soft grit of lake silt left over from a morning swim, the tickle of downy hair.

Michael shakes his head. "You're not. You think you are, but you're not."

I look at my hand on his arm and then glance at the cameras. What exactly is he going for?

"Michael, my hand is right here on your arm." But even

as I say it, I realize he's right. There's my hand and there's his arm underneath it, but now I don't actually feel anything. No silt, no sun-warmed skin. Nothing. It's like my fingers are hovering a millimeter above his arm. I press down, hard. Still nothing. We're magnets with repelling poles.

"What the hell?" I say. "What's going on?"

He pulls his arm away. He huddles in his corner of the booth. "Maybe this isn't such a good idea after all."

I frown at him, frown at my hand, flex my fingers. What just happened?

As quickly as my confusion spikes, it recedes, like a flame suddenly smothered with a blanket. *His arm is not repellent. That was an illusion. Chalk it up to the power of suggestion.*

He hunches like a wounded animal. I reach to touch him again, to show him there are no hard feelings about his weird trick. He leans away. Boy, he's moody.

"I'll go get some soda," I say, and slide out of the booth.

The cluster of girls has thickened; I have to elbow my way past them to get to the kitchen. Another flicker of confusion distracts me as I'm filling the cup at the root beer dispenser. Was I touching Michael's arm or wasn't I?

Lola bounds into the kitchen and says, "That guy is gold. Did you tell him to say all those weird things?"

"He came pre-loaded with a script," I joke.

"Here, take this." Lola holds up Dylan's notebook—she must have swiped it from Michael's table. "Tell him he can only have it back if he pays you for it and then let him decide how to pay you."

"Uh . . ." says the Other One from where he's fixing the jammed dishwasher.

I yank the notebook away from Lola. "Very classy."

"And find a way to bring me into this," she says. "Tell him I'm willing to pose as his sister. Tell him I can cry on cue—I'll just stick some hot chili flavor gel in my eye."

"Uh, that's not a great idea about the hot chili gel," the Other One says, circling his eyes with an index finger.

I walk out before they can give me any more suggestions. As I head back to Michael's booth, I riffle the pages of the notebook with my free hand. I notice a passage underlined in red ink.

"Here you go." I hand the root beer to Michael. "More sugar, to calm your nerves."

He takes a long pull from the straw. I swear he's putting out misery and guilt like radio signals. I open the notebook to the underlined section, then backtrack a bit to figure out the context. It seems a boy has discovered his lost pet rabbit in a magical wood and is pretty unsettled by the changes it's gone through. It had been an ordinary rabbit, but now it can talk and think and appreciate clever riddles and can't very well be a pet anymore.

"I may not be your kind of rabbit anymore, a tame, huddled kind of rabbit. You might not like me as I am, a wild one who knows the smell of leaf litter and the give of pine needle carpets. You cannot understand a rabbit that will not shy from cold, open, loud. Who will not be touched by human hands. No, I am not your garden-cage rabbit anymore. Is it enough to know me from a distance, since that is the only way

we can meet? Or will you leave me now and never return?"

Pretty heavy for a story about a magic rabbit. "You underlined this?" I ask Michael.

He nods, twists away so he doesn't have to read the writing.

This is why he wants to return the book. So Dylan will read this part. "What's the deal with the rabbit? He changed, and the boy couldn't handle it?"

"Something like that," Michael mumbles.

"What does that have to do with Dylan?"

Michael looks down. "I'm not the person he thought I was."

"Want to tell me what happened between you two?" I ask quietly, but not so quietly the mic can't pick me up.

Michael bends the end of his straw back and forth, sucks in a long breath. "He showed up in the woods behind our house nine years ago and immediately decided he was in love with my older sister. I think she liked him too, really liked him." His gaze flicks to the girls watching him. He turns away from them but they just shuffle into a better viewing position. "I thought he was fascinating. He could make a fort out of anything. He made up stories I only half understood but could listen to for hours. He said, This *is how brothers should be.* Then it all started falling apart. He started to realize . . ." His voice falters. He clears his throat.

"What?"

The straw's going to break the way he's bending it. "Do you ever feel like you know things about a person you couldn't possibly know? That you can . . . sense something about them?"

You mean like if a guy's planning his future with you but you get the sense he's really going to leave you to learn how to paint perfect circles around other girls' belly buttons? If only.

"Look at me," Michael says.

I drag my gaze to Michael's face and see only worry—that I won't understand him, maybe. It makes lines around his eyes in an intricate pattern I'd like to transcribe.

"With me, you see what you *want* to see," he says. "Attractive, harmless, whatever. But this isn't what I really look like. It's all an illusion." His voice cracks. "Dylan figured that out and he couldn't get over it."

I try to follow what he's saying, but I'm flooded with confusion again.

"I can influence the way you see me," Michael says, and I lift my eyebrows. "I can influence the way you feel."

I think back to the way I felt a minute ago—utterly confused and then suddenly not. But that wasn't Michael's doing. That was me, sorting things out.

I'm pretty sure that was me sorting things out.

"So you can make me attracted to you even if I'm not?" I ask him with a teasing smirk.

"If you're hoping to have an attractive customer, then that's how you'll see me."

I lean back and study him, trying to figure out if he's just having fun with me or if he really believes what he's saying. It's true that he's everything I'd expect from a rich out-of-towner. The golden complexion, the wind-tangled hair. But the eyes are all wrong—not enough boredom, not enough arrogance. Not nearly enough eagerness to look down my low-cut shirt.

I cross my arms. "What do you really look like, then?"

"I could show you, but you wouldn't understand."

"Why not?" I say with a disbelieving snort.

The cluster of girls has turned into a horde, all hanging on Michael's words. Michael notices. He looks to the door.

"Because I'm too different from you." The lines around his eyes get deeper. "I'm not from around here."

A teenage girl steps past our booth and brushes her hand along Michael's shoulder. He flinches at the touch. She scurries on, staring at her hand, no doubt asking herself if her fingers truly made contact.

"Where are you from?" I ask Michael.

Another girl walks by and whisks her hand through his hair, giggling. Michael blanches and I want to shout at the girl.

"I don't want to do this," he tells me. He braces to scoot out of the booth and my heart seizes. "I'm sorry—I know you need money. I've heard about debtors' colonies."

Who hasn't? Anyone who's ever browsed FeedBin has seen inside one.

The TV screen cuts to a new feed—my face fills the frame. A younger, more plaintive version of my face. Mr. One, master manipulator, is controlling the feed from the booth. Michael freezes, eyes on the replay of my Flavor Foam training. I look panicked and desperate, clenching the trigger of the flavor foam gun like I'm hoping dollar bills will shoot out.

"You want Dylan to come here, don't you?" I ask Michael, trying to lay it on thick so he'll stay. "You want him to see that you're here waiting for him?"

Michael sinks back into the booth. He turns to me, sad-eyed, and nods. I force down a wave of embarrassment at his pitying expression.

Michael fidgets with the cover of the notebook. "Dylan could do what I can do—influence people. And he could see things no one else saw. He figured out how to use this special ability that not many people can use. A vorpal, he called it."

"A *vorpal*?"

"He said it was from a poem."

"'Jabberwocky.'" That crazy mess of a poem—written by a mathematician, so maybe there's hope yet for my poetry skills.

"He used it to find the place where I'm from."

"The place where you're from," I echo, utterly lost.

He looks up, his lake-water eyes startlingly green. "Another world. Another universe."

That's when I notice it's not just teenage girls gathered around our booth. It's their moms, some annoyed at the delay in heading home from the Feed-Con expo, some just as riveted as their daughters. It's also college boys, a middle-aged man in an expo uniform, the cashier from the shop next door, and a couple of elderly women from the salon across the plaza. Most are dutifully pointing e-frames at Michael and me, and glancing at the TV screen now and then to see if it's their camera providing the current view of our restaurant.

And in the corner of the screen—three different logos for three different companies advertise on my feed.

My palms sweat. My tired calves quiver. It's working. I must have made hundreds of dollars already, maybe even a thousand.

All because Michael is convinced there's something wrong with him. All because he's so crazy, this Dylan guy cut out and is never coming back.

He's never coming back, is he? He knows Michael is crazy, and he might feel sorry for him, but he's not driving out here just to get back a cheap notebook, or to hear Michael's jumbled explanations.

People don't come back just because you want them to.

Even if they owe you, even if you owe them.

People don't come back.

Pain blossoms in my gut. Somewhere, Griffin's standing on a pier, paint-speckled in the wind.

Missing me like crazy.

But he's not coming back.

I look at Michael, at the crowd pressing in around him. He doesn't get it, he can't understand.

His angst isn't buying Dylan's forgiveness. It's only giving people something to gape at, adding a feed to the Bin. Mr. One will probably make a mold of Hottie Convinced He's An Alien and then he'll loop footage of Michael's misery for teens and tourists.

I know how that goes.

I search out Lola among the crowd. The Other One is trying to be discreet about wrestling the chili-tinted flavor gel gun away from her.

"She's got a gun," I tell the crowd, and point to Lola.

They shriek and scatter.

"Come on." I pull Michael out of the booth and around the long way to the kitchen. "Through here."

I open the back door, which leads out to an alley lined with Dumpsters.

"Michael." I put my hand on his shoulder. "It's okay. You don't have to tell me any more. Leave the notebook here. I'll give it to Dylan if he comes." *But he won't, he's gone, you're pining for nothing.* The words sink deep into some pit inside of me.

Already, some of the crowd has found us; a string of girls follows us into the alley, armed with outstretched e-frames. Mr. One appears, his expression entreating me to come back inside and use Flavor Foam as a backdrop for my conversation.

"Just go," I plead with Michael.

"But your money," Michael says. "You need the money."

"I'll be fine. This'll be at the top of FeedBin for ages." Or a day maybe, or an hour. Not enough time to make ten thousand dollars, but enough to delay a transfer a little longer, maybe, if MyFuture's feeling generous.

He senses my hesitation. He looks at the girls with their e-frame cameras. "Let me show you," Michael says to me. "So you can understand."

I'd like to understand, I really would. I'd like to understand why a guy like Michael would bother waiting year after year for someone who left and probably never looked back. I'd like to know why people leave in the first place. Even when they love you, even when they owe it to you to stay. But all I really understand is that people have all kinds of debts between them that are never going to get paid.

"You don't owe me anything," I tell Michael.

Michael's lined face is a maze of anxiety and disappointment. "Just let me show you."

"It doesn't make any sense," I say. "You look perfectly normal to me. You *feel* perfectly normal." I move my hand down to grip his.

He grips back. "I'll show you."

And then I'm not holding his hand and I'm not looking into his face. I'm sensing him with something other than my eyes or my skin. His face is not a normal face but a screen of flickering images, a loose collection of colors, like dust motes caught in a shaft of light. His hand is warmth and light and energy, but nothing solid.

He's a cloud.

And then he's back to normal, back to real. His lake-water eyes search mine but how can he expect to find anything there other than shock and disbelief and confusion, and I hope not revulsion, I really hope not.

"I told you it wouldn't end well," he says. "Do you believe me now?"

Overhead, the tufted clouds are hands of loose molecules reaching for each other, stretching and stretching.

"Happy endings are for movies," I say.

He smiles, the first smile I've seen on him, and it looks good. He hands me Dylan's notebook. Then he turns toward a shimmering wave of heat roiling up from the cement and he steps through it and he's gone.

I feel the horde of viewers at my back. I sense a million clicks on FeedBin as my revenue rockets up to ten thousand and more.

3.

WHEN WE WENT
HIGH-CONCEPT

(thirty years from now)

EPONY

Cole and I come from a town in Iowa with one main road—
one way in and one way out. He was Colburn then. Now
he's Cole. They made him do that.

Any time I walked past his house, his chickens would
follow me to the edge of the yard like I was their mother
hen. They were partial to me. I understood the feeling—
more than once during the summer I was sixteen I found
myself following the siren strum of Cole's battered guitar.
He'd sit on his porch and play rage-rock tunes slow as love
ballads, crooning about oil wars, his anger locked tight in
his throat.

He'd play at the creek bend where the small boys swung
from rope lengths over the water like pendulums, arcing
through the air out of sync with his staccato rhythms. They
had yet to learn the reality of coaxing corn out of soil so
desiccated by chemicals you had to use more chemicals to
make anything grow. Cole sang it to them.

I listened, out of sight. Half because I was fascinated Cole had started caring about anything other than trucks, which he'd drawn on the back of every school assignment when we were in the fifth grade. Half because hearing Cole's voice was like waking up slowly and listening to someone tell you where you are.

Once last August, he stood in the creek, guitar abandoned on the bank, and called to me, "Did you come all the way here to lurk in the trees?"

I startled. At school he hardly talked to me, mostly because he hardly talked to *anyone*. Rumor had it there was a sign-up sheet going around for people who wanted to have a full conversation with him. But I knew that was just teasing. I knew because I was the one who'd started the rumor.

I kicked off my shoes and moved in knee-deep. The shock of cold water stole my breath. Cole was dark from the sun, his yellow hair like parched grass. He cocked his head to the side like my grandpop used to do; I swear it's a gesture taught to all farm boys who plan on growing up to make trouble. I fought to stand my ground against the current pushing at the backs of my legs.

"Can't you swim?" Cole had asked.

"I learned in this creek. They threw me in and I declined the opportunity to drown."

It surprised us both that we had anything left to laugh about. The price of seed had gone up that year like it had every year. We got patented seeds that were supposed to withstand the pests migrating from places where it was even hotter, but the patent meant we weren't allowed to store the seed for replanting.

Cole shivered; the water around him rippled. "Can't you come any closer, then?"

I took a few hobbled steps forward, unsure whether to brave the icy temperatures. The current and his smile soon convinced me.

A few days later, I was walking toward town to buy a Coke when the sound of Cole's guitar floated to me over stands of late-summer witchgrass. I stopped to sit on the fence he had propped himself against and asked him if he ever watched feeds about people visiting from the Other Place. "You look half vanished, standing in that grass," I told him. "Ever seen them do that? Just step between worlds?"

Everyone had seen those videos, so Cole only smirked like we were sharing a joke. "I saw a video of one show-ing up at a dentist's office. He just stood there, bug-eyed, watching a woman get her teeth cleaned."

I laughed. I had seen a lot more than that—had actually met one in person, which wasn't that common, except in big cities. But Cole was studying me like he didn't much care to talk about other people at the moment. I stared back. His county fair T-shirt was too small for him, and the date under the logo pinpointed the start of his growth spurt at two years earlier. Why had it taken me so long to notice?

"It's hot as hell," Cole said, pulling at his shirt.

"I wouldn't know, personally," I joked. "But I'll take your word for it."

Cole laughed, and he left his guitar right there propped in the grass so we could walk to the creek.

We met at the creek all through September—after school, weekends. We sunned ourselves on gravel bed islands and hoped the younger kids didn't watch us kissing. When the rainstorms finally came and the creek swelled, our islands disappeared, so we sat in Cole's barn instead. I missed the sound of the world rushing past us, the water surging over rocks.

That spring, just after my seventeenth birthday, the government blew up the levees protecting southern Louisiana and let the area flood so that New Orleans wouldn't. The government had stopped footing the bill for relocating people after hurricanes had destroyed so much of Florida's coastline that they had to let Disney buy out the entire state. So just before the levees blew, the mega-corporations swooped into southern Louisiana to promote their new townships and evaluate everyone for sponsored relocation. Unlike all those poor people in *China's* floodplains. Google was never going to knock on *their* doors offering to move them to drier parts. I kept my eyes glued to the newsfeeds because Grandpop had warned me that our farm, so close to the Mississippi River, was in a floodplain too.

At first, my dad said the government wouldn't let our land flood, that the country needed every bit of corn it could get, because the heat and wind were hard at work turning places like Nebraska and Kansas into sand dunes, destroying farmland and cattle ranches.

But when the Mississippi started swelling, it was a choice

between cities, with their people and businesses, and farm-land. The farmland would have to go. Ours included.

We heard a rumor that Microsoft-Verizon, which boasted the most luxurious townships in the country, had plans to come around and evaluate everyone for relocation. "What are they going to do with a bunch of farmers?" Cole said. "They're not going to relocate us. We don't have anything they want."

He took to hanging out with some older boys who itched to make someone else feel as desperate as they did. On a hot day at the creek, I saw one of them hold a little boy under the water until he stopped thrashing and then let him up just in time. At night, Cole would slip away to meet up with them—in the attic room of that girl whose parents go to town most weekends, or at that guy's half-done house where the front is mostly bare plywood. Cole and his friends would get so drunk so fast, Cole told me, it was like someone was holding their heads underwater and their day had come full cycle.

Sometimes I'd go with him and we'd all watch feeds from different townships and talk about relocating. Or Cole would play his guitar along to the radio and change all the lyrics to swear words. Sometimes he and I would lie in the attic bed together and kiss, and wonder if we should do more than kiss, but then other times he'd be far away, staring at the ceiling, barely acknowledging the brush of my kneecap. "No one cares about this place," Cole told me. "We don't count for anything out here away from the big cities. We might as well be ghosts."

Microsoft-Verizon showed up in town. They asked how many hits we usually got on our feeds. We had to tell them that we weren't blanketed with cameras like cities were and that corn planting wasn't all that entertaining anyway. I mentioned Cole had a solo coming up at a Woodbury Prep choir competition. They weren't impressed.

The Mississippi went on rising. Our days were numbered.

Cole stopped playing his guitar for me. He started spending all his time with the older boys and forgot to tell me where they were going. Rare days I did run into him, he could hardly look me in the eye. I wasn't sure how to tell him that just because Microsoft-Verizon saw reason to reject him didn't mean I felt the same.

I holed myself up in the attic with downloaded school assignments that I ignored in favor of online stories about the Other Place. People were always posting their own made-up adventures with the Girl Queen. But I liked the original stories best, the ones Brixney had transcribed from Dylan's famous notebook ages ago. I read about Dylan and Hunter passing into another world and wished I could do the same. What would it be like to find a lovely land, all cool greens and blues instead of the thermostat stuck on high . . .

I had posters of the Other Place tacked up on my walls, created by artists who mixed descriptions from Dylan's stories with information we'd gotten from the people who actually lived there. Snowcaps and grasslands; swaths of forest, like farms for shade. The posters were like those old-world travel ads designed by hucksters that urged people to *See the New World!*

But the truth was, we couldn't go to the Other Place. According to the stories, that other world overlapped with ours, and to visit it you had to be able to tune out our sights and sounds and tune in to the Other Place's—an ability we had yet to evolve, except perhaps in a few rare cases like Dylan and Hunter. It wasn't that the rest of us didn't have vorpals. It was just that a vorpal strong enough to sense the Other Place was a rare trait, something that would crop up only when the right genes came together.

So until our DNA worked a little harder, we weren't going anywhere.

Cole and I and some other kids from our valley made the three-hour drive together to the Woodbury Prep competition. We competed a few times a year because it was our best shot at college scholarships. Cole sat in the back with the other boys and slept and listened to his headphones, but once I felt him touch my hair and once he caught me staring at him in the rearview mirror. I remembered our days at the creek, and sheltering in his barn, and got moony all over again because I don't know when to quit.

In a city like Woodbury, it wasn't just our clothes that were wrong (everyone there wore disposable stuff they could trade for the latest fashion). We carried old wireless devices while all the other kids had flexi-screens molded around their arms that chirped with constant notifications.

I would stare at the ones decorated with images of teenage boys and wonder why anyone would want to wear a face on their arm.

Cole had tanned skin and a strong body, something you can't easily find in the city, where all the boys are espresso-steamed and pale. The girls at Woodbury Prep loved it when he mentioned anything *rustic* like collecting eggs from a chicken coop. They had no idea how gross fresh eggs are—usually completely covered in chicken crap. Cole was a fascinating artifact, with his cotton shirts and his farm chores back home. I guess I was fascinating too. It was fascinating how I pined for Cole across so short a distance as a coffee shop table.

The Woodbury concerts are about as famous as prep school competitions get, so the coffee shop was crowded. Cole was leaning on the table, striking this strong-arm pose as if he'd studied online clothing catalogs. Really, he was trying to hide the hole in his shirt and that's the real reason he was clutching his elbow. I was trying to get a good look at the flexi-screens stuck on the arms of some nearby girls. One frowning boy seemed to dominate the displays. His shaded cheekbones and blown-back hair made me wonder if he was from the Other Place, but you only ever heard it said that aliens looked just like everyone else.

I'd only ever met one, so I couldn't say if that was a fact.

What I could say is that I wouldn't prefer to meet another one, unless he had more apologies to offer than the last one did.

I kept staring at the face on the flexi-screens until Cole told me, "He's in a band. Stop gawking."

"Why is he so upset?" The boy was scowling but still prettier than I had ever seen a boy.

Cole smirked. "All of his songs are about how he and his girlfriend got relocated to different townships. It's high-concept."

I'd heard of high-concept groups. My friend Willer had a poster of one called Warehouse Burn, a group of boys who supposedly couldn't stop themselves from setting things on fire and then singing about it.

"Or he's suffering an allergic reaction to all that hair gel," Cole said.

I glanced again at the frowning face, the hair standing practically on end. "Could be he regrets signing his contract without reading that clause about eyeliner." Cole smiled, a rare sight these days. I thought about reaching for his hand, which was toying with the handle of his coffee cup. Did he still want to do things like that with me—hold hands? Kiss?

It'd been a long time. I kept my hands to myself.

The girls saw us looking at their screens and came over to ask Cole if black coffee was considered a food group back home. He shrugged because we couldn't tell them that we didn't have money to order anything fancier. The girls leaned on his chair and talked up the choir competition and asked Cole if he was nervous about his solo. They started touching Cole's collar, pulling at the sleeve they didn't realize had a hidden hole. They marveled at how thick the cotton was. One girl said, "Are you like those boys in Warehouse Burn? Can't wear anything too flammable?" and winked at him. But he got all bothered because he couldn't stand to feel like anyone was making fun of him, especially when he didn't have the money to stop it, which was always. He said, "Would you please stop *touching* me."

"Geez, Colburn," I said once they'd hurried away, "they were just trying to flirt with you." Though really, I was glad his glower had scared them off, considering girls back home collected Cole's moods like kids collect trading cards. (I had them all, from Charmingly Blunt to Lost In Self-Pity.)

"They can't see me sitting here with a girl already?" Cole said.

I again considered reaching for his hand, but he had it wrapped firmly around his coffee cup. And he wasn't even looking at me. He was watching the girls walk out of the shop, a defeated look in his eye.

"Thanks for the coffee," I mumbled. He'd spent his last few dollars on me. He could have spent them on one of those other girls, but what girl wants just coffee? Besides me, I mean.

He laid his hand over the tips of my fingers, tentatively. "Great idea, right? Getting you coffee before the performance. Great for the throat."

I shrugged. "It warms me up." But that was a lie. I was already warm—in the tips of my fingers and everywhere else.

I realized the woman at the next table had been watching everything. She saw the hole in Cole's shirt too, I think, because she kept looking at his hand after she came over and he clamped it on his elbow again. I recognized her from the Microsoft-Verizon interviews and went numb with surprise. What was she doing in Woodbury?

First she said to Cole, "Doesn't it feel terrible to be misunderstood?" I thought, *Cole's not exactly some big question mark—he's just moody as hell.* But I kept my mouth shut and Cole couldn't figure out what to say, so the woman added, "And a guy can't help wanting what he wants." It was like a line from a play, so we didn't say anything to that either. "I'm looking forward to the concert," she said to both of us and smiled at the rip Cole was still hiding.

I realized a girl at the counter had been watching us. Even before glimpsing the red tag that circled her wrist, I knew she was from the Other Place. She'd been watching Cole too.

Three years earlier, I had stood on the back staircase looking into our kitchen, where a much older boy drank straight from the tap. He was a farmhand Grandpop had hired for the season.

A creak on the stair gave me away. He turned, drew the back of his arm across his mouth. His face was exactly as I had imagined. Olive-green eyes and fine eyebrows that might knit together in interest over whatever a fourteen-year-old girl might have to say. A streak of dirt bronzed his jaw.

That afternoon, Grandpop took me to look at the collection of junkers he kept in the north pasture and while we were out there alone said, "The people from the Other Place usually stick to the big cities." I knew. Mostly, people spotted them sitting in cafes and parks, or driving down the street, ordinary as you please. They lived in houses and apartments and hotels, usually hosted by government officials but sometimes by volunteer families. "But the best way to know a people," Grandpop continued, "is by studying their food."

I understood what he was trying to tell me—the farmhand was from the Other Place.

I had already guessed it. I knew about vorpals, and that so many people from the Other Place had especially strong ones. They could make you do things they wanted you to do. But they never used that ability. They only ever watched us.

"Why doesn't he wear the tag?" I asked. I had seen some of his kind on TV before, always with a red tag around their wrist that recorded their location and whether they came into physical contact with anyone. I never thought I'd meet one in person, not in a small town in the middle of the country. I couldn't guess how Grandpop had gotten one to come here.

Grandpop reached into the nearest junker and popped open the glove compartment. Inside lay a red metal bracelet twisted out of shape. I gaped at it. "Maybe the government doesn't need to know that a person like him is interfering with a sly fox like me," Grandpop said.

"No interference, only observation," I said automatically.

Grandpop's eyebrows lifted at my conviction.

"I mean—they never do interfere with anything, do they?" I said. "It's a rule. It's why they have to wear the bracelets that tell the government what they're up to. They only watch us, they only want to learn."

"Oh, I suspect they've got bigger hopes than that, Epony," Grandpop said, gazing out over the blond heads of cornstalks, endless and identical.

I saw something in his faraway gaze, the way it lighted on the distant row of trees that marked the creek where he and everyone else had first learned to swim. I saw his throat move as he swallowed the emotion that tree line brought up: equal parts pain and possessive joy.

That was the first time I got a hint it would all be gone someday.

"You've got bigger hopes too, don't you, Pop?" I said. "You think the people from the Other Place can help us somehow?"

"They can. They have ways of making people see things differently, making people agree. They could help us fix this country." He shut the glove compartment, hiding the red bracelet from sight. "We live how we want to—use up resources like they'll last forever. But there's a price for everything. We'll have to pay it, one way or another. Maybe they can help us agree on how."

The farmhand used the name Hayden, which was really just my mother's maiden name. They never gave their real names—I guess because we'd have a hard time pronouncing them. His accent was subtle enough to prove our language didn't give him too much trouble, although I wondered if his vorpal helped him understand what people meant even when he didn't understand their words.

He stayed in the spare room, where a shelf held paper copies of the Girl Queen stories that my little sisters had gotten before the movie adaptation came out. Afternoons, I'd sit on the sacred bed where Hayden slept and I'd pull down volumes to read. I pretended if I read them enough times I could find a way there. Hayden would go too. In the Other Place, there would be no worry about interfering. No government fines, no stares or whispers. He could interfere with me all he wanted.

Once at dinner I watched in awe as he shoveled down creamed corn. Was it only an illusion or could aliens really eat solid food?

The newsfeed blared from the wall monitor, coverage on the latest climate conference. Dad was ready for the usual argument over carbon taxes.

"We make good money from corn, shipping it around the world," he said. "But who's going to buy it with a carbon tax attached?"

I waited for Grandpop's usual response. My little sisters were pressed into the back of their chairs like they wished they could escape through the wooden slats. Mom passed around the bowl of blackberries like a peace offering.

"There's enough demand for corn right here in the U.S.," Grandpop said, so that he and Dad sounded just like the politicians who always popped on the nightly newsfeeds. "We can't keep shipping it. How much farmland will be left in this country in twenty years when it's too hot to grow anything? Taxing carbon's the only way to restrict people from using corn to ruin our country."

"No point in arguing with you on this one." Dad pointed his fork at the newsfeed playing on the screen. "They'll never agree on anything—carbon taxes included."

But to everyone's surprise, the newsfeed wasn't going to address carbon taxes at all. The feed cut to an image of the delegates at the climate conference. *"The World Meteorological Organization has confirmed that allowing the Other Place to funnel energy from our sun's solar activity would stabilize global temperatures ..."*

"What does it mean?" I asked Grandpop while everyone else sat in stunned silence.

"It means the people from the Other Place are going to help us cool down this planet after all," Grandpop said, and turned to Hayden as if waiting for him to confirm it.

On-screen, the report continued. *"Scientists say a small amount of energy has been passing from our universe to the Other Place for decades, but world leaders will now work to find a way to increase that flow."*

I listened in awe. My little sisters tried to explain it to each other: "They're going to fix everything!"

But I noticed concern creeping into Grandpop's eyes.

"It'll take years to reverse the damage that's already been done to the planet," he said. "Decades, maybe."

"But it means no carbon taxes," I said. "That's better for the country, right? For everyone."

Grandpop looked to Hayden, who met Grandpop's gaze

with steely stoicism. "They seem to have the delegates at the conference convinced, anyway," Grandpop said. I knew, then, what was really going on: The aliens had finally used their vorpals to make us all agree on how to fix our problems.

During the next week, we kept the newsfeed on at all hours. The Energy Transfer Deal, as they were calling it, made everyone happy—world leaders, senators in slick suits, hosts of talk shows. There was only the matter of finding a way to open the floodgates and let the Other Place swallow the heat we'd been baking in for too long.

And then the answer came: We'd have to cross over into the Other Place. The more of us who did, the more channels would open to let solar energy slide through.

But that seemed impossible. You had to have a strong vorpal to cross over, and that was all a matter of genetics.

"How will we manage it?" I asked Grandpop one day while we watched the newsfeeds together. "How will people cross over into the Other Place?"

"I don't know if we will." He kept his eyes glued on the screen, but his gaze was unfocused. "Or if we should."

"What do you mean?" I asked. "You think it might be bad for us to go there?"

"Everything has its price."

And he was lost again in thought.

"What will it be like for us, if we cross into the Other Place?" I asked Hayden later, when I found him alone in the kitchen marveling over a loaf of walnut cranberry bread. "Will it be like it was for Dylan? Forests and rivers and palaces?"

He shoved the loaf of bread back onto the cutting board like he'd been caught stealing. "You will find what he found."

I leaned on the counter and tried to read what was in his gaze. He was always so cryptic. He almost never said anything about the place he'd come from. He just referred us to Dylan's stories, as though a child's understanding was all we needed. Maybe he thought he couldn't explain it any better.

"And if we don't want to go in the end, will you make us?" I asked.

"We will only do what you want us to do."

"But you can change what we want, can't you?"

He looked away. "No—we can't change you. Only influence you."

The dim twilight made him beautiful in a blown-glass way that my seventeen-year-old self now knows could never rival Cole's rugged charm. I leaned closer, glad he didn't have a tag and I didn't have a flexi-screen, that no record would show if I reached out and touched him. But he still seemed impossibly far away. I had seen the old video of Brixney and Michael—I knew I could as easy as not put my hand right through him. It wasn't fair for him to be so beautiful and not beautiful at the same time.

I nudged the bread back toward him. "Is there anything solid in your world?"

"Much of it is solid. We just interact with things a little differently than you do." And as he was talking, I saw in his mouth a single star, resting in the entry to his throat. But it was not a star. It was a tiny globe of light he had drawn in with his breath, and now he pushed it out so that it floated away like a bubble.

I touched his shoulder. "This isn't who you really are."

"A person can be many things."

The Microsoft-Verizon rep found us after the competition, while Cole was still holed up in the sound booth because he hadn't placed and wasn't going to get any scholarship. I was camped outside the door, silently willing him to get over it—silent because there was nothing to say. The rep had another line for us, which Cole had to hear through the sound booth door: "Those levees can go to hell. How'd you like to live in a premier township?" It was followed by the *click* of the door unlocking.

She was going to make me and Cole high-concept. Our families and ten others in the floodplain would move into the best township in the country and wouldn't pay a cent for anything. She talked about our energy, about this tension she sensed between us. But I knew it wasn't really about energy or tension—it was about the coffee shop and how girls were drawn to Cole like moths to a flame.

Cole kept smirking at me on the drive home and asking, "What do you think she has in mind?" like he wasn't sure yet he wanted to do it, even though his eyes gleamed with triumph. At first, I cared only that he was happy again, that he leaned close to talk to me, put his chin on my shoulder as though he did it every day. But then I thought about that new band that refused to leave Disneyworld and showed up at random places in the park to play impromptu concerts. It was dumb because everyone knew Disney had to be in on it or else the band would have gotten kicked out forever ago. I hoped Microsoft-Verizon had better ideas than that for our concept.

It turned out they did.

The rep stood in my kitchen the next day and told our parents she was going to take advantage of the fact that I'd hardly ever been on camera and would be relatively easy to scrub from the web. "Teen love is about wanting what you can't have," she said. "What you *shouldn't* have."

My dad adopted Grandpop's rumbling drawl. "Just what are you proposing?"

"Cole's a small-town charmer—any girl would want him," the rep said, and Cole pressed himself into the kitchen wall so that I half expected he'd leave a dent. "But the only girl he wants is the one he can't have. His cousin."

"But I'm not his cousin," I said stupidly.

She had a stage smile to match all those lines. Broad and disarming. "Which is why there's no reason for you to object, Epony."

It took a moment to sink in, and then the air went heavy as lead. I would pretend to be Cole's cousin and he would pretend to be in love with me. It seemed more gross than sexy. But she was right about forbidden love—the girls I knew couldn't get enough of it. That's why they all had those Warehouse Burn pyromaniacs plastered on their arms and T-shirts.

My parents exchanged grimaces across the table. Cole's

parents started sputtering about small-town stereotypes while Cole himself looked like he'd just swallowed the world's bitterest medicine.

In the next room, my sisters had the wall monitor set to CelebriFeed. The male lead in the latest Girl Queen movie—the tenth movie in the series—was taking a ribbing from the host, who kept insisting he must be from the Other Place. "How else can one boy be every girl's dream? You're some kind of illusion—you're on another plane of existence."

The star played at being bashful and laughed the question off. "No, no, I'm solid through and through."

I suddenly had an image of Grandpop in his cracked leather chair, narrowing his eyes at the far end of his pipe. "Exactly when did the existence of an alternate universe become a mundane thought? It doesn't seem normal not to put up a fuss." And then moving his narrowed gaze to me as if he suspected I had the answer.

I did have the answer later, after years of thinking about it. The aliens had a special ability to influence the way we felt about them, to manipulate our emotions. Those vorpals. It was why they inspired only fascination and not fear. Hundreds of them had positioned themselves in the most concentrated parts of our country, thousands had gotten themselves into the most important areas of the world. They were courting governments and the public alike. Their vorpals made everyone love them, even while they remained mysterious to us.

Or did we love them *because* they remained mysterious?

I turned back to the kitchen and said over the escalating noise, "We're not going to do it."

Cole's head snapped up and he hit me with a glare as cold as creek water. It went straight to my heart. At least now I knew his true feelings on the subject—he was in, no matter what he had to pretend about. And he wouldn't take to me screwing it all up.

The silence pressed in on me. I let my own silence press back. Then I said, "We'll do it like this: Cole's in love with me . . ." I gave him a searching look. He dropped his gaze to the scuffed floorboards. "And I want him too. But the reason we can't have each other is that I'm from the Other Place."

The rep had a real smile after all, a smug sort of smirk that left something gnawing at my stomach.

We packed up the house in a week. My sisters said good-bye to every shelf, window, and baseboard, as if they believed the new town house in Chicago wouldn't have such things. I cared more about Grandpop's junkers and spent a couple days mourning with each one in turn. Friday, my parents went off to auction animals and furniture, and to trade information with the other families who were moving too. I couldn't take one more snicker from Willer or any of my other friends about my upcoming metamorphosis, so I stayed home. I sat in the empty room where Hayden had slept the summer I was fourteen, the summer before Grandpop had gotten cancer. I thought of the time Hayden had come in to find me reading on his bed.

"Is the Other Place really like this?" I'd showed him the book cover of Dylan's stories: two boys running through the forest toward a palace in a clearing, on the verge of discovery. The stories within told of strange creatures that grew and shrank at will, of a Girl Queen who glowed with magic, of trees that formed doorways into secret spaces. "Is it so like a fairy tale?"

Hayden's face darkened. The little bedroom was full of his presence, and I thought I might be sensing his vorpal, the way you sense rather than hear the sound of a cat's tail brushing over floorboards. I wished he would sit on the bed next to me and then he did. "You've become enamored with us," he said. "But what you know of us is only what you've invented. Only an illusion."

I leaned against him, and this time I knew my own vorpal was there too, right alongside his. "The illusion is the part we like best."

They scrubbed me from the web, every last image of me, my entire online profile. It depressed me that it was so easy to do. I'd never had a solo in any choir competition, never been named queen at the county fair. I was the one turning away from the camera while everyone showed off blue ribbons at the poultry show, the girl huddled under a sweatshirt at the Friday night bonfire. It was easy to convince people to crop me from their online photos, to delete me from their social media pages. Afterward it felt like not existing. I couldn't even walk into a store and buy a pop. Cole would have to come in with me so the system could scan his image and charge the Coke to his online account.

They messed with Cole's profile too, changing his name from Colburn and adding photos of him as a doting older brother and protector of small animals. His new outfits were a farce of a farm boy's wardrobe—white T-shirts and blue jeans thin enough you could almost see through them. Soft boots that laced halfway to the knee and were good only for padding through coffeehouses and carpeted lofts.

I wore black, always black, a ghost in negative.

We drove out to Chicago to meet our producer, who came packaged with a songwriter barely older than me and Cole. The songwriter had played the bass in a high-concept band that had fizzled out a year ago when it was revealed that the members weren't actually dying of a solar allergy.

"His concept's dead," the producer told us by way of introduction, "but his songs are hot. Melodic as heck."

The songwriter seemed self-conscious only about not having been the front man. "The bass is the gateway that links the guitar with the drums," he said in his defense.

The producer was in his forties and too well-fed and a little bit manic. He took us down to his basement studio, which was papered with burger ads featuring supermodels. I was hungry the whole time we were down there. It'd been months since I'd tasted beef. I mean real beef, not the substitute.

He played some different beats for me and Cole and

asked for our opinion and then told us which one he'd already picked out. "I want it to be effing ethereal," he said, smoothing his paper-thin shirt over his paunch. "Dreamy synths like fireflies on helium."

I had no idea what he was talking about. Could music even sound like that? He must have thought it was his euphemism that had unsettled me, because he explained, "I'm trying to cut down on swearing. For the kids," and gestured vaguely at the models in the posters.

He and the songwriter had already scribbled some lyrics on a paper placemat.

"This is the story." The producer directed his acetone breath at me. "Cole's not supposed to get involved with your type—it's against the law but he can't help himself. And you can do what you want with him, can't you, because your powers of persuasion are sort of superhuman. Your vorpal, yes? So here we go. The first part is Cole's and the second is Epony's."

The songwriter read the lyrics off in a monotone:

I know what you are,
how you watch me.
If I go too far
will you stop me?

"Effing ethereal," the producer cut in to remind us.

I know what they say,
how they watch me.

If I want your heart
can they stop me?
They won't understand this.
They can't come between us.

I stole a glance at Cole. He raised his eyebrows at me. I remembered laughing in the creek together and then quickly pushed the thought away. The creek was just another current in a morass of currents now.

"Right, let's try it in the booth," the producer said, and handed the paper placemat to Cole. "Sing it like a girl would, Cole, like a sweet effing innocent girl."

While they mixed the final track, we went to a movieplex to watch Girl Queen movies. We rented a space that was nothing but a shelf on a stack of shelves facing a huge screen. Footrests rose up from the floor; pops rolled down from a fridge hatch.

On-screen, a river pooled around a city of sun-dazzled glass, and an actor portraying Dylan called a silvery creature out of the water. It was the seventh Girl Queen movie in a row we had watched.

"Watch out for the stinger!" I hollered at the screen, because I knew this movie by heart. It was based on a popular story someone had posted online about Dylan's adventures with the Girl Queen and her brother. There was no telling if it had gotten the look of the Other Place right, but it seemed close enough to what Dylan had described in his own stories, so I was willing to go along for the ride.

During a lull in the action, Cole told me, "They shouldn't have turned your vocals down on the chorus. I was drowning you out."

"We aliens don't like to be loud," I said, poking him in the ribs. "We're a shy bunch. We're really only here to make humans like you sound better."

"Seriously, though," Cole said.

I shook my head. "It's *your* voice that's good. They'll have to do all that thickening with mine. I never heard you sing so high."

"Sounded like a mosquito in heat." He climbed up on the back of the seat and popped open the fridge hatch to use as a headrest. The chemical smell of refrigerant reminded me of ice-cream bars and frozen lemonade. "Ethereal my ass."

"Looks ethereal from this angle," I joked, and prodded him so he leaped off the chair back.

He dropped into the seat and leaned against me. "If I had known they were going to try to turn me half into a girl, I might not have done this."

"Yes you would have." I slipped an arm around his shoulders, praying he wouldn't pull away. My heartbeat was an overproduced version of itself, all bass notes. "Those tween girls like the non-threatening brand of angst. Get used to it, girly boy."

He laced his fingers through mine so that his arm was across his chest. "Those lyrics . . ." He grimaced at the distant movie screen. "I hate acting that way around you."

I stiffened. "Like you're in love with me?"

"No, like I can't do anything about it."

The light from the screen lent his face an early-morning, dirt-streaked window kind of glow.

"You can do something about it." I brushed my chin against his shoulder.

He shifted in his seat so that I thought maybe I was bothering him. But then he turned and kissed me, and the sound of river water from the movie reminded me of our islands in the creek.

Then he jerked away, scowled at the armrest. "You like doing any of this?"

"Kissing you?" I almost laughed. Was there some other reason to do it?

"No, I mean my non-threatening high notes." He flopped back in his seat. "And these pants that are about three sizes too small."

I touched the back of his shoulder, trying to coax him closer again. "It's what everybody wears."

He reached to pull his guitar out from under his seat. "Never mind." He started strumming, and that was the end of that.

We ordered hot dogs and a case of designer candy that made smoke pour out of our mouths. Cole riffed on his guitar despite protests from the other shelves. *"I've tasted sorrow, salt, and sickly sweets,"* he sang. *"Hate it all, but a boy's gotta eat."*

I passed in and out of sleep for the remainder of the movie. I kept seeing my kitchen wallpaper in the Girl Queen's palace, faded and curling. Cole's hens scrambling for the fence line. In the dark nighttime scenes when blue light washed over us, I pretended the world was flooding and I was safe up on a high shelf with Cole and candy, and pretended that was enough.

"Will they buy it?" Cole asked, his thumb hitting an errant note that jolted me out of dreaming.

He meant the girls, the tweens with their lust for high-con. Would they buy that I was an alien? That he was in love with me? That was what he cared about. What kept his mind occupied even while he kissed me, so that he could hardly remember to enjoy it. His shrill tone set my teeth on edge. "They'll eat you up."

We stayed at the movieplex all night and into the following day. Just watched movie after movie and dozed during the boring parts and tried to remember if we existed beyond our shelf. I came to the conclusion that we kind of didn't. The context for every moment of our lives was gone, underwater. Me with no profile, like some mythical creature exiled from Atlantis.

After they'd finished the track, they had us come down and listen to it, and I forgot it was me singing and got goose bumps from the shimmering synths and the bass notes like a heartbeat. Cole's voice was a prepubescent version of itself and so sweet I could almost cry. Effing ethereal, after all.

The plan was that when the single hit the airwaves, every flexi-screen within range of a signal would light up with an image of Cole's haunted expression. Anyone who clicked through to the webpage would discover a forlorn Cole reaching for me as I faded away. Below the image, a single line of text: "They won't understand this."

It was almost the exact pose from that most viral of ancient feeds, the moment Michael faded away from Brixney. Despite what the lyric said, everyone would understand it.

I was wheedling the guy at the grocery counter to let me take some tomatoes and a head of lettuce when the single dropped. His flexi-screen lit up. He tapped on it in a way he thought was discreet, arm below the counter. His gaze went to my wrists and found no screen or red bracelet. Wide-eyed, he waved me on. I thought, *See? Who needs credits?*

On my way home, past house-fronts painted white against the early summer heat, it hit me: I was an alien now.

I started running.

Cole was fidgeting in the entryway of my family's premier town house, his boots smearing dirt on the new white premier tiles. I pointed at the brand-new flexi-screen on his arm, which was spouting our single. "Take it off, what are you thinking? Before they get here."

He jolted. Tugged it off. Then paused, the music echoing, his screen still lit up with the image of his own face. "Wait, who's *they*?"

"I don't know, *they,* people. Fans. Turn it off, they can track your location."

Cole swiped at the screen and our singing stopped. We looked around. We waited. I kept staring at the door. "Should we barricade it?" Cole asked. He cracked a smile. I chucked the lettuce at him.

"Turn it back on." I nodded at his screen.

He made a swipe, tapped through to our website. "Six hundred eighty-seven subscribers." His face went premier white.

The tomatoes slipped out of my grip. "Turn it back off."

A sound of thunder on the stairs and then my sisters barreled into the room. "Come see—you're on CelebriFeed!"

I stamped up after them on shaky legs.

"Stop running!" my dad called from the kitchen. "It's hot enough in here and the a/c won't turn up."

"Dad!" I said.

"Did you get the groceries?" he called.

"Dad!"

"What?" He poked his head in. The wall monitor caught his eye. There was the image from our website, large as life on the screen. "Well, what in the world? I never saw a boy's hair look like that." He turned his gaze to Cole's yellow thatch, nothing like the gelled nest of hair on-screen.

"Are you going to get in trouble?" my younger sister asked.

"For what?" Cole said.

She sidled up to him, as eager to bask in his annoyance as in any other form of his attention. "For interfering with an alien."

"She's not an alien, she's your sister," Dad said, and slumped back to the kitchen.

"Besides, she doesn't have a red bracelet," my other sister said. "She's supposed to have ditched it. How will they know anyone's interfering with her?"

"They'll know from CelebriFeed!"

Cole scooted away to leave them to their shrill bickering.

"*Are* we going to get in trouble for this?" I murmured to him.

"In trouble with who?"

"The FBI or someone."

"The FBI won't believe that an alien could want a human. Aliens and humans aren't even the same species. Only high-con fans believe crap like this."

He was right—I knew it firsthand. Aliens didn't fall in love with silly fourteen-year-old girls or even glammed-up seventeen-year-old girls. "The aliens, then. They'll be mad. They don't like to draw attention to themselves."

"If they didn't want attention, they wouldn't wear those bright red bracelets."

"They have to." My younger sister had inched close again and stood inspecting the way Cole's sweat-dampened clothes stuck to him. "The government said so."

Cole went to the a/c and tried to override the peak-usage sensor. "Anyway, the aliens can just go ahead and kiss it; they're not the ones whose egg is in the frying pan."

For the next few days, CelebriFeed cycled our photo through a hundred times, each with a different headline. *Close Encounter Leads to Illegal Love . . . Vorpal Abuse: He's Under Her Spell . . . Does She Have a Tail?* Cole and I hid out in the township and let our mystique build. Then we flew out to L.A., city of camera angles.

I found out what heat was. The heat of the desert, the

press of the crowds, heat from the tailpipes and the gleaming hoods of cars. The heat from Cole, coming close for a kiss in direct sight of a streetlamp camera. The burn of humiliation at realizing he was only mooning over me because he'd spotted a line of camera lenses embedded in a shop awning. It was the same game over and over: Pull close, pull away. Disappear around a corner, into a waiting car, to leave Cole feigning heartbreak. All for the cameras, for the act.

By the third week, when the cat-and-mouse thing started to get old, our new fans made it easy for us to evolve our act. When Cole went out, they'd swarm him like flies. I'd appear at the right moment, cutting a wide swath through the frightened crowd. *Is she really?* they'd whisper. Or, *Save him from her!* Later, Cole would get me alone with the cameras and try to tell me he didn't want those other girls. I'd tell him he should be with them, that it'd be better for him. A few tears on my part and then I'd leave. We kept it short. We always kept it short. They couldn't get enough.

When the temperatures soared, the rolling blackouts were a relief. The power to the city's cameras went out, giving Cole an excuse to be offline for a couple of days. He ditched his flexi-screen so no one could track him and we drove out to Santa Monica. From Ocean Avenue, we took in the sight of the storm-wrecked pier still in splinters, the Ferris wheel motionless above the dark water like a giant eye peering over the edge of an abyss.

= ≠ =

"Don't care how they see you, I'll never leave you."

"I'll keep us together, stay with you forever."

Cole and I took turns singing over a thumping beat, crouched in an abandoned warehouse whose cameras couldn't be traced. The same building Warehouse Burn often used, according to our producer.

"Stay with you forever." Cole whispered into my ear, "Or at least until I get feeling back in my legs." He shifted into an easier crouch, flashed me a quick smile. I hoped the mic hadn't picked up his joke.

Our producer stood out of sight, flapping his arms at us and mouthing, *More effing intensity!*

"Stay with you forever!" I belted. Then the breakaway wall crashed in and I slipped out of sight, leaving Cole to gape at vaguely threatening forms. The dark, hulking men could have been FBI or some kind of alien task force but were really day laborers in black turtlenecks. The cameras went dead on cue. The producer checked his flexi-screen and reported that we were already number forty-three on FeedBin.

"Intense as heck," the producer said of either our performance or the ad revenue.

Forty-three didn't sound great to me, but he seemed confident we'd topple the teen mini-shows and the clips of skateboard tricks. I figured he knew better than I did.

He pointed a thick finger at Cole. "We need to talk before you go."

I started to follow them but the producer waved me away. "No, Epony. Just Cole. Vocal issues," he said, pointing to his throat. "Don't worry about it. Separate cars out of here, and if you two are going to meet up later, for eff's sake make sure you've disabled any cameras. You're completely offline until prime time."

I swiped Sheetrock dust from my shoulders and shook it out of my hair.

Cole was standing frozen, a spray of white dust turning half his face pale. I gave him a questioning look.

"Cole, did you hear me?" The edge in the producer's voice made me look up. Cole snapped out of whatever spell had held him, jerked his gaze away from me.

"Yeah," he answered. "Alone and miserable and crying into a camera lens at eight o'clock tonight."

I rode to my hotel. The driver tuned the car radio with his flexi-screen since I didn't have my own. All the songs were the same anyway. Girls singing about falling asleep in their party clothes, about glamming up their profiles. Boys singing about cycling through disposable shirts, about their screens too tight on their arms. Lyrics about things I'd never experienced and didn't understand. They'd fake alien accents, something I'd gotten good at in the last couple of weeks, or they'd affect drunkenness and slur their lyrics. The song would build to a climax, there'd be that moment, that one bit of emotion I could grab on to. And back to talk of hairstyles and camping out on high-speed trains.

Not like when Cole sang—when he sang a song *he* wrote, anyway. The whole thing so charged through with feeling, the emotion so palpable it made ladders in the air.

One day I was going to reach out and touch them and climb up to somewhere.

At the camera-free suite I had come to call home, it was a ration day—no air-conditioning. The balcony doors let in smog and not much else. The same news story kept looping on the wall monitor: *"The taskforce will attempt to train people with strong vorpals to cross into the Other Place, which will strengthen the link that allows solar energy to flow into the alternate universe."* I'd already heard all about it, already wondered how they'd find anyone with a vorpal strong enough to sense the Other Place. They'd been trying for years now. I switched it off.

Cole came in. He had his own apartment where we sometimes moped together for the cameras, but we could only drop the act here in my suite. He dragged out the battered guitar he kept stashed there, clipped a guitar string, and used it to override the a/c controls.

We collapsed in front of the a/c unit and lay where we had fallen, looking like a fashion spread of third-world heat casualties. *"I've lived L.A. by camera light,"* Cole sang lazily, strumming his guitar, *"swelter days, blackout nights."*

Then his fingers left the guitar strings and trailed to my arm, my hair. He traced circles and lines on my neck as though mimicking some foreign and complicated pattern. My heart tried to follow it, surging in time with his movements. When he leaned in for a kiss I reminded him there weren't any cameras around. He reminded me not to be an ass. We added a little more heat to the world.

Until Cole stopped mid-kiss, pulled away as usual, that

defeated look coming into his eye again—same as when we played for the cameras. It had gotten to where I couldn't tell when that look wasn't real. "I'm not actually an alien," I told him. "I've got all the right anatomy and everything."

He didn't laugh. "They didn't go for your idea."

"What idea—the thing where we run away together?" I tried to angle myself close to him again, missing the weight of his arm around me. "Preferably to Europe. I could use a vacation from this place."

He rolled onto his feet, fiddled with the a/c knob again. "Yeah, I just said they didn't go for it."

I huddled on the couch, stung. "Is that what you and the producer were talking about? Did you tell him London is completely blanketed with lenses? All those old surveillance cameras are connected to the Internet now."

"They said it would cut all the tension we've been building."

I sat up. "Who's *they*?"

"Producer, rep."

"She's in town? When did you talk to her?" I leaned forward until I could put my hand on his back. "What if, like, we can't get passports—nobody can get entry to England right now—and then we have to get smuggled in—"

He turned to face me. "We don't have a lot of choice here. If they don't want to do it, we can't do it." His arms were trembling. What wasn't he saying?

He pushed my hair behind my ear. I ran my fingers over his arm, inviting him closer, but he didn't budge. I thought for a moment he was about to confess something, his expression was so rabbit-scared. "I'm sorry," he said.

"This whole thing was our idea to start with," I said. "*My* idea."

"And it's *their* money."

"I didn't know you had so much loyalty to Microsoft-Verizon," I said sourly.

He twitched. The floor was suddenly so fascinating that he couldn't look me in the eye. "It's *their* town houses our families are living in, in case you forgot."

"I didn't."

He let his shirt balloon around him with cold air from the unit. "That's how it works, Epony. Someone else sets the price and we pay it. SeedBank, the governor with his damn levees. That's how it always works."

He left to go down to find some fans who could crowd him, crowd out his thoughts, while I watched his feed on the wall monitor.

At eight, I showed up at his place, right on schedule. I knew what scene I'd find on the other side of his door: Cole crushed and lonely, afraid we'd never be together because the FBI was watching us now. They weren't really watching us. But our fans believed what they wanted to believe.

What's next? I wondered while I waited for him to answer the door. We'd given our fans forbidden romance, underage lovers, police in pursuit. And we were only a month into the act. What else would we have to do to hold their interest?

Cole yanked the door open, surprise registering on his

face. Not the good kind of surprise, not relief. A moment of confusion on my part while I waited for an embrace that didn't come. And then I saw her. And thought, *Those bastards.*

"It's better this way," Cole said. "Better for *you.*" Then he stepped close, close enough that I could see the transparent mic clipped under his chin. "They're watching us," he said in a stage whisper.

I pulled out of his grip, stumbled back. *What the hell?* Nobody had told me about this new direction. Why hadn't they told me?

Because they wanted this reaction. Genuine shock. Hurt, humiliation.

I fled down the hallway, downstairs. I heard him loping after me in his soft boots, shouting some line they'd fed him.

I barreled down the street and finally into a cafe. Every table monitor was playing Cole's feed. He was already back inside his air-conditioned den, reveling in the new girl's method of consoling him.

"Fake kissing is still real kissing," I shouted at the screens.

I shot back out into the street. The late-night traffic crawled past, weary drivers peering out at the girl with bare arms and tear-streaked face. The thrum of idling engines was nauseating, the streetlights sad, dirty yellow.

Visions flicked through my head of Hayden. He'd sat next to me on the bed while I was reading, and I'd leaned into him, thinking he might kiss me. I pictured now the puzzled tilt of his head. *"I couldn't ever feel that way about you,"* he'd said. *"Don't you know? The way you look, the way you are, it's nothing like what I could ever want."* It was the last time I'd seen him. Even now, I could feel the stifling heat of the attic room that had been my hideout those final sweltering weeks of September.

One of the cars in the line of crawling traffic had stopped altogether. The driver craned her neck to get a good look at me. A horn blared. The woman went on staring. Had she seen Cole's feed? She was too old to care about high-con.

Her gaze was fascinated, piercing. Her arm resting on the steering wheel was encircled with a red bracelet.

When I was fifteen, cancer made Grandpop's skin dull, his eyes bleary. I felt like I was always seeing him through fogged glass in those days. His hair grew in patches. I could never get a good look at him. He cowered.

I didn't realize it was indecision weighing on him. The cancer was just one more stone on the scale.

Grandpop showed me a map with a red scrawl encircling a large area of Washington State, including the Cascadia parks. "Almost time for me to head out."

I slumped in the backseat of one of his junkers, legs dangling out in the long grass. "Why are you going?" It was my way of saying *Don't.*

The insects buzzed as if to lend sound to Grandpop's wry smile. "The world has already started saying its goodbye. Time I caught up."

My heart crumpled.

"I won't be able to come back to you." He squeezed my chin. The bugs made the evening air sizzle. "Maybe someday you'll follow me."

I looked up, finally, unsure of what he meant. But the two of us only ever exchanged questions, never answers. I tried to hand him the map but he pushed it back toward me, and this time I noted the million red dots concentrated mostly in the circle he had drawn. Pinpointing locations. Locations of what? Before I could ask him about it, he loaded his old, failing body into the most serviceable junker. A minute later, it coughed away down the road.

For two days after I saw Cole kissing someone else, I refused all calls: Cole's, the producer's, the rep's. I think our songwriter even tried once.

I lived off room service and watched newsfeeds and willed my heart to stop sinking like a stone. I tried to put it all together: Grandpop's map with the red dots, and the way people from the Other Place sometimes stared at me—on the street, and in the coffee shop in Woodbury, where I'd thought the alien there was staring at Cole.

I watched Cole's feed, like all his other fans did. Admired the clever love triangle they'd set up, even while I fumed over the betrayal.

I decided it was time to get back to playing my own game.

They paid the new girl to go in and out of grocery stores while Cole pined for her near the cart return. The two of them were supposed to be fighting. Over me, I suppose. Sometimes when she walked out, he looked at her like he was missing something and she had it in her shopping bag. I didn't think he was in love with her. In fact, I happened to know that he hated that pouty city look, the fake needle marks, the black-smudged under-eyes. But there were a lot of things missing in Cole's life and it was probably easier for him if he could put them all in one bag.

I ambushed Cole while they had an actual cameraman camped in view of the fluorescent storefront of the grocery store.

Cole was stunned to see me, in a five-million-volt stun gun kind of way. "Are you—what're you—?" he sputtered. "Are you okay?"

I waved away his *We shouldn't be meeting like this but I'm so glad to see you* attempt. "I have to talk to you. I'm going back."

"Back?"

"Home."

He shook his head, genuinely confused. Home was underwater, along with busted-up levees. But I wasn't talking about *home* home. I was playing for the cameras. I was giving us a way out.

"I'm going to the Other Place," I said.

Cole shrank back, surprised. I almost reached for him. Even now, hurt as I was, I felt he was a magnet and I was metal.

"I want you to come with me," I said, and almost grimaced at how my voice cracked.

"How—how can I? What're you—"

"I'm leaving tomorrow morning." *Leaving L.A., even if you don't come with me. Quitting this act.*

He pulled me aside, as if the cameraman couldn't change angles. "What are you talking about?"

"I won't do this anymore." I lowered my voice to a tone I hoped his mic wouldn't pick up. "I know you hate it too. Come with me." I touched his arm, slid my hand down to twine my fingertips in his.

I knew he wanted to say it: *Come with you where, exactly?* He didn't believe, of course, that we could go to the Other Place. But he couldn't break the act while he was wearing a microphone and the cameraman was behind my shoulder. He wouldn't go that far off-script.

And I hardly knew myself how serious I was. I wanted to leave L.A. and leave the act. Something inside me stirred when I thought about trying to cross into the Other Place. But was it adrenaline, or my vorpal, long dormant and finally coming to life?

I tried to find it, tried to reach out with it and make Cole listen to me. I slipped Grandpop's old map into Cole's hand. "There's a train. Tomorrow morning."

Cole glanced at the map and thrust it into his pocket before the camera could get a good view of it. "What the hell is this all about?"

I glanced through the window at rows and rows of boxed food—rice and pasta and powdered salty cheese mix. Cole's other girl was there, oblivious to what was happening out on the sidewalk. She was scrutinizing a package of instant rice. I remembered Grandpop's comment about knowing a people by learning about their food. I imagined the girl as a student of the L.A. species and almost laughed. Funny how a person's jokes can outlast him.

Cole was waiting for me to say something.

I touched his hand again. "Just come with me."

"You know I can't." Was he saying it for the cameras, because he couldn't cross into the Other Place? Or was he saying it for me, because he wouldn't leave the act?

Nothing in his gaze would tell me. I pulled my elbow out of his grip and strode away.

The Microsoft-Verizon rep was waiting in my hotel room when I got back. Her smile had widened into a shark's grin.

"You've decided to go off-script," she said.

The wall monitor was tuned to Cole's feed, as always. He was alone in his kitchen with a stack of canned black beans and his guitar. I spent a few moments listening to the low tone of his song, letting his voice fill up the dim space of my hotel room: *If the world is a creek bend, you're my city. It's pretty to pretend. Then it ends.*

I turned to the rep, my insides full of daggers. "Remember? I wrote the script in the first place."

"And Microsoft-Verizon financed it. Your whole act." She smiled at the pleasantly poignant sight of Cole singing to his empty kitchen. "I wonder where your parents are going to live after you and Cole have run away together."

I imagined my sisters sighing over Cole's feed, urging

him to come back to me. Would they be surprised if I disappeared? They might believe I had been an alien all along, and then someday a month or a year from now they'd look up from the screen and say, *Wait? Wasn't she just our sister?*

"You know Cole's not going to come with me." The words tasted bitter in my mouth. "He can stay and play out the act as the jilted lover. I'm sure his fans will love it."

"And that's what you want—to leave Cole?" She frowned down at my belongings scattered on the coffee table: some crumpled candy wrappers, an envelope that had once held Elixir guitar strings, a book of Girl Queen stories. "I think I've come to know you better than that."

She touched the Elixir envelope and I cringed. I debated telling her that I'd only saved Cole's trash because he'd scribbled lyrics on it that I couldn't bear to throw out.

The rep laughed. "I think I had you figured out from the beginning. That's my job, figuring people out."

"Then you knew from the beginning I didn't want this as much as Cole wanted it." That day in my kitchen came back to me: the cold-water glare from Cole, and the rep looking on with her smug smile. "That's why you set this up the way you did, isn't it? Giving us that terrible idea in the beginning about us pretending to be cousins. Letting me think that our alien act was really my idea when that's what you were hoping for all along."

She didn't deny it. She seemed almost pleased I had figured her out, happy I had become an apprentice to her art.

I crossed my arms to try to stop my trembling. "Well, now Cole can go on just as well without me." It hurt me to say it. But I had to admit it: Cole wouldn't leave with me. He'd stay and play the game. "You made sure of that. You roped in that girl so you could keep the act going even if I left it."

I started toward the door, but she angled herself to block me. "Isn't that why you chose the role you did? So you could give Cole a good reason to reject you?"

I shook my head, mired in confusion.

"You knew Cole wouldn't stay with his small-town girl-friend," she explained.

Something in my stomach bucked, but my anger was like sand running through a sieve. "You don't know anything about us," I said weakly. "You're like those high-con fans who trust everything that comes through a camera lens."

"I know what I saw on Cole's face when he looked at those girls in the coffee shop in Woodbury." She leaned closer. "Your hold on him might be strong. But it's not strong enough. Not when you remind him of everything he wants to leave behind."

My insides turned molten.

I smelled the sharp smell of black coffee. Felt Cole's finger-tips touching mine. Saw that hole in his shirt, the only thing that kept him from walking out with those girls— the only thing that kept him stuck, sitting there with me.

I ducked around her and left to find Cole.

= ≠ =

He'd gotten halfway to my hotel by the time I caught up to him on the street. His flexi-screen was gone, and so was the cameraman. He ducked into an alley and motioned for me to follow him away from the street cameras.

I turned the corner and ran right into him. He caught my wrists, my freakish bare wrists with no screen and no red tag. No way to tap into my credits in a store, no profile to prove my identity. I had come all the way to the camera capital of the country to be invisible.

"They wouldn't let me tell you about her," he said, his eyes wide and mournful.

"You don't have to go along with it."

He didn't say anything to that. I felt the slow, weak pulse of his heart, the tepid blood ebbing through it. Things impossible to feel, but I felt them. Was it my own pulse, beating against his fingers wrapped around my wrists?

I felt his vorpal, withering in the smoggy heat.

I knew the feeling well: I had felt it before, a vibration on his skin. I'd heard it. In his music—that hum beneath his voice that made the air rise.

How could I have not recognized it before? All along, I'd felt the pull of his vorpal on mine. But I'd never known it until now.

And I knew something more: My vorpal was stronger than his.

"You can't leave." He pulled my arms against his chest, against his slow-beating heart. "You don't have a profile. How are you going to live? Making wildflower salads in the park?"

"Come and see."

He pushed away from me. "And our families will do what exactly? Live on Microsoft-Verizon's generosity?" He gave a derisive laugh. "We've really screwed this up, haven't we?"

His hollow voice made me sick with dread. I sank back against the cold metal of a Dumpster. "We shouldn't have done any of it in the first place."

Cole's expression darkened. "We had to. What else were we supposed to do? We were nobodies. The state flooded our whole town to save cities better than ours."

"And to save people better than us?" I asked, because I knew that was how he felt. "Funny how it works: They put a camera on you and suddenly you exist." I glared at him, daring him to deny he believed that.

He pulled at the neck of his thin shirt, as if stifled by the rotten-alley air. "This whole act was *your* idea in the first place. I went along with the script *you* wanted."

My stomach churned.

I could convince him to come with me without saying a word. I could overpower his vorpal with mine.

I almost said it again: *Come with me.* And he would have.

But then I looked at his neon-white shirt, at his soft boots so thin I could see his restless feet flexing inside them. "I wish we could go back home," I told him instead.

Cole gave me a slow shrug. "There was nothing there, really." He turned toward the mouth of the alley. The streetlights shone in his eyes. A thousand unblinking cameras waited for him.

I wouldn't try any longer to change his mind. And I wouldn't stay.

So I did the disappearing thing I'd gotten good at.

When I was fourteen, Grandpop told me to keep my eyes on the newsfeeds. Watch the waves of famine, the mass migrations, the border wars. The green bloom of algae in the dead zones at the mouths of the Yangtze and the Mississippi alike. He said, "The world is shrinking. It's drying out. We've lived how we wanted to live, and now we're paying the price for it."

"The people from the Other Place are going to fix it all," I said. "Once we find a way to cross over into their world, things will start to get better. It'll take time, like you said. But everything will get better."

Grandpop peered at me from his leather chair. For a moment, I thought the creak of springs was the sound of his weary bones shifting. "Yes. They get some of our energy, we get a solution for our problems. And all we have to do is visit their world of wonders. It's more than fair, isn't it?"

He settled back in his groaning chair and narrowed his eyes at his pipe. "It's a nice story, anyway."

I took the high-speed. The guy at the ticket booth was a fan, so I didn't have to explain why I had no credits.

One brief glance around the station and then onto the train alone to bullet through bushy Oregon to Washington State.

I used the seat monitor on the train to navigate to a website I'd discovered while I'd been holed up in my hotel room. A forum where people posted maps like the one Grandpop had given me. I left a message there.

Epony   9:56pm

maybe someday you'll follow me

If you can't meet me, send someone who can.
Seattle high-speed station, tomorrow morning.

I left it for Grandpop. Or not for him exactly, since there wasn't much chance he was still alive. Really, I left it for Hayden, in the hopes his people knew about the map Grandpop had passed on to me.

Grandpop must have sensed about me what I had only just begun to realize myself—the reason people from the Other Place stared at me in coffee shops, on city streets: It was my vorpal. Grandpop's had been special, strong, and so he noticed it in me too. The way anyone with a strong vorpal noticed another strong vorpal, like a huge red blossom on a radar screen.

And all this time, Grandpop had been trying to decide between encouraging me and warning me.

He had given me his map, covered in a million red dots. Each dot representing the signal from a red bracelet—information he had gotten from a website like the one I'd found, maybe even the very same site. A curious concentration of those signals spread over Washington, parts of Oregon, up into Canada. The overlap between two worlds. The fact that he had never come back to tell me what he found meant he'd probably died at the end of his journey. So I wouldn't know what he'd found until I encountered it myself.

At the Seattle station, I had hours to mull it over. There could only be one reason the aliens were so keen on advertising themselves with their bright red, government-issued bracelets even while they watched our world go into decline. One reason they let us create stories about the Girl Queen and their world, let us spin illusions.

They knew our fantasies would always have more power than the truth.

Everyone loved the idea of stepping into a better world. And if your own world started shrinking enough, you just might put your vorpal to the test. The aliens didn't have to convince us to come. We would convince ourselves. More and more of us would cross into their universe, strengthening the bond between two worlds, opening channels that would let energy flow from our world into theirs.

It's what I was doing now—searching for a world from the stories I loved. And I knew more people would follow.

The only problem was, the stories weren't all true. We were giving in to an illusion.

And I knew now from experience: Illusions end.

Still, what else did we have?

Hours I waited, and then there he was. Dark from the sun, hair like parched grass. A bit taller in thick-soled shoes. Broader in the chest so that I was surprised to find I ever thought much about his chest. I felt the calluses on his hand when he slipped it into mine. For a moment, I let my palm hover against his, afraid it might push right through. But no, it was solid as long as I wanted it to be solid, and he was silent waiting for me to make up my mind.

I made up my mind. I gripped his hand hard and walked out of the station, glanced a good-bye at the snow-naked mountain, and found my way into another world.

4.

WHEN WE COULD HARDLY CONTAIN OURSELVES

(sixty years from now)

REEF

The closest eighteen-year-old Reef ever got to the alternate universe was through a massively multiplayer virtual-reality role-playing game called Alt.

When he walked the streets of Seattle wearing his digital goggles, ordinary buildings changed into sleek alien architecture. But he wasn't really seeing the Other Place— he never would, with a vorpal as weak as his. It was all a mirage, a virtual game for people like him who were left out of the real fun.

Decades ago the government had tried to help people cross over into the Other Place. Then one day, someone famous figured out how to do it on her own—a pop star named Epony. She had an act going where she pretended to be an alien, but it didn't take long for people to figure out she was just an ordinary person who'd found a way into the Other Place. After she left, her boyfriend Cole kept singing about it until pretty soon everyone was heading to Seattle, escaping withered farmlands and flooded coasts to try to cross into a new world. And when that first wave of newcomers died down, when everyone forgot about Cole's songs—there came Alt.

Alt was played in every major city in the U.S., a game/ travel ad. People lost themselves in that virtual world, in a fabrication of the Other Place, and then they wanted the real thing. So they came to Seattle to test their vorpal's strength. The Seattle sprawl was now a dense jumble of miniaturized, pre-fab "container" homes jammed between old buildings. All squares and rectangles, a pixilated city. The place everyone flocked to and no one wanted to live in, the overlap between our world and a land of opportunity.

Those who made it to the Other Place found the same sights Reef saw through his digital goggles when he played Alt: a glass city threaded with silvery canals, studded with trees, surrounded by mountain peaks vaulting over all. An alien city the aliens specially renovated to host denser beings. Those who couldn't cross over made do with Seattle instead. They lived like Reef did—sheltering in container homes, fighting over government-issued food tickets, collecting rainwater in catch basins. Playing Alt while pining for the Other Place.

Reef had seen people enter the alternate universe. Sometimes he could tell when someone was trying to go to the Other Place, could see the glaze in their eyes that meant they were glimpsing another world. He would shadow them as they stumbled down a Seattle street. When they disappeared, the air would waver for a moment, and Reef would try to step through the distortion and into the Other Place. It never worked.

He had seen them return too. They came gray-faced and gasping, to collapse on the sidewalk, in a cafe, in the middle of the street. They couldn't stay more than a few months in the Other Place without getting sick and confused, no matter how the aliens worked at making their world hospitable. The nature of that universe made every human visitor miserable in time. So they returned to Seattle to wait out their sickness and cross over again.

The smart ones came back to Seattle before the sickness overwhelmed them. They crossed quietly, using their vorpals to push away anyone who noticed their sudden appearance. They brought back money from work they'd done in the Other Place, jobs ranging from menial labor to consultation on improving the alien city that hosted them for months at a time. The ones with the strongest vorpals took temporary houses in gated communities, along the waterfront, on the Floating Isle in Puget Sound. The rest huddled into the cracks of Seattle, waiting for their next chance at a payday from the Other Place.

Men were much more likely to have strong vorpals, thanks to a genetic pattern involving X-linked traits—so it was mostly men who came to cross back and forth, to make money to send to their wives and children. But crossing over in the middle of some Seattle street with alien coins jangling in your pockets meant inviting trouble. Reef had once seen a man materialize on Beacon Avenue, blink in confusion at his miscalculation, and before he could disappear back into the world he had exited, crumple under the attack of three other men. You *had* to attack someone like that quick, before he could use his vorpal to dissuade you. Before someone else jumped him and stole your payday. It was a common sight in the sprawl: blood on the asphalt, bodies in the gutter.

Reef found other ways to make money.

"Sir, will you listen to my tale of distress?" A holographic woman in a low-cut silvery dress stepped from a doorway. "An infestation of trolls plagues these parts."

The façade projected behind her was tiered, swooping glass slick with a bright sheen of rain—an alien sight if Reef ever saw one. The holographic woman was straight out of a Girl Queen movie, complete with a pair of tiny wings that marked her as a sylph. Reef seriously doubted that elves and sylphs and slavering beasts roamed the Other Place, but they lurked in every corner of Alt's game world. Apparently, the aliens weren't interesting enough to make for video game characters.

"Their filth is everywhere, our children are sick," the sylph woman continued. "Do you know how to send the trolls back to the woods?"

Olly came up behind Reef, goggles in hand. "Sure—go to one of their spawn points, unleash a Desiccation Spell to strip their defenses, and call down a Siege Flame," he mumbled, fidgeting with the strap of his goggles. He was always making the strap too tight, which explained the deep circular impressions around his eyes—and the nickname Owl Eyes, Olly for short. "But that's not what we're going to do."

Reef raised his eyebrows. "Why not?" It was as good a way as any to send trolls running back to the Seattle park that served as the Warped Wood. It would take all of four minutes, and Reef could return to the sylph to receive a Health Elixir as his prize.

"I've read about this quest on a forum," Olly said. "If you tell her you don't know how to get rid of trolls, she'll send you on a quest to score a Banishment Spell. Do you know how much money people will pay for a Banishment Spell?"

"Yeah, I have an idea." Reef's heart sped up as he did some quick mental calculations.

"Whatever number you're coming up with—divide it by two."

"You're just going to cut in on my quest?"

The sylph shifted on the sidewalk, waiting for Reef to interact with her again. Olly powered on his goggles and now Reef saw him overlaid with an image of his avatar, a muscular Warrior in a shell of armor. Reef's own avatar was a Knight in sword-nicked chainmail.

"I'm going to *help* you on your quest." Olly grinned at Reef. "You're welcome. Good news is, this is the easiest way to score a Banishment Spell you ever heard of. She's going to send you to the Immigration Office and then you just have to answer some riddles."

Reef frowned. "Too easy. Probably hiding a virus."

"No virus. I checked the forums."

"A leech, then. Those are worse."

"Who cares? You only have to hold on to the Banishment Spell long enough to sell it to the highest bidder. It'll be out of your hard drive within an hour, and the leech with it."

Reef turned up his jacket collar against the rain-flecked wind. "I'm not selling someone a spell that's infected with a leech."

"Would you like to eat breakfast today?" Olly said grimly.

"I'll get rid of the leech and take the government bounty instead."

"And get half the money you'd get if you sold the spell."

"I'm not selling it, Olly." Reef bowed his head against a gust of wind. He tried not to notice the gouges in the holographic leather of his Alt boots, or the muck on his sneakers underneath the projection. "You know what leeches do?"

"Sit in your hard drive and don't bother anyone at all?"

"Until D-day. Then they use your network to wreak havoc on government systems."

The rain distorted the projection of the sylph so that she rippled as though with impatience. "Sir, will you listen to my tale of distress?" she asked Reef again.

Olly spoke over her. "What do you care about government systems? You don't even have running water. You pee in a bucket."

Reef shot him a resentful look. "I use the bathroom at McDonald's."

"When they let you in."

Another gamer was coming up the street, ducking under awnings and searching for a quest to take on. His Mercenary's belt bristled with dagger hilts and he looked like he'd be as happy to steal loot as to earn it from questing.

"An infestation of trolls plagues these parts," Reef prompted the sylph, itching now to move on.

"Do you know how to send the trolls back to the woods?" the sylph asked.

Reef eyed the approaching gamer. "No," he told the sylph. "How do you get a troll back to the woods?"

Olly grinned and leaned toward Reef. "Sounds like a joke I know. How do you get a troll to—"

"The sphinx can help you with this quest," the sylph cut in. She hadn't registered Olly's presence. "Seek out her lair in the Immigration Office."

Reef dug out a tin and retrieved a bit of gray-green resin thin as a matchstick and stuck it in his mouth, then wished he could spit it out. It tasted awful. "You need to work on your punch lines," he told the sylph.

He shoved the tin back in his pocket. Two pitiful sticks left. Running out of resin would mean a trip to the hospital, but he tried not to think about that. He pulled Olly on toward the hotel that served as the game's Immigration Office.

The Roosevelt Hotel, a brick column slowly darkening in the rain, looked ordinary enough when Reef wasn't wearing his goggles. He peered up at a dozen rows of windows and wondered how many of the guests inside knew the place served as host to Alt's holographic Immigration Office.

Several huddled forms detached themselves from the building to ask for food, coins, cigarettes. "Don't give up your food ticket," Olly warned Reef. But Reef already had it out of his pocket and was passing it into a pair of wind-chilled hands.

"He lent me one last week," Reef explained to Olly.

"Is he going to lend you one tonight when you've got no dinner?"

Reef shrugged and pushed his goggles back into place. The hotel was transformed into the coppery Immigration Office, supposedly a mock-up of the one found in the actual alternate universe. For a moment, Reef could pretend he was in the Other Place, a new arrival looking for housing and a job. But the sound of car tires cutting through rainwater, and of transients squabbling over food tickets, anchored him in ordinary Seattle.

"Now we just need to get inside," Olly said.

The "Immigration Office" wasn't as easy to get into as it had once been. The managers of the hotel that housed it were sick of gamers invading their lobby and carrying out imaginary swordfights in the hallways. You couldn't get through the doors anymore until a hotel guest went in or out, and even then you had to be quick.

Reef peered through the glass, trying to gauge whether any of the hotel guests was thinking of leaving. He watched a father in a long raincoat tie his little son's shoes. The rich always had sons: They paid for gender selection prior to conception instead of losing sleep worrying about the weak vorpals daughters usually inherited. The only places Reef ever saw wealthy men with daughters were in government propaganda posters like the ones plastered over the interior walls of the hotel. They showed a man toting a smiling young girl on his shoulder with the caption *Daughters Bring Joy*. Reef could hardly take his eyes from the smiling faces, the crown of sunlight behind the girl's head.

"Never seen a girl before?" Olly joked.

Reef looked away from the posters. Actually, he couldn't remember the last time he'd seen a girl walking the streets of Seattle. Even the prostitutes kept to their container homes and let work find them.

Olly was studying one of the posters now, peering in through the hotel's glass door. "If the government's so keen on getting people to cross over into the Other Place, they should let the rich have their sons and stop worrying about it."

"Sure, it's not like we need girls for anything," Reef said dryly.

"Think about all the money the president makes from taxing everyone who comes back from the Other Place with pockets full of alien money," Olly said. He glared at the copper globe hanging over the door. The two continents of Mega America shone silver; the span of Great China, gunmetal gray. "Wish I had the president's vorpal. Smug bastard. Why didn't someone mess with *my* genes?"

Reef shoved his hands deep into his pockets while he waited for the father and son to leave the hotel. Even with his electronic gloves on, Reef was cold. The wind went right through his threadbare clothes. But at least with fall settling in he wouldn't have to worry about water shortages. He'd already set up the rain trap on his container home.

He adjusted his goggles and looked up at the Immigration Office's glittering façade overlaid on the tall column of the hotel. It awakened unexpected feelings in Reef. Envy for those who could escape the sprawl and live in a better world. A vague sense of dread he couldn't quite place.

"Do you think it's weird that the aliens don't seem to mind all those people coming into their world and funneling out their money?" Olly said, pinpointing the source of Reef's uneasiness. "What if they get tired of us?"

"We're giving them some of our solar energy," Reef said. "It's fair enough." But deep down, he wondered how long that deal would last. It seemed to him that the solar channels between the two worlds had already opened wide, and the aliens had no need to keep people crossing into their universe.

A holographic character with a bright yellow exclamation mark hovering over his head watched them from the corner of the building. He rocked on his heels expectantly, red sleeves fluttering under a battle-scarred leather vest.

"What quest is he offering?" Olly asked.

"Don't—" Reef started to say, but Olly was already flexing his electronic gloves.

"Have you heard tell of the Fated Blade?" the man said in response.

Olly groaned. "Not this crap again."

"I could have told you," Reef said.

"We continue to look for the Fated Blade." The man clasped his hands together in distress.

"But where *is* it?" Olly said. "How are we supposed to find it?"

"Alas, I wish I knew."

"What kind of quest is that? What *land* is it in?"

Reef noticed that the father in the lobby was approaching the front door. "Olly, come on."

"What *spell* do we need?"

"Olls." Reef caught the door and scooted inside before anyone could protest.

Olly slid in after him, shaking his head in frustration.

"It's just some top-level gamer playing a joke," Reef said. "That's the trade-off when you give gamers editing privileges."

"Stupidest game edit ever," Olly said. "What's the point?"

Reef worried the grip of the digital sword in his belt. "Just making fun of the Girl Queen stories." He shrugged off the uneasiness that was creeping in. He concentrated instead on evading the concierge who was busy shooing the transients who had slipped through the door behind Olly.

"There's no Fated Blade in the Girl Queen stories," Olly said as he and Reef hurried out of the lobby.

Reef raised his eyebrows. "You're telling me you've read all the thousands of books people have posted online and seen all the hundreds of movies and three-D movies and four-Ds, and you can say for sure there's never been some Fated Blade?"

Olly grunted. "Maybe. But if I had that kind of editing privilege I wouldn't waste it on an impossible quest."

"When's the last time you made *any* changes to the game?"

"I revert edits all the time."

"That's changing things back, not making up something new."

"Game doesn't need to be edited, in my opinion. Fewer people editing means fewer people adding in all these bugs that are screwing up everything."

Reef shook his head. "Editing the game is half the fun—you get to make Alt the game that you want it to be. Who do you think makes up half the quests you go on? High-level gamers with top editing privileges."

"And who do you think plants all the viruses and leeches you spend all your time trying to get rid of?" Olly said.

"Gives me something to do," Reef said with a smirk.

They headed into a vestibule to find the sphinx guarding the entrance to the men's room. Its great tawny haunches were pressed up against a door that managed to look ignoble despite the brassy sheen Reef's goggles lent it.

"Hey," Reef said in greeting.

"Holding up against the smell?" Olly added.

The sphinx peered down at them with yellow eyes set in a woman's face and launched into its programmed speech. "Beyond this entrance to a den of wonders lies a valuable treasure of great power."

"Ever hear anyone get so sentimental about automatic flushers?" Olly asked Reef.

"You'd feel the same way if you had to sit outside a bathroom all day," Reef said.

"If you wish to enter the den," the sphinx went on, its voice striking a balance between mystery and condescension, "you must answer my riddle."

"If it's about a troll in the woods, we already heard that one," Olly said.

"Wasn't very funny," Reef added.

The sphinx ignored their comments and launched into its riddle: "Men ride upon my back, though I cannot be tamed—"

Olly chuckled. Reef rolled his eyes.

"—I surge and rush over ten thousand graves."

"Man," Reef said. "Now that we're here, I really have to take a piss."

"It's not a real sphinx, dork," Olly said. "Just take off your goggles."

"And come back into the game to find my character being gnawed on."

"Well, what surges and rushes and . . . dies?" Olly was already using his goggles to check the web for an answer.

"I'm only thinking with my bladder right now. I thought you said this was supposed to be easy."

"Easier than it used to be. Until yesterday it was three riddles randomly generated from a who-knows-how-long list. And the sphinx was supposed to give us a time limit before eating us." Olly kept searching the web for an answer, flicking his gloved fingers to scroll through a forum. "Someone definitely edited this quest: They did a sloppy job with the dialogue. The sphinx kept bobbing its head after it was done talking."

"Told you. There's a leech in there." The sound of a flushing toilet echoed out from the bathroom, somewhat dampening the solemn effect of the setting. But it lent Reef inspiration: "The ocean."

The sphinx closed its oval eyes at Reef's answer. "Your intellect is keen. Retrieve your treasure."

It shuffled its haunches to make room for them to pass. Reef glanced at Olly.

"Only enough leech-infected loot for one of us," Olly said. "And I have no desire to supervise your bladder functions."

Reef passed through a doorway made coppery by the illusion of an alien façade. The effect inside the men's bathroom was not as impressive. Chipped tile showed through where the digital overlay was patchy with bad edits.

A businessman at the sink gave Reef's goggles a look of mingled surprise and distaste. Reef used the urinal and then found the item he was looking for in the sink: a Banishment Spell, his reward for answering the riddle and a tool for sending trolls scampering. It hovered inside a glass globe, a silvery blue swirl that betrayed no threat. But accepting the item into his inventory would invite a leech into the hard drive that ran his goggles. The leech wouldn't do much harm. Just curl up and wait for a chance to spread to other computers. Until one day, when whoever created the leech finally called upon it to do whatever malicious work it had been programmed to do.

Reef stretched a hand toward the swirling globe. He wondered when he'd have another chance to find a Banishment Spell. He should take it and sell it, like Olly had said. Not worry about the leech.

He hesitated, thinking. Then he hit the globe with a Revert Spell, reversing the edits the creator of the leech had made. The leech was gone.

Reef tried to close his fingers around the spell, hoping against all odds. But the globe vanished. Whoever had inserted the leech had made sure the Banishment Spell would vanish the moment anyone destroyed the leech. Reef was left with the hollow feeling of groping for something only to come back empty-handed, a feeling he experienced all too often.

A ping from his earpiece told him a decent sum of money had been deposited into his account—the government's way of thanking him for getting rid of the leech.

He met up with Olly again in the vestibule. "Breakfast is on me."

"You want to hit up your dealer first? Only two sticks left."

Reef stiffened. He wasn't hiding things as well as he thought he was.

"Go do it," Olly said. "I've got a long list of dungeons to raid when you're finished with all this white-hat business. It's not going to help me if you're dead in two days."

"That might set us both back," Reef joked, his gaze any-where but on Olly. "Think we should revert the edits to the sphinx first?"

"I'm guessing the spell was destroyed when you ousted the leech?" Olly's stiff stance said he was still hoping Reef hadn't gotten rid of the leech, that he had picked up the Banishment Spell and left a copy behind.

"Yeah, the spell's gone," Reef said.

Olly sighed. "Then forget the sphinx. There's nothing left for it to guard."

Reef gave most of the money to a dealer.

"I'd offer you some," Reef said to Olly afterward as he pocketed his tin.

"But then you'd have to keep offering every day? Thanks, you can keep it. I'm not fond of fatal withdrawal." Olly chewed thoughtfully on a thumbnail as they headed toward Pioneer Square in search of breakfast. "Playing Alt must have been mind-blowing back when that stuff still gave you a high."

They passed boarded-up windows and gated doorways and tried to dodge puddles on the sidewalk. "Can't remem-ber that far back," Reef said. A lie. He recalled the feeling of sinking into color and light as he passed through holo-graphic buildings. Wandering for hours in the Warped Wood just to hear the leaves move. Forgetting the real world altogether, forgetting there was anything to forget. But the drug never made him high anymore. He tried to tell himself that he didn't care, that it was a waste to be high all the time and that it had only messed up his reflexes and made his gameplay worse.

But the truth was he missed the feeling of being completely immersed in another world.

"It was stupid ever to start taking it," he said, and that was honest at least.

"You were a kid," Olly said. "If I'd ever gotten my hands on that stuff when I was kid, I would have taken it too."

Reef pulled his goggles back on to avoid Olly's gaze. The wet, gray buildings of Seattle turned to bronze and silver and mottled green glass. He didn't like to think about how his addiction had started. Using resin had seemed normal to him—he'd seen his mother do it. She couldn't hide it from him in their tiny container home. And it hadn't taken long to get dependent on resin to the point where stopping meant damaging his organs.

"What does it feel like now when you take it?" Olly asked.

Reef scanned the street for new quests. He registered the flutter of sylph wings, of elven gowns, of fairies circling the streetlight like moths. "Hurts my stomach."

"That's called hunger."

"Feels like my organs are waging wars over supply routes they've mapped out on my nerve system."

"Now you're being dramatic." Olly nudged him into the street to avoid a group of men Reef had been too distracted to notice. "They look like they wouldn't mind scoring a couple pairs of goggles."

Reef ducked his head to hide his goggles. He'd had to

part with a really rare Impenetrable Cloak to buy this set. Plus, if someone stole his goggles, they'd probably loot his Alt account.

He and Olly headed into a narrow alley made narrower by huddled forms crouching over food scrap breakfasts. Reef spotted a troll peering over the edge of a Dumpster. He decided he couldn't bother to stop and attack it, considering how his stomach was rumbling.

"What do you think all these leeches are going to do?" Olly asked. "Come D-day?"

"Crash our communications, energy networks, governmental defense systems—"

"Forget it. I don't need to hear your Great China conspiracy theories."

"Why do you think the government pays a bounty for every leech cleaned up? You do understand we're at war?"

Olly peered around as though searching for evidence of violence. "It's a very quiet war."

Reef snorted. "Until China finishes planting enough leeches to create a huge botnet—"

"Not every leech is controlled by the Chinese."

"—and then once our systems are down, they'll finish us with a nuclear warhead or two—"

"I said forget it."

A white blur made Reef stop in his tracks and grab Olly by his grimy jacket sleeve.

"What?" Olly said.

"White rabbit." He scrutinized a pile of old pallets. "In there."

Olly pulled on his goggles and kicked the rotting wood aside. "You're seeing things, bud."

Reef tried to squash his disappointment. A white rabbit gave a free help to anyone who caught it.

Olly laughed at Reef's glum expression. "It's not like it's handing out money. What were you going to ask it for?"

"The username of whoever keeps editing in that crap about the Fated Blade."

"I thought you didn't care."

"It's bothering me."

"You said it was just some top-level gamer playing a joke."

"It's annoying, is all."

"A Queen's Mark would be better. Then you could get into the palace at the harbor."

Another white blur. Reef scrambled after it. He saw a flash of fur, long ears pricked forward. Just as he rounded on it, the rabbit squeezed through the closing door of the embassy. Reef yanked the door open, stepped inside—

And the illusion abruptly dropped. Instead of the holographic alien embassy, he found himself inside the tiled lobby of a Seattle bank. A line of text flashed across his goggles: MINIMUM REQUIREMENT: LEVEL 300.

He swore. He was stuck at Level 299 and had been for a year. Without a big fat payment to the Alt franchise, he'd stay stuck.

He'd lost his white rabbit.

Olly was waiting for him out on the sidewalk. "Paywall," Reef explained.

Olly gave him a sympathetic smirk. "I swear those rabbits pull crap like that on purpose. I followed one into a *private house* once and almost got arrested. Broke my ankle jumping out the window."

"What'd it give you?"

Olly reached over his shoulder to pull out an elven ax that shimmered in Reef's display. "Worth it too. This thing deals twice the damage of a war hammer."

A muted clatter of dishes greeted them at their usual haunt, where only a few of the scuffed tables were occupied. They elbowed in at the counter next to a scrawny kid cloaked in a black hooded sweatshirt. Reef always ate at the counter. The jostle of elbows and the buzz of conversation swept away the hollowed-out feeling he awoke with every morning alone in his container. *The spell of arms and voices,* he called it—a phrase his mother had gleaned from one of the antique paperbacks that had doubled as insulation in the cracks of their old two-person container.

Except that when his mother said it, she was thinking of the call to adventure. Namely, heading north out of the sprawl, up into Canada, where green things still grew and the air you breathed hadn't already been breathed by eight million other people. *"The white arms of roads, their promise of close embraces,"* his mother would read over the patter of rain on the roof, *"and the black arms of tall ships that stand against the moon, their tale of distant nations."* Reef had promised her, over and over, that he would get them out of the overlap. He'd level up until he was raking in money and then he'd take them away from their reeking container and the men who owned it for hours at a time.

But he hadn't done it. Especially once his mother, and then he, had become dependent on resin to stay alive. And then, one day . . .

He'd come home to find black-oil blood and twisted sheets. Her chalk-white arms reaching for nothing. Silence and death so thick in the air that he couldn't breathe.

He shook away the memory, jostled the boy next to him a little too hard. A spill of long, golden brown hair slipped free from the hood. Not a boy after all. Reef couldn't see her face, but it didn't matter because his gaze was locked on that long fall of hair, glinting a dozen different colors in the morning light. He reached to touch it, though he felt the same as when he had reached for the Banishment Spell in its ephemeral bubble—that it was impossible, that she would only disappear . . .

She turned sharply. "Not for sale," she said, as if he couldn't tell the difference between a prostitute and someone with regular access to a shower and no taste for a drug that would forever alter her body chemistry. She took in the sight of his goggles perched on his head, the rings around his eyes, the stain of the drug on his shirt where flakes of resin had dropped and left green-gray spots. "Couldn't pay me enough to be with a filthy raccoon like you anyway."

She snatched her bag of food from the counter with a trembling hand, her face white with fear of whatever violence she imagined Reef would do to her. Reef caught sight of the bracelets on her wrist, engraved with her husbands' names, and then she darted out the door.

"I think you mean *owl,* not raccoon," Olly said after her. "And if you wait for the afternoon rainstorm, we'll be cleaner than whatever's stuck up *your* ass."

Reef tried to laugh but his throat seemed to have swollen nearly shut.

The owner of the diner, Maksim, came by then and set down two bowls of their usual: potato and Tabasco soup. "What trouble have you two been into today?"

"No trouble," Olly said. "Just saving the continent from a looming digital war." He rolled his eyes.

Maksim shook his head in disapproval. "It's always that game. You need to find a girl."

"You going to provide the map? The one who was just in here doesn't seem eager to come back."

"Don't need a map." Maksim winked. "Just a little money."

Olly stared into his bowl, but not because he was embarrassed. Reef knew he'd been with girls before, and what other girls were there besides prostitutes?

"What level you boys at now?"

Olly gave him a glum smile. He was far below Reef. "Two ninety-nine," Reef admitted.

Maksim whistled. "No. Really? How does someone your age get so high up there?"

"Start as a little kid. Got to have something to do while your mom's with clients."

The comment didn't throw Maksim at all. "They'll be surgically attaching those goggles to you someday. Owl Eyes is already half there." He nodded at Olly.

"Better than having them snatched off my head like my last pair," Olly muttered.

"When'll you hit level three hundred?" Maksim asked Reef.

A fresh surge of frustration mixed with the soup in Reef's stomach.

"He's stuck at a paywall," Olly said. "One that requires a pretty serious amount of cash."

"Ah." Maksim grimaced in sympathy as he turned to help another customer.

Olly gulped the last of his soup and hopped down from his stool. "I got to go meet with a raiding party, Two Ninety-nine." He pulled his goggles back on and looked at Reef. "Think you can delay the digital war on your own for a while?"

Reef frowned. "Do I take names first and then kick asses, or is it the other way around?"

Olly chuckled and strode out the door.

Maksim returned to the counter and said to Reef, "You seen this posting? Could help you get past your paywall." He tapped a monitor on the wall.

Reef squinted at the screen. It was an ad for a worker husband. Posted by someone with two husbands already and looking for another income. The photo showed a young woman with the wide-set eyes and rounded chin of a doll. The ad said she was only nineteen, but Reef suspected it was a lie. Ads like these were always too promising.

"You get the money you need for level three hundred, she gets a little slice of your income."

"Any slice is a slice too big." But Reef's gaze wandered to the photo of the girl again. Underneath her sweet expression were hints she had lived in Seattle too long: the tilt of her mouth, the flinty black of her pupils. The way she side-eyed the camera seemed to say he could fix all of that for her.

"Photo's nice." Maksim leaned one elbow on the counter and flashed a fatherly smile that made Reef look away. "Fairy-tale characters can't fill up the space in that empty container of yours."

Reef nodded, mostly to put an end to the conversation. In his mind, he went back to the days when he'd come home to someone who was happy to see him, who would tousle the rain from his hair and give him tea warmed with a heat sleeve. And then he couldn't stop his thoughts from returning to the day when he'd come home to that terrible sight: black-oil blood, his mother dead.

It wasn't really true, what the stories said. About how you'll find the Other Place when you look for what is lost.

He answered the ad.

He used the rest of the money from the government bounty to buy a new shirt and pay for a shower. He wished he had enough to buy a new jacket too, considering how cold it was despite the sunshine. It was one of those rare days when Mount Rainier was visible, a purple smudge on the horizon, getting ready to shrug off another layer of rock in the winter rains like a creature shedding its skin. The rivers would get choked, Puget Sound would flood. Everyone would grumble: *Too much water in winter, not enough in summer.* The government would respond by reminding people that everything was slowly getting better now that the Other Place was eating our excess solar energy. Or anyway, that everything was at least not getting worse.

Outside the deli where Reef was supposed to wait, a water nymph lounged in a tiled fountain. She winked at him and flashed a gold-green fishtail. He ignored her. Nymphs parsed out rare potion ingredients, but only in exchange for actual human hair. Shaving his head probably wouldn't make the best first impression on a potential wife.

Reef rubbed his wrist, imagined a bracelet there engraved with someone's name, a *wife's* name. He kept scanning the crowd in front of the deli, searching for the face from the ad and trying to do it without drawing attention to himself. Several men eyed his goggles in a calculating way.

"What I am doing here?" he muttered to himself. He'd never spent much time thinking about how he might look to girls, and that was suddenly the only thing that mattered. He thought his hair was nice enough: dark and kind of longish around his ears. And even though he was too skinny, he was on the tall side and his skin stayed brown all through the winter instead of going ghost-pale like a lot of other Seattle natives. But his grubby pants were ripped at both knees, his shoes held together by duct tape. He was careful to brush his teeth every day to ward off the yellow tinge the drug lent them, but he spent all of his time outdoors and knew he must look weathered.

The nymph was still winking at him. At least he impressed *someone*.

A muffled voice came from under the hood of a huge raincoat. "Are you Reef?"

It was her. Reef could just make out the rounded chin. She pulled back her hood enough to show wide aquamarine eyes and a spray of dark curls. The rest of her slight frame she kept wrapped inside the overlarge coat. She hadn't been lying about her age.

"I'm Reef," he answered, tugging his goggles down to hang around his neck.

She looked him over, stony-faced. "Are you high?"

"No." It wasn't really a lie. He woke up every morning craving the drug and held off as long as possible before giving in. He barely registered its effects anymore, never felt the floating euphoria he had once experienced when taking it.

"Planning on stabbing me?" she asked, her gaze level. She was at least a foot shorter than he was, the shape of her shoulders completely lost inside her huge sleeves.

"I don't think an imaginary elf sword would do you much harm."

She scanned his frame, her gaze stopping on the bulge created by the real knife strapped to his ankle.

"I don't use that on people half my size," Reef said.

She frowned, maybe not believing him. "What's that scar along your cheekbone?"

"From a fight." Reef shuffled his feet, forced out the admission: "And made with my own knife, if you have to know."

She lifted her eyebrows. "At least you got it back." She glanced through the glass front of the deli, where the owner was trying to oust a band of street youths. "I already called the cops, just in case you *were* planning on stabbing me."

Reef whipped his head around, searching for any sign of them. They didn't much like grubby street gamers.

"So we'd better get out of here." She turned and headed down the side street.

Reef blinked at her back for a moment and then hurried after her. She led him to an apartment building with a chipped colonial façade. Reef reached reflexively for his goggles, wondering what sight Alt's creators had designed to overlay the building. But the *clunk* of a bolt sliding aside jolted him back to the real world, where the girl was passing through a door that led to a flight of stairs.

She's taking me to her apartment?? Panic flared in his belly. He'd been so busy worrying she'd reject him on sight, he'd had no time to consider what he'd have to do if she accepted him. He'd never been with a girl before. He figured things pretty much worked themselves out once everyone took off their clothes, but what if he was wrong?

An agonizing minute later, he was standing in the front room of a cramped apartment that nevertheless made his container seem like a glorified closet. The girl put several feet and a couch between them and watched his every move. "Sit there," she said, pointing at a table shoved into the corner of the kitchen space. Reef sat. The new angle gave him a view of the bedroom, where a haggard old man lay dozing in the bed.

The girl followed Reef's gaze. Her face tightened. "That's Croy," she said in a soft voice. The man looked to be forty or fifty, with deep lines etched into his forehead and around his mouth. His head rocked back and forth in delirium. Gauging Reef's distaste, the girl added, "He brought me to the overlap when I was fourteen. My parents had sold me to a matchmaker, and he rescued me."

Reef squirmed in his chair. "I didn't think . . ."

"He doesn't hear us." The girl closed the bedroom door. "It's the drug that did that to him. Once you start, it's a slow death with it and a quick death without it."

Reef fingered the tin in his jacket pocket, his mouth dry. He'd never let himself get up to such a high dose. He wondered how old the man really was. Thirty? Thirty-five?

The girl took off her coat and laid it down. Reef tried to keep his gaze from roving all over her. He pushed back his jacket sleeves and tried to guess where the other husband was. *Home any minute to show me out at knifepoint.*

The girl came and sat across from him, still keeping a wary distance. "I'm Cadence," she said.

"It didn't say in the ad." He'd been wondering.

She shrugged. "Guess that part's not for sale, then."

Reef chafed at the word *sale*. This wasn't about money. Not *just* about money—he wasn't going to marry a girl just so he could get past a paywall.

Cadence held out her palm, expecting something. "You're at two ninety-nine?"

He'd told her in his message, when he'd answered the ad. He pulled his goggles over his head and handed them over so she could check his stats for herself.

The sheen on the goggles lent her blue eyes an underwater look, especially when the images began to shimmer on the lenses. He'd left his inventory up and he watched her eyes move over his items. It was like someone opening up his rib cage and rummaging in his chest cavity. Her hand closed around his sword, although Reef saw only her delicate fist waving through the air. He suddenly regretted the snarling wolf's head he'd had "etched" into the blade. It seemed stupid and boyish now.

"This is nice," Cadence said. "I never had a sword like this. Don't play enough."

"I could help you level your character." Footsteps in the hallway claimed Reef's attention for a moment. He prickled at the thought of husband number two with a knife, a gun. The footsteps went on past the door, but he couldn't take his eyes off it.

"I really only play to use the chat function," Cadence said. "Cheapest way to talk to someone out of the province."

"You still talk to your family?" *After they sold you to a matchmaker?* Reef guessed that's who she meant.

"My—sister," Cadence said haltingly. "Some nice Canadian man bought *her* from the matchmaker."

His focus went back to Cadence, the tightened corners of her mouth. She was glaring at some holographic item he couldn't see.

"And visas are expensive," he said as the realization came to him, "which is why you put out the ad."

She gave him a polite smile. Her fist made figure eights in the air—she had moved on to admiring his crystal dagger. "How'd you get up to two ninety-nine?"

"Play all the time." He couldn't tell her what he'd told Maksim at the diner. "Since I was a kid."

She went on trying out his weapons. He listened for more footsteps while taking manic inventory of her apartment: tins of coffee lined up on the speckled counter, scribbled crayon drawings papering the fridge, a sticker on the kitchen faucet that said their water came from the desalination plant. He thought he detected the faint scent of apples and he filed it away for future dreaming. He couldn't ask for one.

On a side table sat a framed photo of a little girl who must have been the artist of the crayon drawings. Not a boy, Reef was shocked to find. Even though just a little money could guarantee one.

He realized that Cadence was staring at him through the digital images. He looked back at her blue eyes behind the blue display. It was like looking down into a well and finding something you'd thought was lost for good.

He flexed his fingers. He wondered if all girls disappeared the moment you reached for them.

"You seem lonely," she said.

"So do you." Her hand was on his arm.

The wind beat against the one little window. It made the apartment smaller. Cadence pulled off the goggles. Her voice was quiet under the howl of wind. "I can't sleep with you. He wouldn't like it."

He followed her gaze down to the back of her wrist, where a name was tattooed in sharp, angular script: Aedric. Something inside of Reef closed tight as a fist.

He slid his arm out from under her hand, then immediately regretted it. Her skin had been so warm. And the hint of sadness he had seen in her face now flooded her expression.

She went to the window and peered down at the street. "You'd better go. He doesn't know I brought you here." She turned back to Reef with a tiny disc that would fit into the side of his goggles and call up some document. "If you submit this, I'll automatically get twenty percent of any money you make."

A marriage license, then. Reef hesitated, his fingers twined in the strap of his goggles.

"You'll get a cash advance, of course," Cadence said.

Reef nodded, but he still wasn't sure if he should do this. "I could come back later."

The hand that held the disc wilted. "You shouldn't come here again."

The glass shook in the window frame, and with it came the first spattering of rain. Reef imagined the container that awaited his return and the sound the rain would make against the walls: like someone knocking to find out if the box was hollow. "Would you come to my place?" Reef eyed the disc. "If I went through with this?"

Her gaze flicked to the window again and her face tightened with anxiety. She nodded.

Reef took the disc.

= ≠ =

A week later, Reef held his jacket sleeve over his nose in Northwest Square as he made his way through the maze of containers stacked two and three high, dodging streams of waste that gushed out of drainpipes without warning.

"Why are we following this guy?" Olly asked irritably. He had a new digital pet—a bright blue owl that opened its beak every time Olly spoke so that it seemed to be talking for him. "Is he planting leeches or what?" The owl added a sharp *hoot!*

They emerged into an open end of the square, where Reef caught a glimpse of a lean guy in a familiar raincoat pushing his way into a store. It was the coat Cadence had worn a week ago at this same time of day. Reef had made a good guess that Aedric kept to a regular schedule.

Olly huffed at the sight of the candy store, turned into a troll's den by his goggles. "I raided this dungeon when I was ten years old. Can we please take your level three hundred ass somewhere it'll do me some good?"

"Level three oh *one*." Reef pulled off his goggles.

Aedric had the relaxed look of someone who was used to winning knife fights before they started. He hadn't even bothered to make sure he wasn't being followed. From across the square, Reef watched him hand down candy to a small girl in a slicker and ski cap. He felt a twinge of guilt at spying on their family ritual. He hadn't really meant to follow them all the way here. He'd only wanted to see who Aedric was, to rid himself of the image seared in his mind: Aedric's name in black ink tattooed across Cadence's wrist.

"Serious here," Olly said. "Let's go."

"Relax. He's just flexing his vorpal. Making people want to leave him alone."

"Then why isn't it working on you?"

"Why do you think I'm not going any closer?" Anyway, Aedric's vorpal was strong, but it couldn't be the strongest in the world—not if he lived in a tiny apartment instead of on the residency isle floating in Puget Sound.

"Just let him plant his leech and we'll come back later for the bounty," Olly said.

"I think he's just buying candy."

In the street, at the far end of the row of shops, another form materialized, stepping from a patch of hazy air as if from behind a curtain.

Olly didn't seem to have noticed. He was rubbing his hand over a bald stripe at the side of his head and examining his forlorn reflection in a rain puddle. "I look like an idiot."

"Don't expect me to argue."

"What a waste. I gave that water nymph some of my hair so she'd give me noxious mushrooms for a Grievous Potion. But right after I used the potion there was a power outage and my wireless connection skipped out. My character ended up all the way back at the beginning of the dungeon. Potion all used up."

The figure that had materialized from the Other Place was walking slowly toward the candy shop, hands jammed in his pockets, gaze flicking all around the square. Aedric spotted the figure and came out to meet him.

"It would be nice if the government could alert us peons before they ration power," Olly said. "Gave me a free digital pet, though, 'cause I complained so much."

"It wasn't a planned outage," Reef said, his eyes on Aedric.

"They confirmed it this morning. Surprise rationing."

"An excuse to cover up a digital attack."

Olly shook his head. "Where do you get this stuff?"

"You don't read anything that's not written in an Alt forum. Great China's pissed because we have better access to the Other Place and all its money. They've been increasing their digital attacks."

Reef strained to hear what Aedric was saying but couldn't make out much. A thought sent fear spiking through his chest. "You wouldn't know a way to get a visa, would you?" he asked Olly. "Even a fake one?"

"To where, Mexico? You looking for family? Mexico doesn't even care if you have papers. You could walk all the way to Argentina if you wanted to. It's all one country now, right? Hey, maybe there are some Alt lands down there we've never even heard of."

"Not Mexico—"

"Where *are* you from, then?"

Reef pushed away memories of his mother telling him the story of "The Gypsy Queen," of the taste of cinnamon in coffee. "I'm talking about getting a visa to go to Canada." Could aliens get them more easily than ordinary people— is that what Aedric was doing here? Cadence had told him about Reef, and now Aedric was desperate to get her away to Canada so he wouldn't have to share her? Reef gripped the metal tag tied to his wrist and engraved with Cadence's name.

"Canada?" Olly scoffed. His owl hooted, as if sharing his derision—the sound came through Reef's dangling goggles. "Forget it. It may be all one country, but Canada's another planet. You think the president wants people like us crowding his cushy headquarters?"

Reef felt a flicker of annoyance. "You keep talking like there's only one of them. There's, like, a whole cult of them genetically conditioned to run this country. You know that, right?"

"I like to hold on to my fantasies." He turned to admire some passing figure Reef couldn't see with his goggles off. A chesty sylph, most likely.

Reef crept along the line of containers. Aedric was too distracted to bother with vorpals now. Behind him, the little girl had come out of the candy store gripping a sucker in each fist. She had dropped a blue glove on the sidewalk, the tiniest glove Reef had ever seen. Aedric went on talking to his friend in low tones. He was speaking some mixture of English and an alien language Reef had heard before, a slur of z's and s's. When the other guy answered, the only English he used was *Floating Isle*. It wasn't hard to figure out what they must be talking about: smuggling goods from the Other Place and onto the elite residency isle that floated in Puget Sound. Not visas after all.

"Nice clothes," Olly said behind Reef. "You're not planning on jumping them?"

Reef grunted. "Think the four-year-old will put up a fight?"

"Wait, I know what this is." Olly snickered. "Those are the guys, aren't they? The ones you're sharing a girl with?" He wheezed with laughter.

"Just the one on the left," Reef muttered. "The other one's an alien."

"Huh, really?" Olly peered at him but quickly lost interest. "Two other guys. You're paying to be the third guy in line." He laughed into his sleeve.

Reef's annoyance turned to anger. "You know prostitutes aren't monogamous, right?"

"Look, as much as I love spying on your boyfriends, there's an Ice Giant at the bus station I'd like to introduce to my new sledgehammer."

"Fine. See you later."

Reef's gaze went back to the tiny blue glove the girl had dropped. The caption on those government posters kept popping into his head: *Daughters Bring Joy*. The girl licked the two suckers in turns, yellow orange yellow orange.

Reef slunk away from the maze of containers and scooped up the glove, held it out while he slow-stepped toward the girl. Her eyes were the wide-set eyes of her mother, round now in consternation. *Daughters Bring Joy*. He wondered how her eyes looked when she was laughing.

A hand slammed down on his wrist, and the next moment Aedric had Reef's arm twisted behind his back, his face pressed against the pebbled wall of the building.

"I'm Reef!" he blurted.

"Who?"

Pain spiked from Reef's elbow to his wrist. "Reef." He held up his other arm so Aedric could see the bracelet with Cadence's name on it.

Aedric let go. Reef turned reluctantly to face him and saw that Olly hadn't left after all. Aedric saw too. "This your friend?" he asked Reef, smiling as if at some secret joke. Olly took a step closer, sizing up Aedric like he could do anything.

"Yeah," Reef said. He hoped Olly had dismissed the ridiculous glowing owl.

Aedric's face was the flat, ordinary face of any other west-coaster. Skin Seattle-pale, but race impossible to discern. He scrutinized Reef's tattered clothes, the goggles around his neck. His smug smile grew. "You're going to get her the visas she wants? Enough for all of us?"

"If I could get a visa, I wouldn't be living here."

"So that's a no? Good. If you had said yes, I would have known you were a fraud."

The little girl watched this all with fascination. She stared openly at Olly's goggle-eyes. Reef handed her the dropped glove and she accepted it cautiously.

A ping sounded from Reef's goggles and he glanced down at the lenses to find that Aedric had messaged him. The intrusion brought his simmering anger to a boil.

"This is a list of Alt items I'm keeping an eye out for," Aedric said. "I've got some clients on the isle who'll pay big for these, so put yourself to good use."

Reef gritted his teeth. But there was no way he was going to fight a guy with a stronger vorpal. And he couldn't in front of the girl anyway. She was still staring at Olly's goggles. She held a round sucker up over each of her eyes and peered out at him.

"You're at level three hundred?" Aedric asked Reef.

"Three oh one," Olly said for him. "How about you?"

Aedric shrugged, dismissing the challenge in Olly's tone. "I don't have much time for games."

Reef didn't believe him. The goggles sticking out of Aedric's jacket pocket weren't the slim design most people chose. They were big, powerful. Built for gaming.

Aedric followed his gaze and shoved the goggles deeper into his pocket. "I help my clients level their characters sometimes."

"You ever figure out the Fated Blade quest?" Olly asked.

Reef shot him a look that said *Are you serious?* But then he noticed that Aedric's alien friend had perked up and was waiting for Olly to say more.

"Can't say I've run into that one," Aedric answered.

"Ask *him,*" Reef said, nodding at the alien.

Aedric studied Reef for a moment. Then he turned to the alien and said something in his language. The alien didn't reply. Just moved his gaze from Olly to Reef.

Aedric shrugged. "I guess that's your answer." He flicked Reef's goggles. "Keep in touch." He walked away. The maze of containers swallowed him up, the alien following, the little girl last of all, waving one blue glove at Reef like an old-world royal waving a hankie.

A burst of curiosity hit Reef, something to do with the Fated Blade and Aedric's alien friend. But Reef couldn't tell if it was his own feeling or someone else's, pressed upon him by a vorpal.

Reaching level 301 gave Reef access to places he'd only read about in forums. The holographic caverns in Pike Place Market, where he fought off crystal-fanged Dark Elves while maneuvering around the crowded stalls. An enchanted glade inside the public records hall, where he safely sealed up his stock of blood rubies to be harvested later for a potion. Even the sage's warren in the old monorail, where he looked out and took furious notes on the marked locations of rare items hidden all over the city.

He sold weapons and spells and information. He sent Cadence her twenty percent.

She had only minutes at a time to give to him—while she ran out for an order of fish and chips, or collected some package or other from Aedric's contacts. Once they met at the harbor, where Reef had to keep scowling patrol men at bay by flashing the bracelet that said he had a right to be with the girl next to him. And then Cadence had to return home anyway, and Reef was left alone to gaze out at the sleek residences on the Floating Isle, yet another world he'd never be given entry to.

One morning, Reef thought she'd finally come to his container, but it was only Olly.

"Want to run an instance on the waterfront carousel?" Olly asked, tossing an apple to Reef after he opened the door. "Should be able to pick up a Dogsbreath Spell."

Reef pocketed the apple and jammed his feet into a pair of grubby sneakers. "I've got to finish a quest that expires in a few hours. It's all the way uptown."

"Yeah, I figured you'd be too busy picking up higher level loot."

Guilt gnawed at Reef. He hadn't gone questing with Olly since he'd hit level 301. He took a couple of food tickets from under the mattress and held them out to Olly.

Olly let out a snort. "Keep it. You don't need to pay me off."

"What's that supposed to mean?"

"Where's all your money going?" Olly grimaced at Reef's disintegrating shoes. "You giving it all to that girl?"

"Not all of it," Reef mumbled, pulling on his jacket. "Twenty percent. Sometimes extra if she needs—"

Something fell from his pocket and hit the floor with a thud.

Olly stared for a moment at the gray brick of resin while blood pounded in Reef's ears. "I guess it'd be a waste to get past level three hundred and not get *high* while you play," Olly said darkly.

Reef's face burned. "I didn't mean to—I suddenly had all this money—" He snatched up the brick from the floor and jammed it into his pocket. "I'm an idiot."

"Don't expect me to argue."

Reef squeezed his eyes shut. It had been stupid to buy so much. But he'd had the money in his account, and then suddenly he was buying enough resin to feel what he had once felt, to escape into Alt with his senses turned up high.

"I'm gonna go," Olly said. "Let me know if you want to run an instance sometime. Free of charge, okay?" He turned and let the door slam shut behind him.

Reef took his goggles down from their hook, frustration and shame welling inside him. A message from Cadence flashed on the lens piece. She had wanted to meet at a nearby park but was gone now. His frustration grew. He sent a message back: *This is crazy. Isn't there some time when Aedric won't notice you're gone?*

A few minutes later her reply came: *Tonight. There's a quest he's been wanting to do that doesn't show up until after nine. I'll remind him.*

Around nine thirty, Reef showed up at a building across the street from the Roosevelt Hotel, where he and Olly had met the sphinx. He pulled out his tin. It was full, the thin gray sticks packed in tightly together. Reef knew his stomach wouldn't stop wrenching and lurching until he gave in. He took out a stick, glared at it before biting down. He was up to a twice-daily dose now and he couldn't go back.

He knocked on the door of the building. There was no sign, no window front. Cadence had told him only about a gray-painted door next to a noodle place. The door opened, and someone squinted at him before leading him down a hallway to a lounge lit by thousands of tiny bulbs embedded in a map of Great China that wrapped around the room. The provinces were outlined in a thin, glowing line, including the constantly shifting European holding and an uncertain chunk carved out of Africa.

Cadence smiled at him from a couch, an open, easy smile he'd never seen on her. Reef felt several pairs of eyes on him as he walked over. He'd never seen so many girls all in one place, in tank tops and T-shirts instead of bulky jackets. He let his metal bracelet slide down over his hand so everyone could see it, so the guys glaring at him would know Cadence was his wife now.

"You didn't bring your goggles," Cadence said. She'd shed her usual oversized jacket and looked almost bare in a thin T-shirt and jeans.

"No, I didn't." He'd had some inflated idea about her seeing him without his goggles and taking him more seriously, so he'd left them with Olly. But Cadence's own slim pair was around her neck.

He sat next to her, anxious to find out how his body would fit alongside hers. He'd only ever touched her hand, her shoulder through her jacket. Now her arm was pressed alongside his. Reef's fingers itched at the sight of her T-shirt half tucked into the waistband of her jeans.

"What's with the map?" As he said it, several more lights blinked on among networks of wires trailing over the wall.

"Do you like it? Took ages for everyone to rig up. It's for the Troll-Kicker Leech: a light comes on every time the leech spreads to another hard drive. The leeches are forming a whole network—"

"A botnet," Reef said.

She smiled again. "It's supposed to come alive tonight

and do its thing, if the command can get through to it. Not sure what it'll do, though—do you have any idea?"

"Probably launch a DDoS attack. Distributed Denial of Service. Basically, overwhelm a network and make things go haywire. Everything's connected to the network these days—power grid, emergency services. Everything." He was working hard not to grimace at the bitter remnants of resin in his mouth. If he kissed her, would she taste it? Could she smell it already? He tried to be subtle about fishing a mint out of his pocket. "One of these days we'll even send a bomb to finish off the job."

She turned her face to look at the wall behind her. The tiny lights made her skin glow like some digital character. "It's a bit morbid, isn't it?"

Reef shrugged. "China's doing the same thing to us." The mint made his mouth cold. "There's probably some bar in Beijing where people are studying a light-up map of Mega America right now."

"And drinking illegally imported American beer." She held up a bottle someone had left on the table and showed him the Chinese label.

Reef let out a laugh. The sound of it floated to his ears through a drug-induced fog. The whole room seemed to be retreating, shrinking back from him as though he were lifting away. He felt lights blinking on inside of him the same as on the map, dark places coming to life.

He took Cadence's hand and pulled her up from the couch with him. She let Reef put his arm around her waist, but the slow, electronic pulse of the music didn't lend itself to dancing. Reef stood stiffly, unsure of how to close the gap between them. He fingered the hem of her shirt where it was untucked and then he couldn't help but pull her closer. The music throbbed in his head, in his stomach. He brushed his cheek against her hair. "Cadence . . ."

He caught her looking toward a corner of the room and followed her gaze to find Aedric's alien friend watching them.

"He sent a spy?" Reef asked Cadence.

"I think he mostly follows us around to make sure we're safe, although most of the people here are familiar faces." She glanced up to a loft, where Reef spotted an older woman playing with a little girl he recognized. "Once, Shasta and I went out to the harbor for the whole day and Aedric never seemed to know. Or anyway, he didn't seem angry, even though he worries about people seeing us and figuring out we're girls. Getting sold to a—a matchmaker or something."

She'd been about to say something worse, but Reef could tell she didn't want to think about it. He measured the little girl's tiny frame as she crouched against the railing with her toys. He rolled her name around in his mind. *Shasta*. Fear for her clutched at his stomach. The gruesome things that could happen to her on the streets of a city like this . . .

"I wish I could talk to him, but I'm no good with languages," Cadence went on, her attention on the alien again. Reef's hand against her back was getting so heated he worried she would pull away, but she slid her palms up over his shoulders like they were dancing. His heart jostled. "Did you know that the reason they used to wear those red bracelets was so people would know they were aliens? That's why you always see them in government posters wearing red bracelets. Even though I've never see one wear anything like that in real life. Aedric's friend has one tattooed on his arm." She frowned. "Or is it just me seeing that?"

Reef looked to the corner of the room again and saw a band of red ink around the alien's forearm. "No, I see it too."

"They can make themselves look like anything they want. Kind of like an Alt avatar." Cadence lifted her goggles to her eyes. "Should I find out what imaginary tattoos you've got?"

Reef's hand went automatically to the digital label that showed under his chain-metal sleeve in Alt's game world. A free add-on he'd gotten for turning leeches over to the government.

"Leech-hunter, huh?" She lowered her goggles again. "A do-gooder."

He felt his face going hot. "It pays." *Sort of.*

She seemed to calculate something in her head. The price of a visa in leech bounties, maybe. She looked around at the lights coming to life on the wall. "Do you think it really does much good in the end?"

Reef pictured the imaginary Beijing bar, the map of the American continents carved into provinces—Canada and the States and Mexico and South America. All riddled with tiny bulbs, a thousand of them lit. A million, more. "I don't know."

He leaned in and pressed his face against her neck. She smelled like ozone, the clean smell after it rains. Her arms tightened around his shoulders. He kissed her lightly on the jaw, shaky with nerves. He kissed her on the mouth and kept kissing her. Her frame was so slight in his arms he was afraid to hold her too close and then he was thinking about her leaving, escaping to Canada without him. The voices that hummed around them echoed wildly in his head. His own voice came in through a tinny filter. "How close are you to getting a visa?"

Her hands tensed against his back.

"It's what you want the money for, isn't it?" Reef asked. She'd never really said, even though they both knew it was true.

She slid her arms off his shoulders, her gaze on the alien watching them in the corner of the room. "You know why they stopped wearing those red bracelets?" She closed her hand around the metal tag on Reef's wrist, hiding the letters there that spelled out her name. "Everyone wanted something from them. They thought the aliens could make anything happen with their vorpals. Could make everyone get along, stop wars. Make neighbors turn down their stereos." She gave a little laugh.

Reef looked down at her hand covering the bracelet. "I don't mind if you want something from me."

She pulled away, her brow furrowed. His arms were left reaching, holding nothing. He dropped them to his sides. "I have to take Shasta home." She half turned toward a staircase that led up to the loft, then stopped to pull her goggles off and hand them to Reef. "Here, take a look around first. It's a waste to come to a place like this without goggles."

All he wanted to do was pull her close to him again, but he dutifully put them on. The room was transformed into a fairy cove, the carpet a sheet of silvery water that broke around his shoes. The lights on the walls, far from ruining the effect, gave the impression that a horde of glowing fairies had infested the place. Only the music and the buzz of voices intruded on the spell. Reef tried to shut them out. He was so dizzy, his brain still clouded. He remembered reading on a forum that valuable fairy sapphires were hidden in this very cove, but he couldn't see them anywhere in the room. He half closed his eyes. The lights were spots of gold, bleeding into each other, spreading over the walls—

Something popped up in the corner of his vision: a holographic creature, a miniature silver dragon with cartoonish purple eyes. He realized someone was trying to initiate a chat with him using a digital pet as a mouthpiece, and then realized that the chat channel was already open.

"Hi there," the dragon piped. "Guess what—it stopped snowing finally. I'm going to send you some pics of me braving the outdoors again."

"Who is this?" Reef asked.

"Who else? Shasta."

Reef frowned at the girl Cadence was carrying down the stairs. He tried to make his foggy brain work.

"I've decided you're going to be in Canada in time for

Christmas," the dragon said. "Okay? Do I have to make you promise?"

It clicked—Shasta must be Cadence's sister's name too. She was the little girl's namesake. Reef looked at Cadence bundling her daughter into a coat while the girl tried to stuff wispy hair back into her ski cap.

"Cadence?" the dragon went on. "There's no one here. You're the only one I have. You and about six lopsided snowmen." There was a pause, and then—"Are you there?"

Someone else was trying to hail him on the chat channel too, but Reef was already tugging the strap off his head. "Here," he said, thrusting the goggles back at Cadence. "Someone was trying to chat you."

He noticed Aedric's alien friend pulling off his goggles too, although Reef hadn't seen him put them on. Had he been the one trying to hail him just now? Reef supposed a translation program *would* be the only way they could communicate. Cadence was already carrying her daughter toward the hallway, her goggles twined around her wrist. Reef abandoned the idea of getting them back. *What would he even have to say to me?* He had only one idea.

"Hey." He caught up to Cadence. "Did you ever read anything in the Girl Queen stories about a Fated Blade?"

"I don't remember. I stopped reading those stories a long time ago."

"Has Aedric ever mentioned it?"

She turned to him in the mouth of the hallway. "Aedric always says nothing is fated, it's just that some things happen in the right place, at the right time."

He looked at her holding some other guy's kid, going home to some other guy's apartment. "And some things don't."

She reached over and trailed her fingers over Reef's arm where his leech-hunter patch would show if she were wearing her goggles. "I wish I'd met you before I'd met Aedric. I think everything would have been different." He caught her hand, moved close enough to kiss her again but felt unsure this time.

A few bulbs winked to life around her. "If I get visas before Aedric does, will you leave him?" Reef blurted.

She didn't hesitate. "Yes."

He must have looked surprised at her quick answer, because she added, "Would *you* want to raise a daughter here?"

The wispy hair escaping from Shasta's ski cap was a halo, lit by a thousand bulbs. Reef's gaze traced the outline of the girl's tiny nose, her rounded chin. "She looks more like you than like Aedric," he said.

Cadence frowned. "She's Croy's."

More surprise, and then guilt for thinking she'd take Aedric's daughter from him if she got the chance. Croy couldn't know anymore that he had a daughter, not in the state he was in.

Cadence looked away, and he wanted to tell her that he didn't really think so poorly of her, but he could only step back and stuff his hands in his pockets and then she was gone, down the hallway and out the door.

Aedric's alien friend slipped past Reef to follow her but

then stopped and turned back. "Aedric," he said to Reef.

Reef was hit with a sudden flash of suspicion and alarm. Not his own. He studied the alien's face, but it was stoic as ever. "He's not a good guy," he said to the alien. "I get it."

The alien disappeared down the dim hallway. Reef stood against the wall, felt the music humming in his bones, saw pinpoint lights whether his eyes were open or not. He thought about Cadence warm against him, and about Shasta needing a father. He thought about what the three of them would look like on a poster all together. He wanted to leave but he waited until his head felt a little clearer. As he walked out, the lights on the map all flashed red. "Your move, China," he mumbled to himself.

The dream came to Reef a week later: His container was perched at the top of a thousand-container stack, so close to blue sky Reef was almost above it, lost to gravity. It was just him and sunlight in a field of vapor and gas and the tiniest water droplets. They were all wrong about the way to pass into the Other Place. This was the way, through color and light. He pulled a lever, released the prongs that clamped his container to the one below it, and lifted away.

A heavy knock on the door dragged him back to earth. He lurched upright in bed and pushed aside a can of soup to peer through a peephole at the back of a shelf. "Olls?" But it wasn't Olly out there hiding under the hood of a huge coat. Reef jolted back. His head slammed against another shelf. He let out a few whispered curses while he undid the locks and popped the door open.

"Too early?" Cadence asked from under the hood.

"No, I'm awake." *Or I am now, anyway.* She was shivering in the cold and he wanted only to pull her inside and wrap his arms around her. But a familiar ache was starting up his bones. He stopped himself from looking around for his resin. Food would take his mind off it. "There's a place around the corner that serves breakfast. Just like eggs, if you close your eyes while you eat it."

A paper bag appeared from under the coat. "I brought egg rolls. Close enough?"

"All right, hang on." His heart zigzagged inside his chest. He shrank inside and hurried to shove aside partitions to make room for another person to fit inside his cramped living space. He pulled down a bench-top over the bed, a table over the basin that served as a sink. Some of his stuff had to come down from their hooks to leave enough head room. *I'll be pissed if this turns out to be a dream,* he thought.

Cadence ducked inside and slid onto the bench. He sat on the table. His knees had never been so close to a girl's knees before, not even the night he had not quite danced with her.

"Is that a real book?" She tugged a paperback out from where it was wedged under a drawer. The drawer tilted precariously. "Looks like you." The cover showed a man with a gas mask dangling over his chest. Reef looked down and realized he'd slept with his goggles around his neck. He let out a laugh and Cadence laughed with him. He reached to move a shelf jutting near her head but his hand went instead to her hair and then to her cheek. He nodded at the book. "That's the *Aeneid*. '*I sing of arms and the man.*'" He spotted his tin on the floor next to her foot and his mouth went dry. "I always thought that would be a good name for a pub—*The Arms and the Man*."

This time she only smiled. He reached for the paper bag instead of the tin.

"The sign could have two crossed arms like this." He held an egg roll in each hand and crossed his arms in front of his chest. "You have to imagine these egg rolls as guns to get the proper effect." He was trying to get her to laugh again, but it wasn't working. He suddenly remembered something she'd said the night before, about how the aliens had stopped wearing red bracelets because they got sick of everyone asking them for things. Why had she told him that? Because she wanted something from him?

Because she was unhappy that *he* wanted something from *her*?

He leaned his legs away.

She fidgeted with the sleeves of her coat. "Aedric got into some trouble on the Floating Isle. He can't go back there without risking his life."

Reef fought to keep his face blank against the surge of triumph he felt. There was no way now that Aedric could steal Cadence away to Canada.

He shifted over next to her and rubbed his hand up and down her jacketed arm, his reservations forgotten. "I'll make sure you have whatever money you need. I'll run more instances—and I've got some Alt items I can sell—"

"I'm taking a fourth husband. He has visas for me and Shasta."

Some invisible force slammed into Reef's chest.

Cadence hurried to add, "Once the three of us get to Canada it'll be easier to get visas for the rest of you. I wouldn't leave Croy otherwise, not like he is." She rested her hand on his knee. He felt angry and excited all at once. "I'll get a visa for you."

Reef put all his concentration into memorizing the feeling of her hand perched light as a bird on his knee. It was the only thing he could do to ignore the acid eating away inside his stomach. He remembered what Aedric had said to him once—that if Reef had claimed he could get visas for all of them, Aedric would have known he was a fraud.

"I won't let Shasta stay here one second longer than she has to," Cadence said into her jacket collar. She couldn't look at him. Her face was lined with regret.

She moved toward the door and he caught her wrist. Her bones were like bird bones. The light coming through the ceiling vent showed the downy hair along her arm where her coat sleeve had slid back.

"Good enough to grace your pub sign?" she asked, waggling her arm in his grip.

He looked from her weak smile to the bed half hidden under the bench-top he was sitting on. He tried to think of some way he could stop her from leaving him.

Her arm went rigid in his grip. "Don't ask for more than I can give you," she said.

He shook his thoughts away. "I'm going to find a way to get a visa. I'll follow you there, I'll find you." He had his arms around her waist, his face pressed against the zipper of her jacket. "I promise."

She moved her fingers through his hair and then stopped abruptly. He'd meant to make her feel better, but he'd only upset her more. The door popped open, but he hardly heard the sound. She left him with the feeling he was back inside his dream, pressed up against some glass ceiling and shut out of better worlds.

Reef waited outside her apartment building while imaginary creatures passed by him unseen. He itched to put on his goggles, but he didn't dare give in to the distraction. An un-enchanting fog hung in the air and left a chilly mist on his face. Aedric finally stepped out through the glass door of the building. He immediately turned to Reef as if he'd sensed him.

"What're we going to do?" The words came out before Reef even knew he was speaking them.

Aedric paused to fit his goggles over his eyes and scan the street, oblivious to Reef's anxiety.

"He's not going to get any visas for us," Reef said.

"No, he's not." Aedric took his time studying something through his goggles. Most likely an Alt character offering a quest. All Reef could see was a huddle of men gambling with food tickets. "Even the kind of money they've got on the Floating Isle can only get a person so far."

"So what're we going to do? She's going to Canada without us. Can't you use your vorpal to get us visas?"

"Don't you think I've been working on getting visas for a long time now?"

Reef's frayed nerves exploded. "Well, where are they?" he snapped.

Aedric snatched off his goggles and glared at Reef. "I think I know how we can get *one* visa real easy. Don't you?" A few of the men had turned to stare at them. Aedric lowered his voice. "Her newest recruit—Breck. He's got a visa for himself as well as for her and Shasta."

"We're just going to take it from him? His vorpal's got to be stronger than yours if he lives on the Floating Isle."

Aedric scowled. A food truck rumbled up the street, and the men in the alley scrambled to meet it, tickets in hand. Reef couldn't help watching the kitchen steam pour out as the truck opened. Aedric didn't even glance at it.

"Breck's been salivating over this epic item in the dungeon inside the Georgetown steam plant," Aedric said. "A silver scepter. I told him I knew a guy with a level three hundred sword who could help us get to it."

Level 301, Reef thought.

"We run the instance with him," Aedric went on. "Let him wear your goggles so he can use your epic sword, kill the Bristle Beast, and get the silver scepter that the beast drops. You'll have to wear his goggles, of course, since he'll be wearing yours. So while he's busy fighting off mages, you're busy searching through his hard drive for that visa." He tossed a tiny disc at Reef. "Save it to disc—"

"Why don't I just send it through the chat channel?"

"How many people do you think have heard him talk about getting a visa? How many of them do you think would like to intercept it when some idiot sends it through a chat channel?" Aedric glanced at the line of men waiting for their handouts, as though they were the ones plotting to intercept stolen visas. "Save it to the disc and then give it to me. I know how to erase Breck's info from it so it'll be good as new."

Reef resisted the urge to roll his eyes. *You don't think I can figure it out if you can?* "And the other visas? For me and Croy?"

Aedric gave him a blank look. "She didn't tell you?"

"Tell me what?"

He let out a huff. "She's in denial. Croy took a turn."

"A turn? You mean he's dead."

"Will be soon enough. Too many drugs, or not enough—I've lost track of it." Aedric put his goggles back on, used his electronic glove to flick through his inventory. "He's in the hospital, but for all I know he's already gone." *Flick, flick.*

Reef's stomach tightened. The bitter taste of resin or fear filled his mouth. *Someday that'll be me,* he thought. *Will anyone care?*

Aedric tossed an invisible item into the gutter— dropping some vial from his inventory, probably. Reef heard a ping from Aedric's earpiece that meant he had completed some task or quest. "I can get another visa," Aedric said, taking off his goggles. "When that silver scepter drops, Breck will want you to pick it up so that it'll go to his account—because you'll be wearing his goggles. Then you can gift the silver scepter to my contact before Breck realizes what you're doing. You and Breck swap goggles back and we get away fast. The money we get for the scepter should be enough to put us just over the edge of what he's asking for a visa."

It all sounded too convenient. And he hadn't forgotten the warning Aedric's alien friend had given him.

He watched a skirmish break out in the line at the food truck. On the back of the truck, a faded poster showed the president frowning with determination or disapproval—Reef couldn't say which. "How do I know you won't screw me over?"

"You talking to me or him?" Aedric joked, nodding at the poster.

"He's already done his share," Reef said. "Moved to Canada and closed the gate behind him. But I guess that's how it goes when you've got the strongest vorpal. Right?"

Aedric smiled so that Reef could see the breakfast still lodged in his teeth. He looked at the poster. "Tough choice to make, wasn't it? On the one hand, you can let the guy with a strong vorpal take over, call the shots. Or you can sit on your hands, afraid, and wait until some outsider takes over."

Reef snorted. "You're saying you want me to choose whether to be screwed over by you or by Breck? Or are we still talking about Mega America and Great China?"

"I'm saying I rather prefer our own genetically created

tyrant. I'm saying it wasn't such a bad choice to make."

Reef shook his head. But what else could he do? He needed a visa and Aedric was right—the easiest way to get one was from a guy they knew already had one.

He still couldn't stifle the unease spreading through him with the chill of the fog. "I'll bring my friend Olly along. We'll need more than just the three of us."

"Four of us. You met my contact from the Other Place."

The alien, Reef thought, and his unease grew. "If this guy Breck lives on the Floating Isle, how did Cadence even meet him?"

"I introduced them," Aedric said. But if he was upset about it, Reef couldn't tell. He only pulled his goggles back over his eyes and turned down the side street. "Georgetown, nine o'clock."

The Georgetown steam plant was a boxy concrete building whose long skinny windows and razor wire blockade lent it the look of a prison. Huge black funnels protruding from the top were sentinels. Reef and Olly shivered in the fog while they waited outside a doorway someone had cut in the nest of wire.

"You're shaking," Olly said.

"I'm just cold." Reef doubled over and tried to resist the urge to puke. He'd been stupid to let himself move up to two doses a day. There was no way he could hold out until after they ran the instance. And while getting high made Alt more immersive, it also seriously messed with his focus.

"I'm not going in there with you like this," Olly said. "I'm not saying I don't really need to grab some items I can sell, but . . ."

Reef fidgeted with his goggles. "Yeah, sorry I haven't been around to—"

Olly cut him off. "If my character gets killed here, I have to run all the way to the metro station and back before I'll be allowed to resurrect."

"A little exercise wouldn't kill you."

"You're right. Maybe I can talk Seattle into installing a few more hills under its streets."

"Give me a second." Reef moved off into the dark by himself and opened his tin. He promised himself that he wouldn't let his focus drift.

A figure emerged into the light from the goggles around Reef's neck. "Level Three Hundred," Aedric said in greeting.

"Three oh one," Reef corrected.

"Ready to swap?" Aedric nodded to another guy who was trudging through the tall grass of the empty lot. "This is Breck."

Breck's wide grin was friendly enough, but his chemically bleached skin and blue contact lenses lent him a spectral look. "Hey there." His vorpal was like an envelope of air holding him apart from the rest of them. Reef thought it was making the grass at Breck's feet ripple, but he couldn't be sure he wasn't imagining it. It was the strongest vorpal Reef had ever encountered, and this was the guy he was supposed to fleece.

It doesn't matter, he told himself. *As long as he doesn't suspect anything, it's not a problem.*

Breck reached to shake Reef's hand like they were old friends. Reef yanked his goggles off his neck instead and handed them over.

"Oh, right. We're getting started?" Breck tugged at a zipper on his form-fitting raincoat and produced his own pair of goggles. "Careful now. New model."

Reef pulled the goggles over his head and gave Aedric a quick glance. Aedric's usually blank face was full of loathing for Breck. He turned to say something to his alien friend on his other side.

"Olly will be the tank." Reef pointed back to where Olly was loading himself up with imaginary armor. "Breck, you hang back and do far-ranged attacks. If anything zeroes in on you, get close to Olly so he can take the damage."

"Right, right," Breck said, wiggling Reef's goggles into place over his eyes. "We'll all get ourselves to Canada in no time." He flashed another smile that made his cheeks bulge under the weighty goggles. Reef bottled his rage. *Save it for the dungeon, where you'll need it,* he told himself.

"I've got an Impervious Elixir in my inventory," he told Breck. "You might want to drink it now."

Olly led the way through the opening in the razor wire to a pair of battered metal doors. A heavy chain dangled from one handle, its busted padlock lying in the grass below. Breck pushed his way to the doors and let himself in first. Aedric's gaze lingered on the padlock. "Think he slept with her?" he asked Reef. The hatred in his eyes unsettled Reef. He was about to answer *no* when a wave of uncertainty hit him. Breck had visas. He lived on the Floating Isle. Why wouldn't Cadence sleep with him before sleeping with a guy whose house wasn't even big enough to stand up in? A new brand of hatred formed in Reef's heart.

Inside, Breck was testing Reef's new sword, swinging it through the empty air.

"Don't forget," Aedric said. "Breck makes the kill. *Reef* picks up the silver scepter."

Reef scrutinized him, wondering at the desperation in his voice, but the next moment their goggles flashed to life. Leafy vines wrapped themselves around the steam plant's huge concrete beams and rickety metal ladders. Flame-colored flowers and fronded trees exploded through every opening in the levels overlooking the main warehouse. The towering white turbines barely visible in the moonlight were transformed into enormous hives shuddering with some inner turmoil.

"I don't think we want to get too close to the dragon nests," Olly warned, staring up at the hives.

The sudden barrage of images left Reef's head spinning. *Get a hold of yourself,* he thought. His breathing had gone erratic. A warm, dizzying sensation spread through his chest and out to his limbs, courtesy of the resin now going bland in his mouth. For a moment he felt pinned in by the chest-high plants projected by his goggles.

He batted aside a spreading branch to find a grimy control bank that shouldn't show while he was wearing his goggles. It was part of the steam plant, not the game world of Alt. *Bad design, or patchy edit?* he wondered. He didn't have long to think about it.

A swarm of fairies came ripping through the leaves, engorged with foul nectar that they spewed over the concrete floor. The effect from Reef's goggles was to make the floor steam as though it were being eaten by acid.

"Watch your step," someone called, and the voice rang in Reef's ears. He took a steadying breath and forced his mind to focus on the game.

Night hares came next, tall as Reef's knee and baring long tusks for teeth. Reef blinded them with a Flash Spell, and the rest of the group used various Mage Blades and Longswords to dispatch the creatures. Olly snatched up the Shield Spell the hares had dropped and then led the way up a clanging metal staircase to where the plants were jungle-thick and blooming with tentacle-like flowers. Just as Reef was wondering if the enormous blossoms were duplicated from the Other Place or if they were from some game designer's imagination, one of them locked on to his leg with its finger-like tendrils. He hacked at it with a dagger while a mage made his entrance with a swarm of toads swollen to the size of dogs.

"Hang back," he shouted to Breck. "Let Olly take the damage." Breck made some useless gestures with his electronic glove and threw out spells that fizzled in midair. One of the toads stretched its blue-black tongue and came back with the crystal dagger that had been strapped to Breck's arm. *Reef's* crystal dagger.

"I said stay back!" Reef cried in frustration. He groaned at the memory of what he'd gone through to get that dagger—defeated a Dark Elf and then assembled the two dozen materials required to turn its fang into a blade.

"Sorry, really sorry," Breck called, and made another attempt at a spell that was too difficult for him.

Aedric's alien friend, playing as a Light Elf, got busy casting healing spells on Olly while the mage attacked. Reef's goggles created the illusion that veins of magic flowed through the alien's skin, and Reef thought to himself that he'd never seen an alien look so alien before. The mage finally crumpled, and they were off to find the stairway to the next level.

Reef hung back. Now was his chance to get the visa off Breck's account. He rifled through Breck's hard drive until he found it, reached for the disc zippered into his jacket pocket—

A flash of white showed against dark green leaves. Reef froze. That was no night hare.

He plunged into the bushes. Another white flash. Reef brought down the flat of his sword, pinning the white rabbit against the floor.

He felt like shouting. He'd done it—*finally*. He yanked the rabbit up by the ears. This was it—one free help was his. *If only white rabbits gave out visas,* he thought grimly.

He considered asking for a Queen's Mark and gifting it to his own account so he could get into the palace on the harbor. But what good would that do him if he was going to Canada?

And there was still that question that haunted him. "Who made up the quest for the Fated Blade?" he asked the rabbit. Somewhere in the distance the others were clanging their way up to another floor. Olly would kill him if he knew he was hanging back for this. "What's the username?"

The rabbit remained silent for a moment, as if considering how to answer. Then it said, "Would you want me to warn you if you were walking into a trap? Should I—if it means harm to me?"

Reef tried to shake the haze out of his brain. Was his mind playing tricks on him?

"What would you do in my place?" the rabbit went on.

Cold dread seeped into Reef's stomach. "What're you talking about? What's the Fated Blade?"

"Do you want to know about fate? You joined your world to another's without thought of what dangers might come. And now the connection between the worlds will be severed. It must be."

More confusion, and then—clarity. Reef checked the bottom of his display and confirmed that the chat channel was open. The white rabbit wasn't a real white rabbit at all but was someone talking to him through a digital pet. "Who is this?" He already knew. He whipped around, looking for some sign of Aedric's alien friend. Only black leaves and riotous blossoms. "I don't know what you're talking about."

"I'm trying to warn you. Are you listening? You have walked into a trap."

"What trap?" Reef said to the rabbit.

The chat channel closed. The rabbit vanished from Reef's grip.

"Whatcha doing?" Breck said from the bushes.

Reef spun to face him. "Uh. White rabbit." Breck couldn't have heard anything the rabbit had said—its voice had come through the chat channel directly to Reef. "Found it a second ago. Gone now."

"I heard you say something to it about the Fated Blade. Said you thought it was a trap?" He pulled up his goggles and their light flashed on a metal bracelet around his wrist. "It's not a real quest. Just the Chinese mocking us."

"What?" Reef's eyes were glued on the bracelet. No doubt it had Cadence's name engraved on it.

"You know the game is riddled with leeches? All waiting for their creator to say the word and . . ." Breck mimed an explosion with his hands, made a noise with his cheeks puffed out. "Down goes all of our infrastructure. The leeches are waiting for the signal. The signal, the attack— that's the Fated Blade."

Reef squinted at him. His head was filling with fog again.

"Think about the character who offers that quest," Breck went on. "Ever noticed the color of his clothes? Red with yellow stars, same as Great China's flag."

A vague memory came to Reef of the man outside the hotel that served as the Immigration Office. A battered leather vest like a second hide, red sleeves showing underneath—

"I read about it on this forum." Breck grinned that harmless grin Reef was coming to despise. "You read forums?

There's a lot of tips that can help you level up. Well, I guess you don't need that." He shook his wrist, fidgeting with the metal bracelet that must still feel foreign to him. The movement dislodged something in Reef's brain.

"You met Cadence . . . how, again?" he asked Breck.

"Aedric introduced us. I met him on the Floating Isle."

Reef's mind went back to what Aedric had said earlier that day. *Don't you think I've been working on getting visas for a long time now?*

Aedric had introduced Breck to Cadence on purpose. Because he knew Breck had visas or could at least get some. He had set up Breck from the beginning.

Reef almost laughed. Aedric was even more of a snake than he had thought.

Then his skin went cold. *What else isn't Aedric telling me?*

From above, Olly's voice rang out. *"Where are they?"*

"Better go help," Breck said.

Reef followed him. He felt suddenly jumpy. The shadowed plants seemed ominous. What had he gotten himself into with Aedric? What was Aedric planning?

As he clanged up the stairs, he remembered he hadn't yet taken the visa from Breck's hard drive. He quickly located it and fumbled for the disc Aedric had given him.

On second thought . . . He left the disc in his pocket and instead sent the visa through the chat channel to his own goggles, the ones Breck was wearing.

Breck jolted to a stop at the top of the stairs.

"I got a transmission on your goggles?" he said, turning toward Reef. "Let me check it."

"No," Reef said a little too forcefully. "No, it sounds like they need us. Look, I can see them over there."

Breck whirled around, sword in hand. Transmission forgotten. He and Reef scrambled through the foliage to where a huge beast was wreaking havoc, a hulking black mass of bristles. Six-foot spikes protruded from its back, thick needles from its arms and legs. Its glinting black eyes, clustered like a spider's, were almost lost in the nest of bristles covering its face.

It chased them down a rusted catwalk that felt like it would give way any moment. Olly drew it down to the main floor where there was space to get at it with swords.

"That's you, Breck," Reef shouted. "Make the kill and I'll grab the scepter the Bristle Beast drops."

A bank of dials on the wall came to life, needles pulsing frantically. The white dragon hives towering over them began to hum. For one terrified moment Reef wasn't sure if it was all part of the game or if the old turbines had come back to life. He ripped off his goggles to find the turbines still and silent in the moonlight. The dials on the wall were rusted over, dead.

"Reef, what're you doing," Olly shouted. "Put your goggles on."

Reef jerked them back over his eyes to find a chaotic scene. Breck was doing clumsy battle with the wounded Bristle Beast, who was trailing sticky purple blood. The hives had broken open and dragon fledglings were shooting out, thin and whip-like and enraged. They circled overhead, dipping uncertainly as they flew with their new wings, shrieking like banshees, blinking blind, white eyes.

Reef shot out spells like crazy, pulling blindly from Breck's inventory. The alien was doing the same, but with fluid motions that suggested he faced dragon hordes every day. Olly had pulled out a crossbow. Aedric was nowhere to be seen.

Until he was at Reef's back, hissing, "The disc." Reef passed it to him with one hand while dealing damage with the other. Aedric pocketed it, turned to go. Reef thought, *That's it, it's done, he won't know it's blank until it's too late.* But then Aedric stopped, jerked on Reef's arm so that a spell slammed into the concrete beams overhead and fizzled out. "You pick up the scepter," Aedric said. Then he slipped away, the blank disc in his pocket. Reef's heart slid back out of his throat.

"Where's Aedric going?" Breck shouted, still fending off the Bristle Beast's attacks with Reef's sword.

"Just get the beast," Reef shouted back. He was desperate now to have all this over so he could get his goggles back and get away before Aedric came looking for him. Aedric could be stopping even now, checking the disc, finding it blank—"Olls, help him."

"No, I want to make the kill myself," Breck cried.

Olly was busy with the dragons anyway. They dove at him with snapping jaws while he aimed with his crossbow. His armor was scorched and battered. Reef knew he should stay and help, but he ran to Breck instead. The drug had taken its full effect now. Reef took in too many things at once: the whip of wind from dragon wings, the vines that furred every surface, the slippery feel of Bristle Beast blood under his shoes. The blood—he hated that most of all. The steam plant's smell of rust and old steam was like the metallic smell of it, and he had to fight off visions of black oil on white sheets.

He searched Breck's inventory for the strongest spell he had.

The Bristle Beast aimed a spiky paw at Breck, ready to knock away his sword. Reef sent a bolt of crackling blue magic at the cluster of eyes buried in the bristled face. The monster howled with pain. Breck drove the sword home. A fountain of purple blood spurted out and the beast dissipated. Reef's jerking vision took in the sight twice: The beast vanished, it flickered back into existence, it vanished again. In its place the silver scepter gleamed, clean and bright against the vanishing blood and banded with cold, clear sapphires. Reef stepped to retrieve it.

"Reef, wait—" Olly called.

And at the same time Breck said, "No, no. Your sword, your treasure." He jumped forward and closed his hand around the treasure, and three things happened at once:

Olly shouted, "No!"

Reef realized that it hadn't been some effect of the drug that had made him see the Bristle Beast vanish twice.

And Breck jerked his head back as though Reef's goggles had given him a mighty zap.

"What happened, what's going on?" Reef asked him.

Breck clutched at the edges of the goggles. "Oh shit oh shit."

"*What?*" Reef cried.

"It's a leech," Olly called. "Didn't you see the edit?"

"It's not a leech," Breck said.

Reef ripped the goggles off Breck's head and shoved them down over his own eyes. He had just enough time to see his screen scrambled into a mess of random pixels before the display went dark.

"It was a virus," Breck said. "Not a leech, a virus."

Reef felt cold cement slam against his knees. Everything was dark. He pulled off his goggles to see he had fallen.

A virus. A virus from the scepter had wiped his hard drive. Aedric must have planted it, hoping that it would wipe *Breck's* hard drive. But Breck hadn't stuck to the plan. Breck had grabbed the scepter while wearing Reef's goggles. And now everything stored on Reef's hard drive was gone.

"Why did you pick up the scepter?" Reef's voice was shrill. It didn't sound like his voice at all. "I was supposed to pick it up. It was supposed to go to your account."

"Cadence told me I should let it go to *your* account," Breck said. "She said you deserved it since it was your sword I was going to make the kill with."

Cadence? Since when did Cadence have any part in this? Confusion pounded in Reef's head. "She said . . . When did she say that?"

"I told her about the dungeon we were all going to do together. I told her Aedric had set it up so I'd get the scepter on my account. But she said you should have it."

"She said . . ." The euphoria of the drug had passed and

now there was only the feeling of lead settling into Reef's veins, into his bones.

"Reef?" Olly said.

Reef pulled off Breck's goggles and flung them away. His own goggles lay dark and empty on the floor. "Everything on my hard drive's gone. Wiped."

He caught a movement in the corner of his vision—the alien pulling off his own goggles, his face a blank mask. Reef waited for him to say something, but he only turned and walked away, headed for the doors at the end of the warehouse.

"We have to get out of here," Reef groaned. "Before Aedric comes back."

"Aedric?" Breck rocked on his feet, confused, nervous.

"He set us all up," Reef said. "It didn't work the way he planned, but he set us up. Your visa's gone."

Reef's feet pounded an uneven rhythm on the pavement. He found himself at Cadence's apartment building, and then thumping up the stairs, his heart thumping to match. Her door was unlocked, but she was gone. No one in the apartment. Just as he left the building he saw Aedric coming around the corner. Reef ran even while his muscles trembled in protest.

Back to his container. She wasn't there. Something was piled on the bed.

He flicked on the light. The something was a mound of gray bricks of resin. On top of the pile lay a note. Reef snatched it up and then backed away again, as though afraid the bricks would come to life under his fingers. Cadence had scrawled, *Sell it—Croy doesn't need it anymore.*

Reef leaned against the wall, trying to understand what it meant, trying to resist the itch in his bones at the sight of the drug. The night in the light-up lounge came back to him. He had asked her if she was close to getting the visas, and she had given him a strange answer: *You know why the aliens stopped wearing those red bracelets? Everyone wanted something from them.* What had she meant? That she was sorry she wanted something from Reef—money, visas? Or that she was sorry Reef wanted something from her? *But I didn't want anything from her,* Reef thought. *Not even the money in the end. I only wanted to be with her.*

And now she was gone and had left all of this resin behind for him. Why? To make up for the virus that had wiped his hard drive? But she hadn't known that Aedric had planted a virus in the silver scepter, a virus meant for Breck. She hadn't known it would wipe Reef's hard drive.

Had she?

He looked at the bricks piled on his bed. *Sell it.*

He pulled on his goggles and coaxed them to life. His system latched on to a wireless connection and spent a minute setting itself up from scratch. He opened the chat channel and tried hailing Cadence, but she wouldn't answer.

He pulled them off again.

She'd known about the virus. She had wanted it to wipe his hard drive. *Why? Why would she want to do that to him? Because she didn't want another husband. She'd only wanted the visas.*

He didn't think, just loaded his pockets with as many bricks as he could and left his container. Aedric would be looking for him, thinking he still had Breck's visa. He had to leave. He didn't know where to go.

He headed to the lounge she'd taken him to. If she was waiting for him somewhere, that would be the place. But that was stupid—why would she be waiting for him? She was probably all the way to Canada by now.

He wasn't the only one on the street, even late as it was. A knife flicked open behind him, a familiar sound that nevertheless sent a fresh surge of adrenaline through his veins. He turned just in time to avoid a swipe from the blade of a pale-faced junkie. Reef tore a brick of resin from his pocket, flung it as far as he could, and ran in the other direction.

He was breathless and shaking with exhaustion by the time he reached the gray-painted door next to the noodle place. He pounded on the door. No answer. He leaned his back against it, tried to catch his breath. Then the dark unsettled him and he crossed over to the other side of the street. The neon sign over the Roosevelt Hotel was like a beacon.

A ping from his goggles told him someone was hailing him on the chat channel. It was Cadence.

Her voice came through, but not her face: "I'm sorry."

Reef bit back his anger. "My entire hard drive is wiped."

"I wish Aedric weren't so good at doing things like that. I only wanted to get rid of the visa. I knew you would have it."

Reef pressed his fingers against his temples. Anger

boiled in his stomach, no matter how hard he fought against it.

"Do you remember that night at the lounge?" Cadence asked quietly.

Reef turned to glance at the dark building. He remembered his hands warm against her back.

"You said there's probably some bar in Beijing just like the one in Seattle?" Cadence went on.

Reef closed his eyes against the blank display of his goggles. "Why did you do it?"

There was a moment of silence before she answered. "I bet there's a place up here in Canada that's just like Seattle, except it's men and not women that there aren't enough of." Shasta's tiny voice sounded in the background. She was saying something about snow.

"Why did you do it?" Reef asked again, barely getting the words out through his parched throat. "You didn't want me to have that visa? Why?"

"I'm tired of being saved, Reef. I just wanted to get free."

"Free of me?" Reef's heart felt made of paper.

"Free of all of you."

She cut off the channel.

Reef sank down onto the sidewalk in front of the hotel. He searched for his Alt program and then remembered it wasn't there anymore. He downloaded it. There was nothing else to do. The bricks bulged in his pockets and his jaw trembled while he thought about them.

Alt finished downloading. Reef halfheartedly logged on while he wondered where Olly had gone after they'd split up. He couldn't remember saying good-bye. He tried him on the chat channel: "Olly?" No answer.

Alt's cityscape flickered to life around him, copper and crystal dulled by the smoggy mist. A holographic man in a leather vest stood near the corner of the hotel. "You going to tell me about the Fated Blade?" Reef grunted.

The man bobbed his head as he had the last time Reef had seen him. But an unfamiliar, digitized voice came out: "One hour, seven minutes, twenty-seven seconds."

Reef got to his feet. "What did you say?"

"One hour, seven minutes, twenty-two seconds."

The back of Reef's neck went hot with panic. Breck's words went through his head: *It's not a real quest. Just the Chinese mocking us.*

Reef raked his hands through his hair, looked down the street as though he'd find someone there who could help him. *You know the game is riddled with leeches? All waiting for their creator to say the word . . .*

Down goes all of our infrastructure.

He opened the chat channel and hailed Olly again.

"Reef—"

"Listen, something bad's coming, something really bad. Get out of the sprawl. Head for Canada. Our infrastructure's going down—maybe in the confusion you'll be able to get across."

There was a crackle that might have been Olly hitting the mic while tightening his goggles. "You sure this isn't one of your big conspiracy theories?"

"Just trust me. Get out."

"All right, I'm at the metro anyway. Wouldn't mind seeing Canada, even if it's just through the border fence." There was a pause and then Olly said, "You coming too?"

Reef slid his hands into his pockets, curled his fingers around the edges of the bricks there. "Just get out."

Reef ended the call. He racked his brains for the username the alien had used to chat with him at the steam plant.

"One hour, six minutes, forty-one seconds."

The alien answered his hail.

"All that crap you told me about the Fated Blade," Reef said. "Your people are going to help China attack us, aren't they? You're going to shut down the sprawl so we'll stop coming into your world."

It took a long moment for the translation program to come back with the alien's answer: "We're not helping the Chinese."

"Bullshit. I just heard the countdown. In an hour all those leeches they planted are going to activate and overwhelm our infrastructure. And then what? Nuclear attack too?"

"I don't know anything about that."

"The Fated Blade. The stupid impossible quest. It's not a quest at all. It's a countdown to a digital attack from Great China."

"I don't know anything about the quest. Or the countdown. Your wars have nothing to do with me. What I told you is true: Your people have become too dependent on my world."

Reef was hardly listening. "You're tired of us coming into your world and funneling out your money. You don't need us anymore now that you've got the solar energy you want. So you're going to wipe Seattle off the map—"

"You do not understand. This is not about your war. The connection between our two worlds is harming both worlds in ways you do not yet know about. Ways which we have only recently discovered."

Reef's breath went cold in his lungs. "What're you talking about?"

"You have joined your world to ours willingly. And we do not want to harm you. But it must end."

Reef balled his fist against his forehead, struggling to understand what was going on. It didn't make sense. The alien was only going in circles. "You want to destroy us, same as China does."

"We never wanted to harm—"

Reef grunted with impatience. "Why are you telling me any of this?"

"Because it cannot go on. We will separate. We must." Another long pause. Reef couldn't tell if it was because of the translation program or something else, but he thought the alien's voice sounded strained: "And I wanted someone to admit . . . *anyone* . . . I want you to admit that you would do the same thing if you were in our place."

"Do what? You're going to cut us off? It'll be chaos, worldwide war. Our economies will collapse."

Silence from the alien.

"You want to know if I would screw you over to save

myself?" Reef went on. An image came to mind: Shasta sleeping in her mother's arms. His throat constricted. "Sorry, I'm not interested in easing your conscience."

"If you understood how the connection between our worlds is harming both—"

"You want to know what it'll be like?" Reef cut in. "Stick around and see what happens to Seattle. See what happens when China sends a nuclear warhead to the sprawl. Take a look at the death and smoke and chaos and then tell me you can keep your conscience clear while you screw us over."

Reef cut the channel. He was shaking.

Smoke and chaos. There was a better way to die. He could go back with the resin to his container and just float away.

His goggles flashed. Olly was hailing him. "Hey, are you coming?"

Reef hesitated, didn't know how to answer.

"You better hope there are at least a few leeches in Canada," Olly said, "or I don't know what you're going to do with all your time."

Reef peered down the dark street in the direction of his container. "I don't think hunting leeches did much good, in the end."

"It was as effective a way as any to annoy China—and me."

Reef grinned in spite of himself.

"Hey, we might need some money when we get across the border," Olly said. "Got anything you want to sell?"

Reef tightened his grip on the bricks of resin in his pockets. He thought about going back to his container, lifting into an electric-blue sky, lost to gravity and to the world forever.

"Reef?" Olly said, a note of concern in his voice.

Reef's tight grip on the bricks of resin was making his hands sweat. He let go.

"Yeah. I do. I'll meet you at the station."

5.

WHEN WE ENDED
IT ALL

(more than one hundred years from now)

DYLAN

On the first day, you will tell your story. On the second, I will tell mine. On the third, one of us will die.

You will choose who.

The First Day

QUINN

My name is Quinn, and it's past time I came of age.

Some of the girls in my band of kin have already married. Even ones younger than me. But I've been busy with my Special Work.

I only started a couple years ago, but I was meant for it. Something in my bones makes me forever restless. When I was little, I would turn over every seashell nestled in the rocks along the coast. "Like you forgot what you were looking for," Truley once told me, "and you'd remember once you found it."

Now I know what I'm supposed to find. But I've no time left for searching. Like the other girls in my band, I must come of age.

Where I live used to be called Canada but isn't called anything anymore. When a land starts splitting into pieces, one name won't work. We live on the move between the great crevices to the north and east, and the Ruined City to the south. Setting up tents and tearing them down, traveling to sanctuaries in season.

Coldest times, we live in the White Hall, a big block building with carved columns all around. We burn wood right there on the blackened floor and let the smoke go out through the high windows while our Eldest tells stories of the Other Place and the Girl Queen late into the night. White Hall goes away before the cold ends, just vanishes like it was never there and leaves behind a big sloping hill you could get buried under if you don't get out in time.

So we go next to the Library, where we have only a month to read before the whole building disappears, and the books with it. You can't burn anything there because you might send the papers up in flame, but we rip the soft layer from the floor and make blankets of it. Do you know, that soft stuff comes back every time the Library does, but if you try to take it with you when the Library disappears, the soft stuff vanishes too. Same with the books, although I don't mind when they go, because our Eldest tells stories about the Other Place all year round.

In burning season when the trees catch fire in the heat, we take shelter in the High Tower, which is a stacked-up building taller than the trees and all covered in vines and crawling with creatures—mice and shrews and raccoons. The creatures come there to get away from the smoke and the heat from the trees on fire, like we do. High Tower vanishes quick—you can't stay for more than a few weeks. If you were standing on one of the tallest stacks of the building when it disappeared, you would fall right to your death, which is what happened to Truley's mom when she went back for something she forgot.

The last part of the burning season, we try to get to the coast, where it's cooler. There are sanctuaries that come and go much quicker than High Tower, like the Room With Medicines, which stays for maybe a day. And the Place Of Soft Seats—cushy chairs lined up in long rows under the trees—which you can only use for about half a day on your way to somewhere longer lasting.

I used to think that the good sanctuaries were created by magic from the Other Place, in order to give us aid. Now I'm older, I understand different: The Other Place doesn't create sanctuaries out of nowhere—our Eldest says the sanctuaries are "ghosts of our ruined past, come to haunt us as much as to save us."

Some of the oldest ones will tell you that they remember a sanctuary—or one that their fathers had told them about—that isn't quite like the others. Because when it vanishes, it takes you with it. It launches you not back into the past but into the Other Place. Into a land of plenty—always enough food, enough medicine. Babies born all through the warm seasons and no one freezing in the cold. Sanctuaries that stay put. Houses instead of tents, and nothing ever torn down. No need to move on to the next place. No need to war with another band over what you don't have enough of.

This is the reason I have put off my coming-of-age until now. I must do my Special Work, which is to find this sanctuary some say doesn't exist, the Transporting Sanctuary.

Once every few years we might travel down to the

Ruined City, to look for quarry if times are hard or we've missed an important sanctuary. But the Ruined City has a bad air. I've never gone very close myself. From a long way off I can see all kinds of High Towers that aren't sanctuaries but just old buildings stuck to the spot and probably ruled by hordes of rats. We only go there if we're desperate, because it's the lair of the evil mages, shadowy men who want only to destroy everything good. Times have happened that some kin who went into the city didn't come back out. That's what tells us the mages live there. That, and the foul look of the place.

The mages are a plague to us, venturing out in secret from their lair and setting spells to work against us. Long ago, they were banished from the Other Place, and they've been in a rage ever since. They know they can never get back there, so they plot to destroy it. In the meantime, they play spiteful tricks on anyone they think has it better than they do.

It was like that once when Artak killed his first wild dog. We roasted it on the spit, but then after we ate it, it appeared right back on the spit again. We said to ourselves it was magic from the Other Place helping us eat our fill, so we ate again, and again the meat appeared back on the spit. But this time we realized some trouble: We'd eaten the meat twice, but our stomachs felt emptier than ever. It was the evil mages—they were taking the meat from our stomachs and putting it back on the spit so we couldn't ever get full. We had to pack up camp and leave that place so the evil spell wouldn't spread to our other food.

Sometimes the mages conjure up not-sanctuaries with food all rotten, or with great machines that grind and scream. Once when I was out scraping bark for medicines, I saw a house appear like a beautiful dream, bright yellow with a peaked roof to let the rain and snow slide off. But when I went in through the door I saw the back wall had been smashed in. There was so much rubble everywhere it was like someone had grabbed the house and shook it and shook it until everything was bits and pieces. There was something under the rubble too, which I couldn't see but smelled rotten. I turned and went out of the house. I ran hard until the bright yellow was lost in the trees.

No good magic would conjure a sanctuary like that.

I told our Eldest about the yellow Dream House once I could bring myself to talk about it. That's when she told me that the evil mages like to torment us with bad things from our past. I asked her what had happened to that yellow house in the past, why it was so terrible inside. Eldest thought for a while. Her gaze went narrow like it does when she's sorting the good dried berries from the spoiled ones. Her clothes were the only ones that hadn't gone to rags, since we always gave her the newest felt to wear, and I started to feel twisty-nervous standing in front of her with my skirt in shreds.

"How do you think the Ruined City came to be?" she finally said. I had never imagined the city as anything else but what it was now—a terrible play-land for angry mages. I started to tell Eldest that it must have been the mages who had created the city.

Except in my heart, I knew that it hadn't been the mages. I knew from Eldest's hard stare. From the way her chin wobbled just before she turned away. Mages never create anything at all. They only conjure things that already exist from other places, or turn good things bad.

It was the people, then.

It might be difficult for you to imagine how *people* could smash up something as big as a city without any kind of magic. But I've seen a whole camp trampled and charred. I've seen the look in someone's eye when he means to kill—like there's nothing that can stop him from tearing the whole world apart. And long-ago times, people made those great screaming machines the mages conjure in their not-sanctuaries. Machines can do about as much as magic can, I'll bet.

So it was people and their machines who ruined the yellow Dream House, same as what happened to the Ruined City.

The evil mages probably sent the Dream House to me to hurt me because they hate my special love for the Other Place. No one else has ever seen the yellow house. Only me, who loves the stories of Dylan and the Girl Queen and the beautiful land they live in. Who has been visited by visions no one else has seen.

When I was a young girl I was once alone in the forest, gathering plants for medicines, when I caught a rare sight: a girl lifting up out of the ground as if out of water, her wet hair shining in the sun. Just for a moment she appeared, only one moment and then gone—vanished like a sanctuary. She was an avatar, a magical sighting sent to us from the past for shoring up our hearts. This avatar was the Water Nymph, a symbol of that which belongs to two worlds—water and land, our world and the Other Place. I am the only one who has seen her since the time our Eldest saw her, as a young girl.

When I went back to camp, our Eldest told me that long-ago times, there had been a stream there where I had seen the Water Nymph avatar, but it had dried up like so many others and filled in with trees and dirt. She said my sighting of the Nymph meant that I had one foot in the Other Place, just as I must have put one foot into that dried-up stream.

Not long after that we went on our way to the Cold House of Bounty Sanctuary, which is a metal room full of icy-cold foods that sits on a wide gravel bank. It's one of the best sanctuaries but also the hardest to get to—not only do we have to pass over the mountain ridge, but we also have to be on the lookout for bands who don't want to share the Bounty.

We were tired and wary by the time we reached Cold House, but still we sought out the avatar that appears near there quite often who we call the Exhorter. When she appears, she looks right through all of us with her piercing stare and says, "When you finish all of your homework, you can play one hour of Mario. Just one hour, don't try to ask for more."

Then she sits down and stares through our torsos, just stares like she's watching to see what we'll do, and sometimes she'll move her wrist or give a snort of laughter and then watch silently again. We children stand with our hands folded before us, contemplating her words. *Finish your work and then play.* It's the simplest of commandments and the hardest to follow.

But this time when she said her words, it was different. It seemed to me she didn't look through everyone. She looked right into my eyes. And so I knew her words held a special meaning for me. *Finish your work.*

Afterward, I told our Eldest that I knew I had a Special Work ahead of me, because I had seen the Water Nymph that few others have seen, and because the Exhorter had looked me right in the eye when she had exhorted.

"What is your Special Work?" Eldest asked.

I didn't know then but I knew it had something to do with the Other Place, that land of beauty and magic that Dylan first found so long ago.

I hardly ate the boxed foods at Cold House of Bounty, where we stayed for less than a day and then ran off before another band might come through. I was skinny and weak when we went on to High Tower to shelter from a forest fire, but I climbed the steps to the tallest stacks so I could be alone and think awhile. I thought about the Dream House.

I thought about how evil could eat up beauty.

And how that isn't the work of only mages.

I thought about what I had seen once from a hiding place in the forest. The look in someone's eye like there was nothing that could stop him from tearing the whole world apart. The charred and trampled camp.

After sunset that night in the High Tower, the sky went

on blazing through the night, orange-red above a distant line of yellow fire. In the morning, the sky would turn to ash and fall down on us soft as snow. But for now, the forest fire was beautiful against the gray-and-black sky. A world of trees was being eaten up by flames, and from a distance there was nothing terrible about it.

I decided upon my work.

"I want to find the Transporting Sanctuary," I told our Eldest. I thought she would say no, that it was a waste of time and no good reason to put off my coming-of-age. That I was too old to believe in stories of that fabled sanctuary. Instead, her eyes went small, as though her vision were sliding into the past. She nodded her trembling head.

Why else might the Water Nymph have appeared to me except for the Special Work of finding a doorway into such a world?

I had gotten very good at going off on my own—I was used to searching for alder bark and shrub berries for my father, who made most of our medicines. So I went off in search of sanctuaries. I made a catalog of the ones we visited and the ones other bands told us about and the ones I found on my own. I kept track of all the avatars in case they might have any clues about how to find the Transporting Sanctuary.

Our Eldest tells us to pick a certain avatar to hold in our hearts, either for courage or for wisdom or to model ourselves after. The boys all like the Moribund, a man who appears near High Tower far too often, his skin black as he suffers through his death throes. Thankfully he goes almost as quickly as he comes, so you only see him for a few seconds at a time. My best friend, Truley, used to prefer the Melodious, a girl with a bright-painted face who sings about a boy she shouldn't love, but when I try to sing the song to Truley now, she makes her much-too-old-for-that face and picks up her baby. I have my own avatar to think on, the Water Nymph.

I would remember her when I was afraid, or just weary and hungry. Always when I was alone in the forest I called her to mind.

I kept up my work for years.

Until our Eldest came to talk to me. Our band had welcomed so few babies in the past year, and fewer had survived the winter. A boy had asked about me—Artak, who I guess is a man now, since he survived the ten-day trek along the crevice. Really, he's no older than I am. Eldest told me it was well past time for my own coming-of-age, when I should travel along the crevice in search of some token to bring back to a husband. Times have happened girls have found bits of gold down in the crevice, revealed there where the earth opened up some generations ago. But Artak would take me even if I failed to find so much as a gold flake.

"My Special Work isn't finished," I told Eldest. "How will I search for sanctuaries when I have babies to take care of?"

Eldest kept her gaze trained over my head and told me, "Your work will be for your band now."

Artak smiled at me for the next three days. He was as nice as any of the other boys in our band. Still had all his teeth. No terrible scars or anything, though his hair had stopped growing along one patch over his ear where he'd been burned. We'd played together as kids. I knew he would treat me nice.

But I'd seen his face set in hatred once over what another band had done—raided our camp and taken all our food. A good enough reason to hate another band, I guess.

I'd seen that look in his eye while I hid—like the whole world was his to tear down. The same as I'd seen on the face of every other man in my band that day when they trampled the other band's camp and burned it to the ground. When they pulled down some of the men in the forest before they could get away and took home the women they could catch. I had seen what Artak had done to one of the women there in the trees.

It will be different with me, when I return to him. I suppose it will be different, because we're of the same band.

My days of searching for the Transporting Sanctuary are over. I've traveled farther along the crevice than any of the others ever did when they came of age. I saw their old campfires along the way, the remains here and there of a shelter or bed. I've come this far in the hope of making up for being so late.

Before I set off, our Eldest gave me a warning.

She told me some who have traveled along the crevice for their coming-of-age have found more than just gold rocks. I asked her what she meant and she said that my Special Work might even now be ahead of me. "There's a rare chance," she said. "But I've been thinking for some time that this might be your real work. And I'm sorry if it is."

It was possible, she told me, that I might meet someone on my journey. Someone from the Other Place.

Times have happened that young ones on their coming-of-age journey have encountered such ones. But they never speak about it. They come back and it's like they're closed in a cloud of their own air—everything about them dims. They are quiet, sad.

I thought to myself that Eldest had that sort of look about her. Closed up. Muffled in sadness. I always thought it was because she was so much older than any of the rest of us. But now I wonder.

Eldest told me that if I should encounter one of the inhabitants of the Other Place, I would have a choice to make. "I can't tell you what that choice is," Eldest said to me. "All I can tell you is the choice is yours alone and you are never to speak of it to anyone.

"But you must be careful—the evil mages are always on the prowl, hoping to find a way to destroy the Other Place, and they can take the disguise of nobler forms, true citizens of that magical land."

"How do you know all of this if no one has ever spoken of it?" I asked. "How do you know I will be given some choice to make?"

"Because I was one of those who met someone from the Other Place." The haze of summer heat went heavy around us, like it wanted to close me in her small, sad world. "I made my choice. And I have never been sure since then if it was the right choice to make."

The Second Day

DYLAN

You have told your story, and now I will tell mine.

I am Dylan of the famous tales, who first found the Other Place long ago.

My first visit there was a tour of wonders. I feasted in the golden rooms of the elven palace, explored jewel-crusted caverns, steered a ship with dragon-wing sails to the misty islands. Every corner of the land holds some puzzle or prize: a ruby lodged in the heart of a ghostly tree, an elixir made from ancient salt dried on moonlit banks, a silver scepter held captive by a sphinx. It broke my heart to return home that first time.

But the queen of the Other Place had given me a golden bracelet that would enable me to find her again, and so I soon went back. On my second trip to that realm, I brought my brother, Hunter. He loved the golden palace, the hidden treasures. He wished to win the Girl Queen's favor, so he vowed to rid her land of the evil mages who so often caused chaos there, draining magic from fairy coves, muddying crystal streams, and bringing sickness wherever they walked.

First, Hunter and I ventured to the sphinx's lair to win a silver scepter of great power. Then we chased the mages all the way to a distant place called the Wasted Wood, where we battled with them and finally used the magical silver scepter to banish them from the land.

The longer we stayed in the Other Place, the more we loved it. Hunter loved the riches of the palace, the thrill of heroic quests.

I loved the Girl Queen.

We soon went home, but I couldn't help returning again and again. I would think of the Girl Queen and suddenly step right into the woods behind her palace. Then Hunter asked to return, and so I took him with me. But when he realized how many times I'd gone there without him, when he saw how the Girl Queen preferred my company and how I had learned the secrets to unlocking the land's hidden wonders—he grew bitter. He lost heart for our adventures and went home.

But I loved the Other Place more than I loved my own world, and I chose to remain in the enchanted realm and never to leave. I made my home in the palace and every morning asked the queen how I could increase her happiness. Her younger brother became like my own brother and wrote tales of my adventures. I quested for treasure, recorded lore, passed judgments, made decrees. I forgot the world I had come from. And I was happy.

Until I realized that some malaise had struck the Other Place.

The malaise crept in so slowly, I didn't notice for some time. How long had it been since I'd seen a forest clearing humming with magic? How long since the drone of fairy nests echoed from a flashing cove? The silver scepter itself lost its glow and its rainbow array of jewels grew dim. No longer could I use it to keep fell creatures at bay. Trolls roamed farther from their dark lairs, mage-crows from their desolate crags.

I set off to survey the trouble, as far as the outlying lands. I was gone for months, documenting my findings. A black island had sprung up in a distant bay and turned the water foul. A terrible stench rose from crevices and caverns, and poisoned streams and wells. Farmers reported sharp black spikes growing up through their fields. A terrified hunter returned from the forest to say that he had seen more spikes jutting up from the soil there. It seemed everyone and every place was affected but none knew the cause. My mind worked endlessly but found no answers.

After almost a year, I journeyed back toward the palace, sick and weary from my wanderings. The land turned bleaker. Even my carriage began to molder, the silk lining turning black and falling away at my touch. I stopped at meeting halls and taverns along the way, eager to learn what had befallen the land in my absence. I heard tales of trees growing brittle and shattering like ice, crops failing and food growing scarce.

When I reached the palace, I saw a face that sent a shock

to my spine. A face I had all but forgotten. I searched my mind for who that face might belong to. *Could it be . . . ?* My head filled with memories that had slipped away long ago. No, not slipped—that I had *pushed* away. As if I'd shoved them all down into some deep place and now they were crawling out again.

Here at the palace was Hunter.

"Brother!" he cried, and smiled at me. But in his eyes I saw the same bitterness that had driven him to leave the Other Place long ago.

"You've forgotten about me," he said. "I had to find the way here on my own."

He opened his palm to show me a tiny jewel, gone black with age or ruin. Then he reached for the gold bracelet on my wrist and turned it to expose the empty setting from which the jewel had fallen. "A bread crumb," he said. "I found the jewel in our own land, and it led me here to you."

Unease slid into my heart. I learned that Hunter had been here in the Other Place for some months but had done nothing to combat the spreading miasma that covered all. I suppose there was nothing he *could* do, but it angered me to learn that he feasted while others starved, that he courted the queen's attention while the stench of death hung in the air. To him the Other Place was a game, a child's plaything. I don't think he believed it was all quite real.

I busied myself in my work, testing out theories that had been offered by the sages in the outlying lands. I sent scouts into the crags to see if the mages had somehow returned, sent spies to watch the ice giants on the far side of the mountains. I applied balms to the sick, said spells over foul wells and withered crops. But the land continued to decline.

One day I was visited by a sage I had once sought council from as a boy. He came to the palace and stood in the receiving room with his dark eyes like smoldering coals, his body so frail I feared the pounding echo of the fountains would knock him down. "You have known what the trouble is," he said to me. "You have known it since you returned from the outlying lands, but you will not face it."

I assured him that I had no such knowledge. "If you know what plagues us, it is your duty to reveal it."

"I do not know," the man said. "I know only that it is something so terrible you will not let yourself discover it."

I had him escorted away, thinking he had grown too old to know his mind anymore. But what he said haunted me. Whenever I saw my brother's face, I felt the sage was right, but I couldn't understand why I should feel that way. I wanted above everything to discover what plagued the Other Place—why should I not let myself discover it?

My brother grew restless in the palace, impatient with the queen's agitation. I tried to make him understand what danger the realm was in, but he would not listen. I realized he had fallen into a deep disappointment, that he had returned to the Other Place in the hopes of finding ease and happiness, but that those things had eluded him. After the sage's visit, he became convinced that I could heal the land but would not.

"See how pale he has become?" Hunter told the queen.

"How sickly? He grows worse as the realm does. It is some spell he has cast in order to drive me out."

"I am only weary from searching for answers," I said.

"There is a look about you of evil magic," Hunter said, and the queen admitted that it was true.

Her suspicion stung me, but at last I had to admit to myself that the sickness I felt was more than exhaustion. I hardly ate anymore, and a terrible pain throbbed in my arm. Something lay deep within the flesh there, something I had kept secret for a long time.

Once long ago my brother and I had sought to rid the land of evil mages, as you will remember. We had chased the mages all the way to their camp in the Wasted Wood and done battle there. The mages were terrible men. Not even really quite men, but shadows of men, as you said, Quinn. They had turned the wood into a foul place.

When Hunter and I had met the mages there in battle, we saw . . .

The wood was full of terrible things.

I'd all but forgotten, but now I remembered. Their dark magic had driven all the animals rabid so that the creatures had gored the trees with tooth and claw, and the stench of rotting wood was thick in the air. The wood nymphs stalked us like we were quarry and slavered for our blood, and we only eluded them by cutting down trolls and tossing them the carcasses. The putrid sap that covered all claimed our boots and cloaks. But at last we drove the mages from their dark hiding places and defeated them with the silver scepter's magic.

Afterward, Hunter and I could barely crawl away. We made camp outside its boundaries, where I discovered that a fell creature no bigger than my hand had latched on to my pack. It was completely black but for a cluster of milky eyes, and covered all over in sharp bristles. We had lost our swords in the wood, and we could find nothing sharp enough to pierce its bristled hide to kill it.

The sage I spoke of earlier had his warren nearby and, seeing our fire, came to find out what we were doing in those parts where few ventured anymore. We showed him the little Bristle Beast and he told us what we must do: Return it to the Wasted Wood, where it would feed on the dark magic there until the wood was cleansed of it and the beast died of starvation.

No worse instructions could he have given to us. We dreaded returning to the wood, even with the mages banished, because of the terrible things that still lurked there. But we knew the task must be done and so we started off, our steps heavy.

On the way, more trouble befell us: The Bristle Beast pierced my arm with one of its bristles. I was so overcome with horror that Hunter promised he would finish our task on his own. I returned to our camp to nurse my wound, but the quill had sunk so deep into my flesh that I could not remove it. When Hunter returned the following night, I told him I had removed the quill. I could not bear for him to know that something fell still lay inside of me. We never spoke of it or the wood again.

Now, years later, I knew I must travel back to the Wasted

Wood. I left Hunter and the queen at the palace and went to find out whether all of the dark magic had drained away, or if some vestige remained and managed to putrefy the whole land. I had only to come to the very outskirts of the wood to find my answer.

The wood was as infected as it had been years ago; no dark magic had drained at all.

This knowledge so sickened me that I lay in camp for days before going back to the palace. Even when I left the wood, I felt that some curse followed me, that I was tainted by dark magic.

I told Hunter about the Wasted Wood and he revealed the truth. He had meant to take the Bristle Beast to the Wasted Wood that day years ago, but as he had gotten closer to the wood, he had been so overcome with dread that he had dropped the beast into a deep cavern, where he left it to starve.

The source of the realm's sickness was now revealed.

We couldn't find the cavern, so we assumed the earth had since closed over it. But it was clear what must have happened to the beast. It had fed not on the dark magic of the distant wood, but on the good magic of the land. The beast was growing so large on this diet that its black bristles had pierced the earth: The spikes reported by farmers and hunters were really the prickled brow of the beast jutting up from the soil. The black island in the poisoned bay was rumored to be the heel of the beast, pushing out from the soft silt of the bank.

I realized that to kill the beast would be to collapse the

whole of the Other Place. To let it live would be to watch it grow large enough to break free and in doing so, destroy all.

I called for the sage, who gave an answer to my dilemma. A very old and almost-forgotten type of magic must be used to petrify the beast. Turned to stone, it would no longer be able to feed on the magic of the land, nor would the beast collapse or decay underneath the land. Slowly, the magic would leak out of the petrified beast, back into the land, and all would be saved.

There was a problem with this plan: The person who petrified the beast must have non-magical blood. Otherwise, the beast would defend itself by sucking all of the magic out of its attacker in an instant, killing the person and preventing the beast's petrification. In the whole of the Other Place, only Hunter and I had non-magical blood, so the task had to fall to one of us. I was ready to agree to this task, when the sage revealed one thing more: The person who wields the spell would petrify not only the beast but also himself. He would give his life for the Other Place.

Still, I was willing. I loved the Other Place with all my heart and would do anything to save it. And yet I came to realize I did not have the strength to wield the spell. The bristle that had been lodged in my arm so long had slowly poisoned me so that I had almost died journeying to the Wasted Wood and back.

I could not save the land that Hunter and I had doomed.

Upon realizing this, Hunter fled the palace, never to be seen again. For him, the Other Place was only ever a dream-land, and he was not willing to give his life for it.

I determined to find some other non-magical person to complete the task. But by this time I couldn't remember how I had first come to the land, or that I had once lived in a non-magical world. The sage revealed to me that there were other non-magical people in existence somewhere, people I had once known but had lost, though he didn't know where I could find them. I set off to search, with the fate of the Other Place growing ever more precarious. I wandered into your world.

Now I must see my task completed. Here, where the earth has opened, someone must cast the spell to petrify the beast and save the Other Place. Whoever is willing must be ready to give her life. If no one is willing, it will mean death to that magical land, and to the queen I love.

The Third Day

DYLAN & QUINN

Quinn made up her mind. She knew what her choice would be. She was surprised to feel disappointment.

Dylan too was surprised at how his heart sank when he saw Quinn coming back from her camp. The crevice where the earth had opened revealing a swath of rock either black or deepest red was too terrible for him to look at straight on. In the corner of his vision, Dylan saw the molecules of the rock shifting and sliding into tangled knots. The juncture of two universes. He felt his own body weaken at the sight of it so that he could hardly keep on his feet.

Quinn took the shining scepter from Dylan while he explained how to use it. He pressed himself against the mossy far wall of the crevice and gave her instructions for how to perform the spell that would petrify the Bristle Beast. The beast's flesh showed through the wall of the crevice, a wound open to the air. Quinn wondered why Dylan wouldn't look at it, why he squirmed now like an agitated animal.

"Will you perform the spell?" Dylan asked, breathless and wincing.

Quinn lifted the scepter, admired its smooth silvery handle, the clear bulb of an eye at its tip. "You aren't who you say you are, Dylan."

Quinn stood before him, brandishing the device he'd given her like a club, brandishing her vorpal too. Here, near the juncture of the two universes, his vorpal was weaker than it had ever been, distracted by the ever-shifting molecules Quinn didn't seem to see. He felt her vorpal pressing at him, testing him.

Could it be that his story hadn't worked after all?

But then, why was she still here?

Quinn hated to admit it: Dylan's story was a lie.

No one had listened more closely to the elders' stories about the Other Place than Quinn had. She knew them all—up to the point where Dylan and Hunter had found the Bristle Beast and had agreed to return it to the Warped Wood.

She turned to find that Dylan had stopped his tortured squirming and was watching her, a faint line creasing his brow.

"You made three mistakes in your story," Quinn said.

Dylan's expression was all curiosity—not what Quinn had expected. Her conviction wavered for a moment.

"First," she said, "the jewels on the silver scepter—you talked about 'a rainbow array.' But everyone knows the silver scepter's power comes from a band of sapphires from the crystal waters of a fairy cove.

"Second, you called the lair of trolls and fell beasts the *Wasted* Wood. But I've always heard the place of trolls called the *Warped* Wood.

"Third, the way you described the Bristle Beast—the creature you hate so much that its image must be seared into your mind. You said its eyes were white. But the stories say they're as black as its body, that its one weak point is almost impossible to find."

She held the scepter out in front of her as if it might offer some protection against whatever reaction Dylan might decide to have. He went on gaping at her.

He was going soft at the edges like something dissolving in water.

Dylan felt he might collapse at any moment. From relief or fear or exhaustion.

She hadn't believed his story. Everyone believed his story.

She lowered the scepter, dropped her stony expression. "I wanted you to be the real Dylan," she said. "I wanted this to be my Special Work." She nodded at the terrible face of the rock. "Now my only work will be to walk away. And cut Artak's meat and wash his pots and hope birthing his babies doesn't kill me."

Dylan studied her. "Why didn't you go home last night?" he asked. "Why come here to face me if you knew I wasn't—if you thought I was a mage?"

She squinted at him. "Are you a mage? You don't feel like what I thought a mage would feel like." Her vorpal probed at his. "But you're not Dylan. So I can't do what you want me to do. I know what my Special Work is now: to do nothing, to go back home." Her voice was heavy.

Dylan leaned against a crumbling wall of rock. The red-black juncture in front of him left a sunspot on his eyelids when he closed them. "I'm not a mage. And my story wasn't a lie. Not exactly." He didn't expect her to believe him, but maybe that was a good thing.

Maybe he didn't want her to believe him.

When he opened his eyes again, here is what he saw: not some poor, stupid native of a world that was lumbering into its last days. But a girl whose tattered felt skirt was still green with moss from the nest she had made for herself the night before, whose weary slouch told him she'd been awake for hours, weighing his concerns alongside her own. A girl he didn't want to hurt.

Quinn knew she must walk away.

And yet—

Dylan wasn't a mage.

He had some secret, but it wasn't that. Her vorpal felt his confusion and discomfort and . . . sympathy. For her. That wasn't something mages felt, if she understood the stories.

And now Quinn realized the real reason it had taken her all night to make her choice when those three obvious mistakes should have made it for her: Despite the proof that Dylan was lying, Quinn believed his story.

Dylan wished he knew what was going through Quinn's mind while she scrutinized the juncture in the rock. She finally turned back to him and asked, "Is there really a beast?"

Dylan only looked at the red-black swath of rock and shuddered.

Quinn charged up the scepter as Dylan had instructed her and gasped when the top turned vibrant blue.

Dylan's stomach lurched. "Turn that off." He was clammy with panic. He couldn't let her do this. "I don't think you're the one who should wield the spell."

She gazed at the crackling blue light, mesmerized.

"Didn't you listen to the story?" he said. "I said you would die if you carried this out."

She cocked her head and gave him a dark smile. "Do mages always feel so guilty when their evil plans work?"

Dylan wanted to grab the device from her hand, but he couldn't manage to take more than a small step. Quinn moved toward the red-black glare in the rock, luring him. His body threatened to turn into a puddle of formless cells. The solid form he had taken was too difficult to keep together much longer.

"Don't," he said, almost choking on the hot dusty air. "It's you. The beast is you."

Quinn froze. The device crackled in her hand.

"It's you," Dylan said again. "It's your whole . . . land."

She blinked at him, confused. She finally lowered the device. "Canada?"

"Your whole world, all of it. Your entire universe."

She looked around at the moss-draped maples, frowned at the sight of a distant dust storm. Dylan wondered how much was in that library she'd mentioned, what she might have studied of cosmology.

"Somehow our two universes got stuck together," he told her. "Yours has been pushing into ours for over a century now. It's wreaking havoc there."

Her body was still rigid, her brow furrowed. "There's no Bristle Beast."

Dylan looked away from her and then back.

"It's *us* pushing through the Other Place," Quinn said. "Destroying it." She folded her arms around herself. She seemed to be shrinking.

"It can't go on much longer," Dylan said. "Even your world is starting to come apart. You've seen the proof: The great crevices that have opened up. Other things."

"What things?"

"The . . ." He didn't want to tell her. He didn't want to ruin *everything* that gave her world meaning. "The sanctuaries. Those places that vanish and reappear."

She shook her head. "Those places are brought to us from the past. To help us."

"No. They come by accident." He couldn't stand the way her shoulders drooped when he said it. He wanted her to go on defying him, refusing to believe him. "Everything's getting pushed around. Pieces of the past are getting jumbled up with the present. It isn't magic and it isn't mages. There are no mages. What you see is merely your own world coming apart."

Her face was pale as death. Her jaw clenched tight as a vise. "And the avatars? Are those just an accident too?"

He was silent.

"Tell me," she said.

"The avatars are just people from the past," he admitted, "getting pushed around in time."

"None of it is from the Other Place? It's not magic?"

Yes, it's all magic, he wanted to say. *All accidents are magic. The fact that you showed up here, the fact that it's me you met and not one of the others who were sent here . . .* "Your world is breaking apart. Like ours has been doing. It's going to get worse. I wouldn't be here otherwise. We didn't think it would be right to *make* you sever the connection between our worlds . . ."

She unfolded her arms to study the scepter in her hand.

"Look, the story I told you—it was as fair as I could tell it," Dylan went on. "I said you would be giving up your life if you did this."

She fumbled to turn off the device but couldn't figure it out. Her hands were shaking too much to find the right pressure points.

"It's only fair." Dylan heard his voice coming out garbled and strained. He took a few steps back from the scarred rock face, as if that would help. "Your planet is going to pieces. You've bombed the whole place. Even if our worlds weren't stuck together the way they are, it's doubtful you could ever build everything back up. The ice caps aren't coming back, even though we've taken so much of your solar energy. Do you understand any of what I'm saying?" None of this was coming out right. "You let everything get so bad that there's no turning things around."

She finally found the right points; the blue light went out.

"Our worlds have to be separated or they'll smash each other apart," Dylan said.

Quinn said what he couldn't.

"And only one will survive."

Quinn's skin went cold even as the heat of the late-morning sun pounded the top of her head.

"You don't have to do this," Dylan said. "I told you we wouldn't make you."

Quinn's grip on the scepter slackened. Dylan lurched forward and caught it. He retreated with it back to the far side of the crevice, away from the wound in the rock wall behind her.

"So that's the decision I have to make?" Quinn said, her mouth dry. "If I save the Other Place, my own world dies?"

"But do you see? That's not even the decision. Your world is going to die anyway. It's a world beyond repair."

Quinn tried to understand what he was saying. *A world beyond repair.* The great crevices, the Ruined City, the food shortages, the animals growing scarce, the summer fires in the unbearable heat . . . But that was what the sanctuaries were for, to help them in their need.

Except—the sanctuaries were really another sign that her world was broken.

"What will happen to my world if no one cuts it away from yours?" Quinn asked.

"The same thing that's happening now. Your world will continue to die. Time will go to pieces. Perhaps something more. If you sever the connection, the same will happen, only much, much quicker. At least, as far as anyone can guess."

Quinn's stomach turned. Her legs buckled in the heat and then Dylan was at her side. He guided her to a shaded spot where a sapling grew out from a deep crack in the rock wall. Quinn lay back against the slope of rocks and grasses, heat pounding in her head.

"I shouldn't have told you all that," Dylan said. "I was only supposed to tell you the story. It was supposed to be a lot easier." He gave her a glum look of apology.

She glanced away. "Do you know about the Transporting Sanctuary?" she asked weakly.

"I told you the sanctuaries—"

"I know. But is it true that there's a way we could get into the Other Place? Into your world?"

"You mean like an evacuation?" He chewed his lip. "We've thought about that. A long time ago a lot of your people came into our world. We tried to make a place where they could live. But it doesn't work. Our atoms hold together more loosely than yours do. Your people can only stay for so long. And when we come here to your world—it's like holding our breath. It's like trying to live underwater. Neither of us is made to live in the other's universe."

Quinn heard him through a long tunnel. She thought she might be losing consciousness. For a moment she had the sensation of swimming in dark water, as though through an underwater cave. She imagined herself surfacing on the far end, breaking into sunlight like the Water Nymph. Finding herself in another world. Dylan's world.

His voice brought her back. "We've tried to work this out for over a century. We've tried to find some other solution." His tone dipped low. "Our worlds are foreign to each other. They weren't ever meant to meet."

A hot spike of anger went through Quinn's chest. She lifted herself, weak as she was. "That's wrong. You're wrong. The Other Place is all I've loved ever since I was young. I saw the Water Nymph, I don't care what you say about the avatars. She came to *me*, only me. She knew I had a Special Work."

Dylan didn't say anything. His eyes were round and startled.

"The real Dylan wouldn't say those things," Quinn said. "He was glad our worlds came together."

He didn't deny it.

"Isn't any of your story true?" Quinn said bitterly. "Hunter going away and coming back, the sage trying to help you remember. Is it the same story for everyone who comes along the crevice and meets you?"

"Different people have posed as Dylan, it isn't always me." He bowed his head so she couldn't see his face. "But I use the same story. Every time."

She heard the heavy sadness in his voice. She'd told him things she'd never told anyone. She suddenly felt sorry for him, sorry they were both locked in this awful nightmare.

They were sitting now almost facing away from each other, both hunched over as if to protect twin wounds. *He only wants to be away from me,* she thought, *away from here.* She felt the same way—she'd only ever wanted to be left alone to do her work. But now she couldn't for a moment think what had been so bad about that idea of going back to her band, visiting the sanctuaries in turn, setting up the tents and tearing them down, having children with Artak. Panic clawed in her belly. She could have found a way to go on searching for the Transporting Sanctuary with her children at her heels, rambling through the forest together. What was so bad about that? Why had she thought marrying would be so bad?

Instead she had her Special Work: to kill one world for the sake of the other.

She took a great shuddering breath. "I can't do it," she said.

"I know." He stood and gently took her hand. He pulled her up and led her away from the terrible red wound in the rock.

They retreated to a copse of pale trees. Dylan sat on a soft carpet of leaves and moss and studied the scepter. It was supposed to repel the matter of his own world, push it away from the heavy tangles of matter that made up Quinn's universe. It would close up the wound in his own universe and leave the wound in hers gaping open. There was no other way to do it. No other way that his people had found.

He turned his gaze to Quinn. Her knees were huddled to her chest, eyes trained on some distant sight. Was she thinking about all of the avatars who had spoken to her? The sanctuaries she'd cataloged? Maybe she was only looking at the tangle of moss and trees in the distance.

Dylan wished he were back in his own world, soaking up heat and energy. But he was beyond that point—no amount of energy would save him now. He breathed in warm air that seemed to leak right back out of his lungs into his loosening form.

Quinn looked at the scepter Dylan was holding. "You're too weak to use the scepter—is that why you want me to do it? You can't do it yourself?"

"It's not exactly true that I'm too weak to do it on my own," Dylan said. "It's just that my people—we can't quite bring ourselves to do it." He struggled to find a way to explain. "There was a time when we felt we could. When we felt we *must* destroy your world to save ours. But then there was a great war between your countries, and it was terrible to watch the suffering that destruction brought on your people. We knew it would be the same if the connection between the worlds is severed, only worse—your whole world would be destroyed."

Dylan remembered the avatar she had told him about,

the Moribund. He hoped the man wasn't really experiencing his own death over and over again, that it was only that Quinn's people were getting a glimpse of him through some window in time.

He closed his eyes for a long moment, trying to erase the thought altogether.

"After that, my people decided that we couldn't bring that destruction on you," Dylan went on. "And when we make a decision together, it's very hard to undo. Our vorpals echo the decision back to us. That kind of resolve can keep a hold on us for generations. But now your world is suffering anyway. It's coming to pieces the way my world is. We can't let things go on the way they are, but we can't bring ourselves to destroy you. We can only hope that you will choose to sacrifice your world for ours."

"But the story you told me," Quinn said. "You said I would die if I saved the Other Place, but you didn't say that my whole *world* would die."

"We're getting desperate." He turned away.

"It's not right," Quinn said. "You should have told me the truth to start with."

Dylan laid the device between his feet. It looked harmless in the leaf litter. "You want to know the truth? My world isn't some enchanted realm. We let you believe it was so that you wouldn't stop us from taking your energy, so you wouldn't look for a way to cut yourselves free from us. We made sure that we would be the ones with the power in the end."

He could see in Quinn's searching gaze that she was deciding whether to believe him. He grew weaker under her hard stare.

"*That's* the truth I should have told you from the start," he said feebly.

Quinn crossed her arms. "You said that you once got people from my world to go into your world."

"It's not a sanctuary that does it."

"The Transporting Sanctuary."

"There's no such thing. It's just . . . some people are special. They can see the Other Place, can walk right into it."

"I've never heard of that happening."

"You have to be in the right place. Even if you're special, you have to come far enough south—here, to where the two worlds overlap."

Quinn drew herself up. "So if someone from my band, someone special, came here and walked into the Other Place with this device . . ."

Dylan's stomach went hard as rock.

"That person could cut the Other Place away from this world," Quinn went on. "*This* world would be the one to survive. Wouldn't it?"

Dylan studied the hard planes of her face. He nodded.

"So the real decision," Quinn said quietly, "is save the Other Place, or save my own land."

"No. Save the Other Place or save a *dying* land. *That's* the choice."

"But still. It's my choice."

Somewhere above them a bird warbled in answer. Dylan himself had nothing to say. He had already told Quinn at the beginning of this: You will choose.

Quinn got to her feet. Her legs trembled. "I don't want either world to die. I only ever wanted to find a way to the Other Place. I thought if I could find it, then maybe things wouldn't be so hard for my band."

Dylan's heart thudded. She was leaving. He'd known she wouldn't go through with this; still, he wasn't ready for her to leave.

She turned and took heavy steps in the direction of her camp. A bolt of alarm went through Dylan's heart. "Wait."

She looked back. Dylan could feel whole parts of him shutting down, over-stressed by exposure to the juncture. It was all he could do to hold together a semi-solid form. "Will you—will you stay with me? For just a little while?"

Quinn stood frozen for a moment. Dylan felt sure she would turn and walk away without saying another word. But she took hesitant steps back to where he sat.

"It's just that you're the first person I've seen in weeks," he explained.

Her expression softened.

"I usually don't mind being alone," Dylan said. *But there's something different about you.* He couldn't say it out loud.

She tucked her hair behind her ears and he saw again how earnest she was, how she always thought so carefully about what she should do. He regretted ever trying to trick her. He hadn't thought he had it in himself to feel so deeply about anything anymore, but he felt such deep regret that if he looked down he might find he had worn a hole right through himself.

Quinn kneeled and touched the device lightly, as if afraid to wake it. "What would have happened to you if I had used this? Would you have been trapped here or could you go back?"

"I can't go back either way." He cleared his throat. He'd left his water at his camp. "I—I'm not going to last much longer. I've been exposed to the juncture too many times, for too long."

Quinn squinted against the sun reflecting off the far rock face. Her lips parted as though she was about to say something, but instead a rush of air escaped. Dylan wondered how there could be any room in her heart right now for sympathy.

"It's all right," he told her. "Really. I volunteered for this. I knew what would happen."

She turned toward him with a questioning gaze.

"I thought I might as well," he continued. "I haven't been the same anyway. Since . . . Since something happened . . ." He shook his head. He couldn't bring himself to say it.

Maple flowers were spilling out of her skirt pocket. The petals were half crushed. They lent a sweet smell to the air. Dylan leaned closer to her.

"I would have liked to have gone to your world," she said.

Dylan imagined himself showing her great glass buildings like she had never seen—High Towers with all their windows still in place. Whole cities whirring with life. "Yes, I think you would have."

"It's not all ruined yet? Breaking apart?"

"Some parts of it are. But other parts . . . Cities in the mountains that move with the snow drifts, crystal sea caves like windows that look into water . . ." He broke off again. More things he didn't want to think about—he couldn't go back home. Already, he felt his insides giving up, shutting down.

"Is there a palace?" Quinn asked.

He supposed there was—plenty of them. He nodded.

"And the Girl Queen?"

"There's a queen. She's not a girl, she's grown. She's not the same person from the stories, really."

Quinn touched his arm. "Don't tell me about the Water Nymph. I'm going to think of her however I want." She closed her eyes. The streaks of dirt on her face looked like misplaced shadows. "Do you really have a brother?"

"I have an older brother who's a bit like Hunter. We didn't always get along." A hot prickle went down Dylan's neck. "When I think about it, it's like being in that Warped Wood . . ."

Quinn opened her eyes. "It's okay. You don't have to tell me more. I've been to a place a lot like those woods. I know what kinds of things happen there."

Some hard knot inside Dylan's chest loosened.

Quinn's hand rested on his arm and it might have been the only part of him that wasn't trying to dissolve.

"Do you really think our two worlds were never meant to come together?" she asked, her voice so low he could barely hear her. "I can't bring myself to believe that my world was never supposed to be this way. I can't believe the Water Nymph wasn't meant for me."

Dylan looked up at the birds skittering through the canopy of leaves. "Our worlds have changed each other in terrible ways."

"Not all terrible," Quinn said.

He supposed she meant the sanctuaries and the avatars, mistakes though they were.

He cared only about her arm against his, the smell of maple flowers, the shifting sunlight that made her eyes flash copper. "No, not all terrible."

She looked at him, surprised. She must have heard in his voice what he meant. She gave him a sad smile. "The funny thing is, I always just wanted to be left alone."

"So did I." A dark memory of his brother threatened to overwhelm him. He pushed it away. "People change you."

Dylan's body felt weighed down—with exhaustion, with a sad sort of weariness. He lay back against a tangle of roots and moss.

"I'm tired," he said. "You should probably go now. You have a long walk ahead."

"No. I'll stay a little longer." She moved her hand into his. Little lines of worry appeared around her eyes.

"Are you going to bring your band here?" he asked. "Find someone who can cross into the Other Place and use the scepter? You can still save yourselves that way."

"I don't care about that just now," she said. "I care about what's happening to you. Isn't there some way I can help you?"

He shook his head. "What will you tell your band when you go back to them?" he asked.

"I'll tell them I met someone from the Other Place."

"Say it was a dark mage." He felt dizzy. He thought he would float away if she didn't keep hold of his hand. "The darkest. And he told you terrible things."

"I'll say it was Dylan, and that he finally came home to his own world."

"To the world he ruined?" He closed his eyes. He hardly knew what he was saying. Exhaustion threatened to overtake him. "He started all of this, the real Dylan. Drew us all together and now we've screwed each other up. We might have been okay if we had walked away much sooner. We could have gone back to how we were before we got stuck together."

He felt Quinn shift in the dirt next to him. "You're wrong, you know," she said. "People don't change you. They can't, because you're never just one thing to begin with."

"They do. They do terrible things and you go to pieces. You can't be put together again."

She brushed a hand over his forehead, light as a falling leaf. "That's what people are. Just all different pieces."

Quinn imagined the tall spikes of the Bristle Beast coming up through the dirt, felt herself speared. The smell of decay kept coming back to her coupled with the memory of running, *running* from the yellow Dream House.

The soft sound of Dylan's breathing drew Quinn's attention. His sleeping form had sunk into the leaf litter, sunk too far. Quinn couldn't tell where his back ended and the ground began. All of his lines and shapes had gone blurry. He was like a Water Nymph: half in, half out of the world.

He was like something being consumed.

Quinn was like something being invaded. Her entire world filled up all the space inside of her. The ruffled lakes, the shadows of moss on trees. The white unspooling rivers, trailing like veils over mountain ridges. Truley gathering up the howling baby, Artak at the fire. The yawning crevices. The charred camp.

She tried to picture it all going to pieces.

Once Quinn had seen her band set fire to another band's camp. She imagined it now as the forest fire she had once watched from the High Tower—red and orange and soft gray—eating and eating at the world.

Destruction wasn't the work of mages.

Dylan awoke when he heard Quinn's soft footfalls coming back to him. She jostled him as she lay down again. He felt the cool smoothness of the device in her hand. He tried to slide it out of her grip and found that he was no longer solid enough to do so. The scepter tumbled into the leaves. Quinn's hand melded into his, pushing right through his loosely held cells.

He found he didn't mind.

Quinn severed the connection between the worlds. She chose death for her own.

Her work was done. She trembled on the cool blanket of leaves, still holding Dylan's hand.

His words rang in her ears: *Your world will continue to die. Time will go to pieces. If you sever the connection, it will happen much, much quicker.*

She thought: *Maybe life will narrow down to a single moment.*

It could be a moment like the Moribund, a pinpoint of agony. Or it could be something lovely, like pulling out of the water into the sunlight.

She listened to the leaves rustle in a warm breeze, the only voice on the air.

Another sound among the trees—

She raised herself up to look.

And saw the oddest sight: A young boy was moving through the woods, confusion lining his face.

And here was a young girl coming to meet him, the sun in her hair.

Quinn shivered with surprise. She sat frozen, watching.

"It's them," she said in awe. "The Girl Queen. And Dylan—the real Dylan."

Time will go to pieces.

"It's the moment they first met," she said. It was like seeing an avatar, someone brought from the past.

Already they were vanishing, like all the other avatars vanished. Sliding back into the time from which they'd come.

But Quinn had seen them.

A magical sighting, sent from the past.

Or, no: a sign of a world going to pieces. And it was only chance that it had been young Dylan and the Girl Queen she had seen. An accident.

But maybe some accidents were magic.

Maybe some people were meant to find each other.

Quinn huddled closer to Dylan and he stirred.

"I wish people could know about the end," she said.

His agitation made the air around them ripple. "About how I lied? How your world will die?"

"No. I wish they could know about the two of us," she went on, turning to face him. She couldn't feel his hand anymore. He was as loose as a cloud. But all of his molecules seemed to be reaching, reaching. "And how one world saved the other."

He and Quinn were both reaching now, lifting away with time and heat and air.

Like water into sunlight.

ABOUT THE AUTHOR

Parker Peevyhouse lives with her family in the San Francisco Bay Area, where she has worked as an instructor and tutor and currently volunteers with teens. She enjoys puzzles and games of all kinds and can usually be found wandering local trails or watching science fiction movies. *Where Futures End* is her debut novel.

Find her online at www.parkerpeevyhouse.com, and follow Parker on Twitter (@parkerpeevy).